Counterfeit Conspiracy

Strike a Match 2

Frank Tayell

Dedicated to my family

Published by Frank Tayell
Copyright 2016

The author has asserted their moral right under the
Copyright, Designs and Patents Act, 1988, to be identified
as the author of this work.
All Rights reserved. No part of this publication may be reproduced, copied, stored in a retrieval system, or transmitted, in any form or by any means, without the prior written consent of the copyright holder, nor be otherwise circulated in any form of binding or cover other than that in which it is published and without a similar condition being imposed on the subsequent purchaser.

ISBN-13: 978-1523659616
ISBN-10: 1523659610

Other titles:

Post-Apocalyptic Detective Novels
Strike a Match 1. Serious Crimes
Strike a Match 2. Counterfeit Conspiracy
Strike a Match 3: Endangered Nation
Work. Rest. Repeat.

Surviving The Evacuation/Here We Stand
Book 1: London
Book 2: Wasteland
Zombies vs The Living Dead
Book 3: Family
Book 4: Unsafe Haven
Book 5: Reunion
Book 6: Harvest
Book 7: Home
Here We Stand 1: Infected & 2: Divided
Book 8: Anglesey
Book 9: Ireland
Book 10: The Last Candidate
Book 11: Search and Rescue

For more information, visit:
http://blog.franktayell.com
www.facebook.com/TheEvacuation

Prologue: Another Dead Lead
(The Investigation So Far)
1st October

"You don't get more dead than that," the newly promoted Assistant Commissioner Weaver said.

"Oh, I don't know," Captain Henry Mitchell said. "Lying in a grave, it almost looks natural."

To Ruth Deering, there was nothing natural about the nearly decapitated corpse. The body didn't bother her, nor did the blood. She'd seen enough of those in the last two weeks that they were almost commonplace. It was the smile that made her stomach churn. Surely the man hadn't been happy in the moment before he'd died, but it seemed a macabre twist of fate that his muscles would curl into that particular grimace.

They were on the edge of the old city of Bournemouth in what was now a relatively poor district of Twynham. Compared to the old-world, there were no affluent districts. Twenty years after the Blackout, indoor plumbing and electric lights qualified as luxuries. For most of the quarter-million people who lived in the metropolis that sprawled along the southern English coast, nights were lit by candle and winters warmed by open fires.

"Natural or not," Weaver said. "What do you make of it?"

"Murder, obviously," Mitchell said. His accent was from the American Midwest, tempered by two decades living in Britain. Like Ruth's adopted mother and many others, he'd been stranded in the UK during the Blackout. "As to the rest... Deering?"

The question might have been vague, but she knew from the increasingly familiar tone what he was asking. "Yes, sir. The victim is male, thirty-five to forty years old." She stepped closer. "His height..." She swallowed. "It's hard to tell with his head gaping back like that, but he's around six foot. Patched jeans, repaired jacket, scuffed shoes – there's nothing special about the clothing, except that it's more worn than most people would tolerate. Either he didn't care about his appearance or he didn't spend any money on it. His neck…" She took a deep a breath. "His head has been almost decapitated. Judging by the blood on the blade, it was done with the shovel. Probably post-mortem because who'd lie still for that?" Ruth knelt down and lifted the body's hand. "There's no rope around his wrists, or marks indicating they were tied. Rigor mortis has yet to set in, so he was killed within the last thirty-six hours." And there was something else, a long thorn caught in the sleeve. Grateful for the excuse, Ruth looked around for the bush or shrub it must have come from.

"Longfield, do you have anything to add?" Assistant Commissioner Weaver asked.

"I suppose we could check the wound for mud," Police Cadet Simon Longfield suggested. "That would tell us whether the grave was dug before the man was killed."

"From his position lying half inside it," Captain Mitchell said, "I think we can be sure of that. But I don't think the decapitation was done post-mortem. I'd say that the blood on the shovel's handle is arterial spray. The killer knocked him unconscious with the shovel, pressed the blade against his neck, and then stamped down on it."

It was strange to see Mitchell and Weaver actually getting along, Ruth thought. They'd seemed to hate one another a few weeks ago. They weren't exactly being friendly, and Mitchell was still ignoring Weaver's seniority, but open hostilities had been put on hold. Ruth put it down to the promotions. In Mitchell and Riley's cases it would be more accurate to say that they had been re-promoted to the ranks they'd held before being demoted and assigned to the Serious Crimes Unit. Quite what had caused that demotion, Ruth wasn't sure, though she suspected Weaver might have had some part in it. The restoration of rank was the result of exposing Commissioner Wallace's conspiracy to flood the fragile British economy with millions of pounds of fake currency, and for their part in foiling the attempted assassination of the Prime Minister. For similar reasons, Weaver had been elevated to the rank of assistant commissioner with specific responsibility for policing in Twynham. Captain Mitchell was still in charge of Serious Crimes, with Riley as his new sergeant, and the unit was being expanded. Ruth, much to her frustration, was still a lowly police cadet. The rules were clear. A graduate of the academy had to serve three months before advancing to probationary constable. Those three months apparently didn't get waived even if the cadet concerned had been the one to shoot the assassin and so save the PM's life. Perhaps if her shot hadn't winged the man they only knew as Emmitt, and if he hadn't then escaped, it would be different.

"Did the killer make him dig the grave?" Simon Longfield asked.

"You tell me," Mitchell said. Simon looked at the body. Ruth kept looking at their surroundings.

Police Cadet Simon Longfield was the first of the new additions to the unit. He'd been in Ruth's class in the academy and had been stationed in Police House. The rest of the new squad, transferring in from postings across Britain, were due to arrive the next day.

"I… um…" Simon mumbled.

"Deering?" Mitchell prompted.

"Look at the boots," Ruth said, remembering one of her first lessons in the Serious Crimes Unit. "They're work boots, but the soles look reasonably clean. The soil here is thick and loamy. If he'd dug the grave, the mud would have stuck to them."

"You can tell a lot about someone from their boots," Mitchell said.

"And as much from the surroundings," Sergeant Riley added. "Like what time of day the murder occurred."

To the south of the grave was a dumping ground of rubble and brick. Beyond that was a warehouse that had lost its roof during the Blackout and two of its walls to weather in the years since.

No one knew how many had died during the seventy-two hours when the competing AIs had fought their brief war. Billions had been killed in the nuclear holocaust that had brought it to an end. Nor did anyone know whether those missiles had been launched by the machines or by people trying to stop them. Twenty years on, it didn't matter.

Thanks to the cargo ships and bulk grain carriers that had come aground on the beaches a few miles south of where Ruth now stood, Britain had weathered the apocalypse better than anywhere else on the planet. Those ships had kept hundreds of thousands of survivors alive during the first, harsh years as they built farms, coalmines, steam trains, power plants, and a vast fishing fleet. As their stores of food had grown, ships could be spared to find out what had become of the world. Because several cruise ships with mostly American passengers had come aground along with the cargo carriers, the new fleet was sent across the Atlantic. In the early years, they took food and pharmaceuticals. Latterly, they had been taking words. To mark civilisation's recovery, a live radio broadcast had been organised. The Prime Minister and the American ambassador had been scheduled to speak, with a response to be broadcast from the across the Atlantic by two of the presidents of the United States. It was halfway through the broadcast that the assassination attempt was made.

Though the Prime Minister was wounded, she'd finished her speech. They'd cut to a pre-recorded version for the remainder of the broadcast, and so the public had yet to learn of how it had almost come to a disastrous conclusion. Nor had word of the counterfeiting been printed in the newspaper. As far as most people were concerned, the radio broadcast meant that the era of music radio wasn't far off, with television close behind. Until then, everyone had to find entertainment wherever they could. For the workers standing on the scaffolding surrounding the warehouse, that entertainment was the police officers gathered around the body.

"The murder was committed at night," Ruth said. "The workers on the construction site have a clear view of the victim. If it was daylight they'd probably have stopped it."

"Or, if they were involved, they would have finished burying the corpse," Mitchell said, "but they would *not* have reported it."

"You know," Simon said as if he was only just realising, "I think that grave's a bit small."

"That's because it wasn't for him," Weaver said. "I'm almost certain of it. His name is Lionel Norton. He was… involved with a woman named Georgia DeWitt. He terrorised her. Norton took great pleasure inflicting pain on women. Five weeks ago, DeWitt had had enough. She stabbed Norton in the arm with a pair of scissors. At the time, she was in a branch of the National Store. The incident was witnessed by an off-duty constable. DeWitt was arrested. Norton didn't want to press charges. He would have preferred to meet out his own brand of justice. I kept her in the cells for her own protection. Four days ago, I had to release her."

"You could have told us that ten minutes ago," Mitchell said.

"Yes, I know," Weaver said. "I arranged for DeWitt to move into a room above a chandler's prior to starting a new life in Newfoundland. Norton must have discovered she'd been released, found where she lived, and brought her out here to kill her."

"You should have told us," Mitchell repeated. His eyes roamed the construction site, and then the murder scene. "There are footprints inside the grave. Around its edge, there's an indentation of a shoe's toe. Someone tried to climb out and slipped. The shoe has a raised heel, and they're four or five sizes smaller than Norton's boots. It's a safe bet that they belong to a woman. So, Norton brought her here and made her dig the grave. She hit him with the shovel and dragged his body into the pit. Do you see the marks on the ground there? Realising he was too large for the hole, she decided to decapitate him. She put the shovel to his neck, stamped down, and probably then realised he'd still been alive. The shock of the blood spurting out of the wound was enough to bring her back to reality. She ran. Have you checked her address?"

"Before I sent for you," Weaver said. "She's not at home."

"Then she's fled. It's a pretty straightforward case, so why are we here?"

"Because DeWitt was in the cell block when Josh Turnbull died," Weaver said.

Josh Turnbull was part of the gang of counterfeiters. He'd been murdered while in police custody.

"Do you think she saw the killer?" Ruth asked.

"No," Weaver said. "I asked her, and she had no reason to lie. However, it is possible that the killer thought *she'd* seen *him*. That killer could have brought DeWitt here with the intention of burying her in this grave, and Norton intervened."

"No, that's not possible," Mitchell said. "Not according to the evidence. There were only two people here, Norton and a woman. The woman killed Norton."

"Look harder and confirm that," Weaver said.

"What about the other possibility?" Mitchell asked. "That she was involved in Turnbull's death?"

"She wasn't," Weaver said. "Whoever killed Turnbull had keys to the cells, and access to a cyanic compound and a syringe. All she had was a bucket, mop, and occasional access to a broom. If you'd ever met her, you'd understand. The woman was in a constant state of terror."

"What does she look like?" Riley asked.

"Five-five, with hair so blonde it's almost white," Weaver said. "Angular nose, green eyes. Never stands up straight, walks as if she's trying to make herself seem as small as possible. Timid. Terrified. She was a seamstress by trade though not a member of the tailor's guild. The hope of finding work brought her to Twynham six months ago. There's no family, and Norton made sure she had no friends. If she were to go anywhere it would be to me, and she hasn't as yet."

"And if we find her," Mitchell asked, "what do you want us to do?"

"I'm not concerned about her," Weaver said. "I just want to know this is the better of two possible endings in another pitiful domestic abuse case."

"Understood. Longfield? Longfield!"

"Sir?" Simon snapped back to attention. He'd been staring fixedly at Norton's almost severed head, and looked a little sick. Ruth supposed that was to be expected. Unlike her, he'd dealt with nothing more gruesome than paperwork since he'd graduated from the academy.

"Longfield, go with Riley," Mitchell said. "Start at the construction site. Confirm whether anyone saw anything. Find out when the last person left yesterday evening, and who was first in this morning. Oh and check whether Norton worked there. He chose this spot for a reason. Do you have an address for DeWitt?"

"Here," Weaver said. "The bottom one is DeWitt's, the other is the address Norton gave at the time DeWitt was arrested."

"Deering, you're with me," Mitchell said, taking the piece of paper from Weaver.

Due to her new rank, Weaver had a horse-drawn buggy to take her back to Twynham. Ruth and Mitchell had to rely on bicycles with studded-leather tyres that offered little grip on roads carpeted with slick leaves.

Mitchell winced as he raised his leg to mount. The foot went back down. "It's not far," he said. "Perhaps we should walk."

"Are you all right?" Ruth asked.

"It's only my side, where Wallace shot me," Mitchell said. "I keep forgetting about the stitches. Now, this murder, what would you do next?"

"Um… check DeWitt's rooms and see if her clothing is missing," Ruth said. "Ask in the chandler's if anyone remembered her arriving and, if so, what kind of bag she brought with her. If that's gone then it would confirm she ran. As to finding her, we could send her description to all the provincial railway stations. But…well, she's probably run home, wherever that is."

"Probably, and if we find out where that is, we'll send a note to the local constable to keep watch for her."

Ruth fell in behind Mitchell as they pushed the bikes between a horse-drawn skip and a scavenger's cart.

"What about Simon?" Mitchell asked. "Do you trust him?"

Mitchell had asked her that a dozen times over the last week. So had Weaver. Simon had been transferred to Serious Crimes on Ruth's recommendation. Weaver had asked Riley and Mitchell whom in the police they could absolutely trust. They'd both suggested a few names. Ruth had added Simon's.

"Yes, sir," she said. "We were in the academy together. He's a friend."

"But he's one of *the* Longfields?" Mitchell asked, again for the dozenth time.

"Yes, sir. He's their only son. Like I told you," she added.

The newspaper described Simon's parents as captains of industry. Ruth thought 'generals' would be a better fit. Their wealth came from having owned a small dairy herd and powdered milk business before the Blackout. During the chaotic years afterwards, they'd grown the herd by rescuing animals from farms where the owners had died or fled. When the power plant was built, the milk-processing plant was re-opened and quickly expanded. From dairy, they'd moved into beef, and then into canned and processed meats. As the economy was rebuilt, and money issued once more, they'd bought the canneries. Now they were a major producer of the food-aid being shipped overseas.

"So why did he join the police?" Mitchell asked.

"I... I'm not sure," Ruth said. "It's something to do with his parents wanting him to know how the real world works. They don't want him to inherit the business without working for it."

"I heard that hesitation in your voice," Mitchell said. "What's the 'but'?"

"Um... well... this is between us?"

"Of course."

"I think it's because he's not cut out for business," Ruth said.

Because of his parents' connections, Simon had been given a relatively safe position in Police House. Ruth's assignment to Serious Crimes had also been due to nepotism, though she'd not known it at the time. Maggie, her adoptive mother, had known Henry Mitchell during the Blackout. When Ruth had insisted on applying to join the police, Maggie had asked Mitchell to watch out for her. By the time Ruth had finished her year in the academy, Mitchell had been demoted and sent to the backwater Serious Crimes Unit, and so it was to there that Ruth was assigned. During her first two weeks, she'd seen a suspect shot, been shot at herself, killed a man – though in self-defence – almost been killed by Commissioner Wallace, and personally prevented the assassination of the Prime Minister. If that was Henry Mitchell looking out for her, Ruth dreaded to think what could have happened if he'd been trying to sabotage her career.

"You mean he's stupid?" Mitchell asked.

"No, not that. I don't think he's cut out for business. He's... well, he's too nice, and he daydreams a lot."

"Ah, then he's probably not suited for this line of work. They should have found him a job at the university. Still, if you trust him, that's good enough for me."

"Yes, sir," she said. Mitchell had said that exact same thing a dozen times before, and experience told her he'd ask again at least once before the sun set.

They continued on in silence. A lingering Indian summer had been replaced by a week of storms. The skies were now clear, but so were the branches of every deciduous tree. They passed a smallholding made up of back gardens where the fences had been removed. The people toiling inside barely spared them a glance as they cleared the tilled earth of fallen leaves. Life went on. But it shouldn't. Ruth didn't think it was right that the newspaper had yet to print anything about the assassination or the counterfeiting. Not that there was anyone to whom she could complain. The paper would cover it, *eventually*, she'd been told. That was wrong, too. The truth was important. Truth. That word echoed in her mind. It had taken on a particularly personal significance over the last week.

"You seem pre-occupied," Mitchell said.

"Do I? I was thinking about the body," Ruth lied.

"I wouldn't bother," Mitchell said. "Riley and I should have the case closed before nightfall. I think, if you cut through this avenue, you should be in the woods in twenty minutes."

"What? Oh, no. You're not serious? Not today. This is a murder."

"And I can handle the investigation well enough on my own. Go on. Don't keep Isaac waiting."

There was no point arguing. Ruth mounted her bike and cycled north.

Every day for the last week she'd gone to the woods west of Christchurch to be taught how to shoot. Mitchell hadn't needed to explain why it was necessary. She'd been standing twenty feet away from Emmitt when she'd shot at him. She'd aimed at his chest, but only hit his arm. He'd escaped. That she'd probably broken his arm was little consolation.

Mitchell had asked Isaac to train her. The strange, secretive man had been there in the woods every day, but it was Kelly who was conducting the lessons. She was a willowy, patient woman who never failed to miss a target. Always hulking in the background was Gregory, a sullen, mountainous man with arms as thick as Ruth's waist. Isaac usually perched on a tree-stump, offering a sardonic commentary.

Isaac, Kelly, Gregory. None of them had surnames, at least as far as Ruth knew. In fact, she knew very little about them at all. Why did they all wear clothing of that same shade of dirty grey? Where did they get the spare ammunition? Where did they go when they weren't loitering around the woodland clearing? She'd tried asking, subtly at first, and then outright. Even so, she'd learned little beyond that Isaac was a strange man, probably in his forties, and that those who followed him did so with an almost absolute devotion.

Most of what she knew about the man came from Mitchell. During the Blackout, Isaac had received a message stating that there would be food on the British south coast. It was on the strength of that message that Isaac, Mitchell, and thousands of other survivors had left the ruins of London and headed south. They'd found the grain ships, and the cargo carriers and cruise ships. That was the seed that had grown into Twynham. As to who had sent Isaac the message, that remained a mystery.

Ruth reached a point where the old road met the new train line. A narrow track ran between the railroad and the regimented row of poles that carried the telegraph from Twynham down to the more rural areas in the southwest.

Frequent traffic had cut a muddy track through the fallen leaves. The railroad, and hence the path next to it, curved around the woodland's edge. Following it would mean a longer journey but an easier one than trying to drag the bicycle through the wild undergrowth. She steered onto the track next to the railroad, cycling as fast as she could without spraying mud and rotting leaves over her uniform.

If she had one word to sum up her brief time as a police officer, it would be 'questions'. There always seemed to be far more of them than there were answers. As much as she was curious about Isaac and the Blackout, if there was one thing she wanted answered above all else, it was to do with her own past.

After Wallace had died, she'd searched his study. At the back of a drawer in his desk she'd found a coin. On it was a stylised backward 'L', surrounded by an inscription that read THE TRUTH LIES IN THE PAST, with each word separated by five stars. When Maggie had found her in the refugee camp, the only word Ruth had known was 'five'. Her only possession was a toy bear. Around its neck was a scorched ribbon, with one embroidered word still legible. RUTH. That had become her name, yet now she was almost certain that the word was TRUTH, and that the T, and the rest of the inscription, had been burned away. That meant that there was a connection between her and Wallace, or between him and her parents. As Wallace was dead, there was little chance she'd… she'd…

There was a small group on the railroad tracks around four hundred yards ahead of her. Two men and two women, wearing shapeless baggy trousers and ill-fitting tunics. She brought the bike to a halt, dismounted, and moved to the cover of a spreading pine. They could be workers going from one farm to another. Or hunters? No. One carried a ladder. Whoever they were, there was something *wrong* about them.

They'd stopped and were huddled in conference. The wind carried a few syllables toward Ruth, but not enough that she could make out the words. The group seemed to reach a decision. A man, dressed more shabbily than the rest, took the ladder and leaned it against a telegraph pole. That decided it. Whoever they were, they didn't work for the telegraph company.

Ruth walked toward them. Pushing her bicycle, she kept her pace slow and casual, acting as if there was nothing unusual about the tableaux. Hoping they would run and worrying what she'd do if they didn't, her hand dropped to her belt. She checked her truncheon, and then her revolver. Doubt flashed across her mind. Had she remembered to load it? There was no time to check.

She was a hundred yards from the group before one of the women spotted her, turned, and ran. The other woman quickly followed, as did the man holding the bottom of the ladder. Ruth mounted her bike and pedalled furiously toward them. The man halfway up the ladder did something strange. He didn't try to escape. He continued climbing. Reaching the top, he grabbed for the lowermost of the metal rungs embedded in the pole itself. He couldn't reach it.

Ruth sped up.

The man stretched. He jumped. He grabbed the metal rung with his right hand, but his feet knocked the ladder over. For a moment he hung there, one-handed, his left hand trying to find purchase on the smooth wooden pole. He fell, picked himself up, and finally began to run.

Ruth was fifty feet away. Forty. Thirty. The man wasn't moving very quickly. Had he twisted his ankle in the fall? Twenty. Ten. Five. Two. She let go of the handlebars, leaped from the bike, and knocked the man to the ground.

"Stop!" she hissed. "You're… under…" But the man was struggling too hard for her to waste breath on words. She pushed a knee into his back and twisted his arm around until he was pinned. "Stop!" she said again, struggling to get the handcuffs out. Even when cuffed, he kept squirming.

"Stop it! You're under arrest!" she screamed. The words sank in, and the man subsided.

"What were you trying to do?" Ruth asked, realising that she wasn't entirely sure what crime he'd committed.

"Righteous work," the man hissed.

"What does that mean?" she asked.

The man didn't reply. Ruth waited to see if he would try to run even with his hands behind his back. He didn't. She looked over at the fallen ladder. Next to it was a pair of very crude wooden-handled shears.

"Were you trying to cut the telegraph wires?" she asked.

"I was doing my duty," he replied, which was no more illuminating than his earlier comment.

The shears were an oddly crude tool, but looked newly made. That was as baffling as his answers since old-world wire-cutters were sold in every hardware shop. Then she saw fresh splinters on the telegraph pole where something had been carved into it. An 'N' and… she stepped around the pole so she could see the carving properly. Her heart froze.

The man, or one of his comrades, had carved a name onto the pole, 'Ned Ludd', except that the 'L' had been written backward, just like on the coin she'd found in Commissioner Wallace's drawer.

"Who's Ned Ludd?" she asked.

"I am," he replied.

"What were you doing?"

"The duty of the righteous," he replied.

Ruth gave up. There was no point trying to question him here. She looked toward the city. That was the direction the man's comrades had gone. If she tried to walk the man back to Twynham, and if those others had stopped, they might try to rescue him. She wasn't sure how that confrontation would end, but it was too much of a risk. Hoping to spot a plume of smoke from an approaching train, she looked behind. The skies were frustratingly clear. She couldn't wait. The other three might return. Then she remembered Isaac. The clearing wasn't far. Leaving her bike next to the ladder, she hauled the man to his feet, and saw the reason he'd been unable to run very fast. He wore backless, wooden clogs.

"Did you make those yourself?" Ruth asked as she pushed the man off the road, and into the forest.

"You should reject the old world, if you want to bring about a truly new one," he replied.

"What does that mean?" she asked.

"Understanding only comes to those who—" the man's words were caught short as he stumbled on a rotting branch.

"Get up," Ruth said, grabbing his arm. The clothing was as roughly made as the clogs and just as impractical. It was too baggy to be warm and had a greasy feel that suggested it had never been washed. From his odour, she doubted the man had either. She stepped back, concern about fleas replacing that of the man being rescued by his comrades, but without her pushing, pulling, and occasionally prodding, he stopped moving.

"Come on," she said, grabbing the man's arm after he'd fallen for the tenth time. "Get—"

She heard a branch break somewhere to her left. She spun around, drawing her revolver. It was Kelly. In each of the woman's hands was one half of a broken stick.

"You make a lot of noise," Kelly said. "Who's he?"

"One of a group of four. I think they were attempting to cut the telegraph," Ruth said. "I wanted to borrow Gregory's cart to take him back to Twynham."

"Then you're going the wrong way," Kelly said, gesturing over her shoulder. Ruth, occasionally prodding the still-stumbling prisoner, followed her.

"Ah, Ruth! And you've brought a friend," Isaac said with his usual bombastic effusiveness.

"I think he was trying to cut the telegraph wires," Ruth said. "And he carved something into the pole. A name."

"My name," the man said. "I am Ned Ludd."

"Then either someone has invented time travel, or you're delusional," Isaac said. "Where did you find him?"

"About two miles that way," Ruth said gesturing over her shoulder.

"It's more like a mile and a half over there," Kelly said, pointing about thirty degrees to the east of where Ruth had indicated.

"There were three more of them," Ruth said. "They ran along the railroad in the direction of Twynham. I need to take this man back to Police House, and then I'll come back to search for them."

"Gregory? Please give Ruth a ride. As to the others, Kelly and I will find them."

"This is a police matter," Ruth said.

"Of course it is," Isaac said.

"I mean that looking for them is something the police should do."

"But you'll be busy taking the suspect into custody," Isaac said with exaggerated patience. "And though we are mere civilians, do we not have a civic responsibility to maintain law and order?"

She could tell him not to, Ruth thought, but he would still go looking for them.

"You aren't to hurt them," Ruth said.

"And when have you ever seen me hurt anyone?" Isaac replied.

That wasn't much of an answer to anything, but Ruth let it go. She pushed the prisoner into the back of the carriage, and climbed up onto the cab.

Ned Ludd, written with a backward 'L'? There was no way it was a coincidence. As Gregory drove the carriage toward the city, she tried to decipher what it meant.

Chapter 1
Ned Ludd

"Sir, we need to talk," Ruth said.

"It's never good when a woman says those particular words to a man," Mitchell said. He was at his desk in the cabin in the yard of Police House, peering at an old-world map covered in pencil and ink annotations. He looked up and saw her face. "It's serious? It'll have to wait. Five telegraph lines into the city have been cut. No telegrams are getting in or out of Twynham."

"None? This is connected," Ruth said. "On the way to meet Isaac I came across a group of four people. They had a ladder. When they saw me, three ran, the fourth tried to climb the telegraph pole. I caught him."

"You did? Well done. Where is he?"

"Being processed. But that's not all. On the telegraph pole they'd carved a name, Ned Ludd, except the 'L' was written backward. Let me show you." She picked up a pen and drew a sketch of the carving.

Mitchell reached into a drawer on his desk and pulled out a small silver coin. He placed it next to the sketch.

"Where did you get that?" Ruth whispered.

"You remember the American ambassador's assistant, Lucas Fairmont?"

"You apprehended him on the beach," Ruth said. "He was selling information on the owners of oilfields in the U.S. That half-eared man, Jameson, was with him. The one who was Emmitt's lookout during the assassination attempt."

"Right, and there was a third man. Donal, the one I shot," Mitchell said. "This coin was in his pocket. What is it? You look like you've seen a ghost."

"Not a ghost," Ruth said. "But I've seen that coin before. Wallace had one."

"He did?" Now it was Mitchell's turn to sound surprised.

"With the same inscription," Ruth said. "I found it just before you… well, before you passed out. I… I sort of kept it."

"Why didn't you hand it in?" Mitchell asked.

"I was going to," she said. "It's…"

"Tell me."

"It's hard to… okay. When Maggie found me the only word of English I knew was 'five', and you see how there are five stars between each word of the inscription?" As she said the words aloud she realised how flimsy a connection that was. "And," she hurriedly continued, "I had a bear. A toy one, you know? Around its neck was a ribbon. Most of it was burned, except for the letters R, U, T, H. That's how I got my name, except I think it was the beginning of that inscription."

"On a ribbon around the neck of a toy bear?"

"I know it doesn't sound like much," Ruth said. "It's… I…" She trailed into silence.

"That coin has to be entered into evidence," Mitchell said. "Bring it to me and I'll deal with it. As to any personal connection between it and you, we'll discuss that some other time."

"Yes, sir. Sorry," Ruth said.

"But you arrested a saboteur. That *is* a good day's work. There are two coins? Interesting. It suggests there is a good deal of organisation behind these crimes. Unfortunately, it also suggests there are more conspirators than we first thought. No one would go to the trouble of only making two, and no other suspects had one on their person. But the coin will have to wait. The telegraph is critical. Tell me about this suspect. Did he say anything?"

"That he was doing the work of the righteous," Ruth said. "When I asked what that meant he sort of repeated himself, using different words to give the same non-answer. He said that Ned Ludd was his name. When I told Isaac, he seemed to think the suspect was lying."

"Because Ned Ludd is a folk hero who probably never existed. The name was used as a figurehead during the early years of the industrial revolution. His followers, or the people who used his name, wrecked the machines and mills that were putting them out of work. In the years since,

Ludd's been used as a symbol whenever some new technology comes along that threatens to destroy a previously secure sector of employment. I suppose it should be no surprise that someone is using it today."

"A rejection of technology? That explains his clothes," Ruth said. "He's wearing hand made clogs, and a rough-cut tunic. The wire cutters he was using looked like he'd made them himself. They weren't old-world make."

"Even more interesting. Any ideas what the connection is between him and the coins?"

"No, sir,"

"Then let's go and ask him."

"Where's Ned Ludd?" Mitchell asked the duty sergeant.

"Interview three," the sergeant replied. He handed Mitchell the file.

"Ned Ludd, five-foot ten. You've got his fingerprints, but no age or address," Mitchell said.

"He declined to give them," the sergeant said with a tone suggesting that was both commonplace and not his problem.

"Take this to Assistant Commissioner Weaver," Mitchell said, scrawling out a note and handing it to the sergeant. Mitchell and Ruth headed through the doors that led to the interview rooms.

Mitchell peered through the small, reinforced glass window, then stepped back to let Ruth see. The suspect sat, eyes closed, with a slight smile on his lips, and his hands together.

"It's almost as if he was praying," Ruth said.

"Interesting, indeed," Mitchell said, and opened the door. The suspect didn't open his eyes, not even after Mitchell sat down opposite him. Ruth stood by the door.

"Nice clothes," Mitchell said. "Did you make them yourself?"

The trousers were little more than two shapeless tubes of cloth stitched together at the waist. The tunic was too long, but the arms were an inch too short. Both garments looked as if they were woven from undyed wool. There were no buttons or zips, just a wooden toggle around the man's neck.

"And wooden clogs," Mitchell continued, seemingly oblivious to the man's silence. "Can't you afford shoes?"

The man's lips twitched, but his smirk quickly returned.

"I think the ensemble would be improved by a button or two," Mitchell said.

The man sneered.

"I see. My name is Captain Mitchell. You've already met Officer Deering. What's your name?"

There was another long pause, and Ruth thought the man would stay silent, but finally he said, "Ned Ludd."

"No, it's not. If he ever existed, Ned Ludd is long dead. What's your real name, the one your family will use when they come here to report you've gone missing?"

"My family knows where I am."

"Then it can't hurt to tell us your name."

He gave a dry, mocking chuckle. "Without my name, you can't find me," he said.

"Find you? You're here," Mitchell said. "We've arrested you."

"You know what I mean."

"I really don't," Mitchell said. "Explain it."

The prisoner threw a look up at the light bulb overhead and shook his head.

"Fine, we'll call you Ned Ludd for now," Mitchell said. "Let's talk about the telegraph. Why were you trying to cut it?"

"Because technology leads us back to destruction," Ludd said. "We have to move forward. Progress means rejecting the old ways and embracing the new."

"By the old ways, do you mean things like buttons and denim?" Mitchell asked.

"Whether you believe it or not doesn't change the truth," the man said. "The telegraph has brought back the radio. Computers won't be far behind. The AIs will be reawakened, and this time they will complete their destruction of the planet. I was doing my rightful duty."

Mitchell glanced at Ruth. She took that as her invitation. "You said we have to reject the old ways. What are the new ones?"

"The ancient path," Ludd said. "We have to... to temper our modern experiences with old wisdom. Thus do we reject darkness and evil."

"So this *is* a religion?" Mitchell asked.

"Religion?" Ludd almost spat the word. "That's just another tool of the machine!" His voice rose to a shrieking crescendo. "Another way of forcing compliance from the masses. You reward them with trinkets and threaten them with damnation. So is *your* will done!"

"It sounds like a religion," Mitchell replied calmly. "And how does cutting the telegraph help in your cause? It wouldn't have taken us more than an hour to fix."

Ludd's brow furrowed. He looked from Mitchell to Ruth. The smile returned as he shook his head. "Another lie from agents of the machine. It will take longer than that. And the next time? And the third? We are legion. Imprison me. Kill me. A hundred more are ready to take my place. You won't listen to reason, and so we will act. We will change your behaviour until..." He paused, as if trying to remember something. "Until you change it yourselves," he finished with far less enthusiasm than he'd begun the sentence.

"I see," Mitchell said. "Let's talk about Ned Ludd."

"He is everywhere."

"So he's not you?" Ruth asked.

"I am he, and he..." And again the man stalled. "He is legion," he finished.

"Why did you carve that name into the pole?" Mitchell asked.

"So that you shall know us by our deeds," the man replied. "And by our deeds shall you know the truth. The name of the oppressor..." Another pause. "The name of the oppressor changes, but the name of our cause... it... it remains the same." He smiled again as if he was happy with what was clearly extemporisation.

"Do you know that you misspelled it?" Ruth asked.

"What?" the man asked, his smug mask cracking.

"Ned Ludd. You spelled it wrong," Ruth said. "It's understandable. A lot of people don't know how to write. I suppose you were trying to copy the letters as best you remembered them."

"I *can* write," the man protested.

"It's nothing to be embarrassed about," Ruth said, keeping her tone patronising and patient. "Here, let me show you." She took out her notepad and wrote Ned Ludd. "You see. That's how you write a capital 'L'. You had it facing the wrong way."

The man laughed. "That's how we write it. To show that though the enemy evolves, only revolution can bring about true evolution."

"And who taught you that?" Mitchell asked.

"Ned Ludd," the man replied.

"And where can we find him?"

"He sits before you."

"I see," Mitchell said. "What about the others who call themselves Ned Ludd?"

"They shall find you. Oh yes. The fifth is coming. Remember it."

"The fifth man?" Ruth asked.

The man gave a hollow laugh. "Remember," he said.

"Remember the fifth?" Mitchell asked. "Remember, remember?"

The smile vanished. Ludd twitched in his seat.

"Tell us about the man who told you about Ned Ludd?" Mitchell asked.

"You shall know soon enough. The fifth. Remember!"

Mitchell sighed. "We'll get you a blanket. You're going to be here for some time."

It took Ruth an hour, and some dictated suggestions from Riley, before she finished her report on the arrest of Ned Ludd. Mitchell took it to Weaver's office, but before Ruth had time to relax, a runner arrived, summoning her, Riley, and Longfield.

Weaver had taken over Commissioner Wallace's old office. The name 'Wallace' had been removed from the sign by the door, but Weaver's name had yet to be added. Nor had anyone added the word 'Assistant' above the title. Inside, the shelves were empty and the paintings were gone from the walls. Even the old leather and wood furniture had been removed, replaced with utilitarian metal cabinets, a small desk, and equally impermanent folding chairs.

"There are three telegraph lines into the city," Weaver said. "One from Wales, Scotland, and the north, another from Kent and the east, a third from Devon and the farms to the west and northwest. Each was cut. Those in the north and east were cut in two places. The western line was severed in only one location. We lost communication with the rest of the country for two hours. Had that sixth line been cut, it would have been longer. The damage however, has been the same. Only priority messages are being allowed on the line, confirming that all settlements, towns, and depots are secure. Normal service won't resume until tomorrow. However, as yet I can see no purpose to this sabotage."

"There have been no attacks?" Mitchell asked.

"None," Weaver said. "An unidentified vessel was spotted off the southern Kent coast, near the ruins of Folkestone, but there were two sightings yesterday so I'm not concerned."

"The suspect mentioned this time, the next time, and the third time," Mitchell said. "Not the time after that, but 'the third'. There'll be another two similar incidents.

"And then there was that thing about the fifth," Ruth said. "A fifth saboteur, maybe? I counted four of them by the telegraph."

"No," Mitchell said. "He said 'remember the fifth' and there was a definite reaction from him when I said 'remember, remember'. I think it's the date we can expect that third attack."

"The fifth of October?" Ruth asked. "That's four days from now."

Weaver sighed. "Remember, remember, the fifth of November, gunpowder treason, and plot," she recited. "Haven't you heard the rhyme? On the fifth of November in 1605 a group of conspirators planned to blow up Parliament. They hoped to kill the protestant King James and install a Catholic monarchy. Do you think there's a religious component to this?"

"I'd need to speak to him again to be sure," Mitchell said, "but I don't think so. His speech is littered with slogans from dozens of competing ideologies. I'd say the words were chosen more for their poetry than for any deeper significance."

"I see." Weaver picked up a sheet of paper. "From Deering's somewhat brief report, we can assume they were all unarmed. If there were four at each location, then we're looking for twenty-four of them. You say this carving connects it to the assassination and the counterfeiting?"

"By the backward 'L'," Mitchell said. "That connects it to Donal, and to Wallace."

"Who's Donal?" Longfield asked.

Weaver frowned. "You are a cadet, Longfield, in the presence of senior officers. Remember it."

Simon blushed.

"Lucas Fairmont," Mitchell said, "was the assistant to the American ambassador. He was selling information to the two men, Donal and Jameson, on a beach near the rusting hulks. I arrested Fairmont and shot Donal. Jameson escaped, but Deering apprehended him after the assassination. Fairmont gave us the two men's names."

"Donal and Jameson. They sound Irish," Weaver said.

"Jameson isn't," Mitchell said. "Not according to the brief conversations I've had with him. Conversations might be a bit too strong. He does nothing but smirk and sneer. We've learned nothing useful from him. What about Fairmont?"

"He is in custody at the embassy so, technically, he's in American jurisdiction. According to…" Weaver picked up a different piece of paper. "Agent Clarke says he has provided information on three different locations where he traded information with those two men. The S.I.S. conducted the search, and none yielded any clues."

"Can we speak to Fairmont?" Mitchell asked.

"I'm due to meet with Ambassador Perez this evening," Weaver said. "I'll ask. But for the moment, Donal and Jameson are both dead leads. Donal, quite literally." She leafed through the other sheets of paper in the folder. "Emmitt's rifle can't be traced. The ink used to print those counterfeit notes could have been stolen by almost anyone in the Mint. The properties they've used were either unclaimed derelicts, abandoned, or vacant. Which brings us back to Ned Ludd. Unlike Jameson, the man is talking. Three attacks, you say, with the third on the fifth of November? We'll increase the guard on Parliament."

"And what if they chose a new target?" Mitchell asked.

"Indeed," Weaver said. "And that is why we are here, isn't it? So how will you proceed?"

"I've sent a message to Rebecca Cavendish of the Railway Company," Mitchell said. "She'll pass the word to all the train stations. Ned Ludd's clothing is highly distinctive. Assuming his colleagues were similarly dressed, they'll be easy to spot. If they used the trains to get to the sites where they cut the wires, we'll know."

"As he professes a hatred of technology," Weaver said, "I doubt they would have used the railways."

"Probably not," Mitchell agreed. "It's worth checking. And that clothing is interesting. It would have taken longer than a week to make. So this group existed before the assassination."

"Or their clothing has," Riley said.

"Quite," Mitchell said. "We'll start looking for Luddites tomorrow, when the rest of the unit's new members arrive."

"Where?" Weaver asked.

"The university, the docks, the power plant," Mitchell said. "Anywhere the adoption of new technologies might imperil employment."

"Then the farms and mines would be the most logical breeding ground for recruitment," Weaver said.

"There's not many coal mines in Twynham," Mitchell said. "Of course, there's another possibility. Though Ned Ludd may think sabotaging the telegraph was part of a grand scheme to halt technological progress doesn't mean he's right. Emmitt might have intended it for some other purpose. Stopping a message getting through, perhaps?"

"Indeed," Weaver said. "I already have officers going through the telegraph messages that were sent before the wire was cut, and those messages that were delayed. If any are suspicious, I should know by tomorrow. Whether they are or not, until these saboteurs are caught, this matter is not at an end. Dismissed."

"Weaver's odd," Simon said.

"So's Mitchell," Ruth replied. "And Riley. I don't think normal people join the police."

"And what does that say about us?" Simon said. "But it's nice being out in the fresh air."

There was a chill wind coming in off the sea, bringing a salty mist with it.

"Personally, I'd rather be in the warm," Ruth said. "It's going to be at least another hour before we get back into shelter." And another two hours and a three-mile cycle ride before she was home and warm.

"Trust me, this is much better than sitting behind a desk all day," Simon said.

He and Ruth were on their way back to where she'd arrested Ned Ludd. According to Mitchell, this was so Simon could see the crime scene first-hand, and so Ruth could confirm that the S.I.S. officer processing the scene had collected all the evidence.

"A ladder, and the wire cutters," she said. "It's not like anyone could miss them."

"What's that?" Simon asked.

"Oh, nothing. I think Captain Mitchell wanted to get us out of the way. But he could have loaned me his bike." Hers was still by the telegraph pole, and that was the reason she had to walk. Her collar already felt damp as she pulled it up, higher around her neck.

"I was wondering..." Simon began after a few minutes of silence.

"Yes?"

"Well, there doesn't seem to be a rota. I mean, I expect that they'll put one together when the rest of the new officers arrive tomorrow," Simon babbled. "But I was thinking, well, I was wondering, um..."

"What?"

"Well, which days do you get off?"

"Me?" Ruth smiled. "I've not had a day off yet, not really. Weekends, weekdays, it's all the same. I think we're expected to work the case, and if there isn't anything to do, we're supposed to sneak away before anyone notices we're not busy."

"Oh." Simon sounded genuinely downhearted.

"I tell you what *is* nice," Ruth said before Simon could say anything else. "Having you in Serious Crimes, and being used as a proper police unit."

"Because it wasn't a real unit, was it?" Simon said. "Tell me again about Commissioner Wallace. Captain Mitchell shot him, didn't he?"

Ruth sighed and began the story she'd told many times before.

Before joining the academy, Ruth had looked forward to the short winter evenings. They'd meant an early dinner and an excuse to curl up with a book in front of the fire. Tonight, it meant a three-mile cycle ride across damp potholed streets back to The Acre.

After re-inspecting the crime scene – which had barely taken more than a minute – they'd caught a train back into Twynham. Simon had headed north, to Longfield Castle, a rambling mansion his family owned to the south of the old village of Burton. Ruth doubted that the roads he'd use on his journey home would be in such poor repair as the ones beneath her wheels. The potholes filled with mud weren't too troublesome. The bicycle's thick tyres could find some purchase, though the wheels sprayed dirt all over her legs. Those filled with nothing but rainwater hidden underneath a coating of leaves were far worse. She was almost jolted from the bike a dozen times before she reached her home.

"The roads are getting worse," Ruth said as she closed the door behind her.

"And a good evening to you," Maggie replied. "Bad day?"

"A busy day made worse by having to walk the last mile. It's not safe cycling in the dark."

"Enjoy it now," Maggie said. "It'll get worse when the snow comes."

"I should complain," Ruth said, pulling her boots off.

"Indeed you should, and not to me. Write to our MP."

"Yeah. Maybe I will," Ruth said, already composing that letter in her mind. "Who is that?"

"Tchh!" Maggie scolded. "Rupert Pine. Now, wash your hands, pick up the masher, and then take your anger out on the potatoes."

"Is there hot water?" Ruth asked, hopefully.

"There was," Maggie said, "and there will be again, just as soon as you fill the kettle and set it to boil."

Ruth sighed, picked up the kettle, put her boots back on, and went outside to the tap.

The Acre had no electricity, but they had mains water thanks to a standpipe in the front garden. If they wanted hot water, it had to be boiled on the stove. To have a hot shower, the water had to be carried up to the bathroom and decanted into a waxed canvas sack attached to an old-world showerhead. Once the spigot was turned it took one hundred and ninety-six seconds for the sack to empty. After being caught waterless and covered in soap too often to count, she'd learned to time it exactly.

She stuck the kettle under the standpipe and turned the tap. The Acre had been a refugee camp. Over the years, the number of migrants reaching Britain had fallen. Most new arrivals now found a home with the fishing crews who'd rescued them, or in the farms where they came ashore. As a result the population in The Acre had dwindled. The camp had been closed, and then re-opened on the other side of the main-road, though it was now called the Milford Immigration Centre.

Maggie ran a schoolhouse in the downstairs rooms of their tumbledown house. She was paid by the government, though never enough, and they now had to pay rent. The Acre had been given to Mr Foster as compensation for a plot of land of similar size on which the main railway station had been built. Foster had installed the water pipe. It was an improvement on having to walk down to the pump, and that had been a revelation compared with collecting water from the river. However, by providing running water, Foster was able to double the rent he could charge.

"It's freezing out there," Ruth said when she got back inside.

"That's the young for you, complaining about getting some fresh air," Maggie said. "I've barely had ten minutes of it today."

"Yours was a bad day?" Ruth asked.

"No worse than most," Maggie said. "We had two new students today. Ahmed and Nesirine. He's fourteen, and she's nine. I think they're from Algeria, but it's hard to be sure. They've only a few words of English, and only a few more of French, which is still about twice as many as I know of Arabic. If I understood them, they came across land, through Egypt and up through Turkey. They were adamant they passed the pyramids. Or," she added, as she lifted a saucepan from the stove, "perhaps they were trying to say that they knew what a pyramid was. But they arrived through the Channel Tunnel three days ago with a trade caravan. Or I think it was a trade caravan. Perhaps it wasn't." She sighed. "It was a long and trying day."

"No one learned anything?"

"Not really. Each day I feel like I'm less of a teacher and more of a babysitter. The two children have gone to the shelter for the night. They'll be in the classroom tomorrow, but within the week they'll have been found a home somewhere else."

"Then maybe *you* should write a letter to complain," Ruth said.

"I already did," Maggie said. "Weeks ago. I finally got a reply. It's in the envelope on the dresser. You read it while I dish up."

It was from the Department of Housing and Employment under whose jurisdiction the immigration centre fell. Ruth skimmed through it.

"They're shutting the school," she said. "That's terrible."

"It's wonderful news, and it's long overdue," Maggie said. "Processing centres made sense when we had thousands of people arriving each week. It was the only way of preventing disease from spreading throughout the country. Now, calling them counterproductive is being polite. Shipping those kids here only so they can be moved on again in a week? Utter madness, and thoroughly disruptive to the children already here."

"You're not angry?" Ruth asked.

"Not a bit of it. Of course, it doesn't say what the new plans are, and they may well be worse, but that's not our problem."

"No. No, I suppose not," Ruth said. "Does that mean we'll lose the house?"

"I doubt it, but the rent has to paid. Of course, there's little reason for us to stay. Your work is in the city, and as for me, well… I don't know. There's the silver lining. You wanted to leave, and now we can find somewhere in town."

"It's… I… well, I suppose I did want to leave, but I didn't want to know that I'd never be able to come back."

Maggie smiled. "Despite what people may tell you, you can always go back. Now, eat up and tell me about your day."

As they ate a meal that came mostly from their own garden, Ruth did.

"And he calls himself Ned Ludd?" Maggie asked. "I suppose that was a natural name for someone to use if they were against technology. Are you sure it's connected with Emmitt and the counterfeiting?"

"I do. There's something else. Something I wanted to ask. It's about when you found me in that camp, when you rescued me."

"Yes?"

"Did you look for my parents?"

"Of course I did," Maggie said.

"And there was no sign of them?"

"No. Why do you ask?"

"Commissioner Wallace had a coin. On it was a symbol, a backward 'L'. And there was an inscription, the truth lies in the past. I think that was the same message that was on the ribbon around the neck of the bear you found me with, except that all the letters except R U T H had been burned out."

Maggie closed her eyes. "I was in the camp," she said, "working with the team who brought the antibiotics. When I found you… well, I heard you first. You were sobbing. I followed the sound to a hospital tent. There were ten stretchers, and on each was a corpse. Everyone was dead. Any of them could have been your mother or father. No one stepped forward to look after you, and it wasn't like it is now. Back then, if you found a child, you took them in. I told everyone I could about you and asked them to pass word to the other survivors. There weren't many of those, and none came forward to identify you. I suppose… I understand that this is important to you. Perhaps the camp's other survivors could be traced, but if no one has come looking for you after all this time, you should ask yourself whether you really want to know who they are."

Ruth realised how ungrateful her questioning must have seemed. "It's not for me," she said. "I mean, it's about the investigation, that's all."

"Of course, of course. Now, be a dear and take the scraps to the pig. I've got to plan a lesson tomorrow that somehow includes geography and maths for a class that speaks a dozen languages, none of which are English."

Ruth had wanted to ask another question, but wasn't sure she dared. She could tell that she'd upset her mother. She grabbed her boots.

"At least these are waterproof," she said, trying to change the topic. "You won't believe what Ned Ludd was…" She trailed into silence as she stared at her boots.

"Was what, dear?" Maggie asked.

"Three of them ran," Ruth said, "but Ned Ludd couldn't. He couldn't run!" She pulled on her other boot. "I have to go. I'll be back soon."

"Back from where? Where are you going?" Maggie asked, but Ruth was already out of the door.

The bike fell from under her twice, and she crashed into a hedge once, as she hurtled through the dark streets toward Twynham. When she reached Police House, her jacket was torn and her trousers were covered in mud. Mitchell had already left. Ruth knew he had rooms in a pub. She didn't know which one, but she'd been to Weaver's house before. A moment later, she was back on her bike, cycling along better-kept roads illuminated by the occasional electric lamp. Twenty minutes after leaving Police House, she was hammering on Weaver's door.

"What is it?" the assistant commissioner demanded, before she'd opened the door. "What—"

Ruth didn't give her a chance to finish the sentence. "The clogs," she said. "He couldn't run in them. He could barely walk."

"Who?" Weaver asked.

"But the others ran. They wore shoes. He didn't."

"Take a breath," Weaver said. "Calm down, and tell me—"

"Ned Ludd! He didn't come from very far away," Ruth interrupted. "It has to be close to where I arrested him. Two miles, or three, but not much further."

Weaver stared at her. "The clogs Ned Ludd wore means he couldn't run? Yes, I see. Yes." She nodded to herself. "Yes, I do. Be at Police House at dawn."

"At dawn?" Ruth asked. "Aren't we going to search for them now?"

"It's dark," Weaver said. "How would we find them? We'd need lights. They would see us coming and disappear. And for something like this, we need more than you and I. Go home. Get some rest. You'll need it."

And so, for the second time that day, Ruth went home.

Chapter 2
Fingerprints
2nd October

Ruth was up before dawn, and out of the house soon after. The night shift was still on duty when she arrived at Police House. Weaver's office was locked, as was the cabin in the yard. Ruth sat down on the steps to wait.

"Couldn't find your bed?" Mitchell asked.

Ruth opened her eyes and realised she'd fallen asleep.

"Sir. I think I know where the saboteurs came from. It's the shoes. The clogs! The suspect could barely walk in them, so he must have come from —"

"An abandoned cottage surrounded by woodland, two miles south, one mile to the west of where you arrested Ned Ludd. Kelly found them. She and Isaac went searching for them. They split up. After locating them, she went to find Isaac. He came to me, and by the time we got back to the cottage, it was empty."

"Oh." Ruth deflated. "They'd gone?"

"But left a lot behind," Mitchell said.

"Like what?"

"You'll see for yourself in an hour or so. The rest of the new members of the team should be here soon. Why don't you see if you can find some coffee?"

"Oh, no, I'm all right."

"I meant for me."

"It's getting crowded in here," Captain Mitchell said. Ruth gave a polite smile at what she hoped was a joke, but the captain wasn't wrong. Besides Mitchell, Riley, and herself, there was Simon, Constables Kingsley, Barton, Haney, and Kowalski, all of whom had been with the railway police. Then there was Sergeant Davis. His accent was Welsh, and he wore the most curious of uniforms. Rather than being made of blue waxed-wool, it was a figure-hugging black with almost as many pockets and pouches as there were patches and repairs.

"Welcome to Serious Crimes," Mitchell continued, "and that's as much of an introduction as we have time for. Yesterday morning, five telegraph wires leading into the city were cut. Cadet Deering stopped a sixth from being severed." He nodded in her direction. "She arrested a suspect, three others got away. During the day, we ascertained that these four came from a property nearby. We located it late yesterday evening. When I arrived it was empty of people, but full of placards with slogans of a technophobic persuasion. The suspect Deering arrested calls himself Ned Ludd. He also gives that name to every other member of his organisation. It's possible he's just doing that for his own amusement. However, for now we'll assume we're looking for a militant group of technophobes, probably calling themselves Luddites. Though no one was injured during yesterday's sabotage, we can link this group to the assassination attempt. You're all up to speed on that?" He looked around at the new faces.

"Sergeant Riley filled us in," Davis said.

"Good. We're assuming Emmitt orchestrated the sabotage. It was done for a reason, quite what that is, we don't know. From what he said, we suspect that this was the first of three similar incidents. The final one may take place on the fifth of November. It might not. Remember that Emmitt was conspiring with Commissioner Wallace. He almost killed our Prime Minister, and came close to flooding the market with enough fake currency to destroy the economy. Kingsley, Barton, Haney, you're assigned to Assistant Commissioner Weaver. You'll join the search for properties near the five telegraph wires that were cut. Davis, I want you to interview Ned Ludd. There's a cultish edge to his mode of speech. See if there's anything you recognise. Kowalski, your file says you went to the university."

"Not as a student," the man said indignantly. "I worked there!"

"And today you return. Take Longfield with you. Start with the library. Get the names of anyone who's taken out books on the industrial revolution, the real Ned Ludd, and the Luddites. I want a list of any classes that are taught where those are subjects. Are any of the students missing? Keep your eyes out for a backward 'L'." He pointed at the sketch Ruth had drawn of name 'Ned Ludd' which was now pinned to the board on the wall. "That seems to be their symbol. Riley, speak to Jameson."

"Again?" she asked. "He won't talk."

"No, probably not, but if anyone knows what Emmitt is planning, it will be him. Get to it. Deering, you're with me. Bring the crime-kit."

"Are we going to the cottage?" Ruth asked.

"First, we're going to the stables," Mitchell said. "The Luddites left a lot of evidence behind, and they might return to destroy it. I won't give them the chance."

Before the Blackout, the building Police House now occupied had been a school. The stables were in what had once been the swimming pool. A horse and cart was already waiting for them. Ruth stowed the crime-kit next to a neat stack of evidence bags.

"What did you find at the cottage?" she asked, as Mitchell drove the horses through the streets.

"Not much, and a lot. It was too dark to do a thorough search, and I was primarily looking for clues as to where they'd gone. I didn't find any. In short, it's a small cottage, with mattresses for six."

"Not four?"

"Precisely," he said. "So why did the other two not join in the sabotage? The biggest find were tunics and trousers. All of rough wool."

"Like Ned Ludd's?"

"Yes."

"So they left some spare clothes?" she asked.

By way of reply, Mitchell clicked his teeth at the horse.

"Or," Ruth added, "they changed out of the tunics and back into normal clothes."

"Which is what I'd do," Mitchell said. "In addition there were some tools, but no weapons. They did leave some placards, and the evidence to suggest they spent their time making them. The slogans all express an anti-technology sentiment, and a few have backward 'L's on them. If we didn't know to look for it, we'd probably assume it was a spelling mistake."

"Placards? So they were planning some kind of demonstration?"

"Probably. That's what you'd expect from a political group."

"But shouldn't they have had one already?" she asked. "I mean, they should have started with the demonstrations and graduated to sabotage, not the other way around. Or have there been demonstrations?"

"None big enough to catch my notice, so I would say no. That's proof that Emmitt is the one pulling their strings. Whatever he's planning, he hasn't wanted their existence to be known until now."

"Then the real question is why *he* would want the telegraph cut," Ruth said.

"Exactly." Mitchell pulled on the reins, bringing the horses to a stop at a busy junction.

"Maybe it was a distraction," Ruth said. "Like murdering Dr Gupta. It has no purpose except to prevent us from investigating anything truly important."

Mitchell flicked the reins. The horses walked on.

"Or," Ruth continued. "Is it a double bluff? Are we meant to think it's a distraction, but in reality it's something critical to his plans?"

"Ah, the game within a game," Mitchell said, giving the reins another flick. The horses began to canter. "And the game within that. I can see you are developing a healthy dose of paranoia. It usually takes a few years for a copper to acquire that. So, if it was a distraction, then what are they trying to distract us from?"

They travelled in silence for another mile. Mitchell had an easy hand on the reins. He had experience with horses, Ruth thought. She wondered if that had been learned since the Blackout, or if it came from before. She didn't know that much about him, but, she thought, the journey to a crime scene probably wasn't the place to ask.

"I like mysteries," Ruth finally said.

"You do?"

"I mean mystery books," she said. "Stories about robberies are my favourites. You know, jewel heists, bank robberies, those kind of things."

"Really? I like comic fantasy, myself," Mitchell said. "Something that takes me away from this time and place."

"Oh. Okay, um… the point I was making is that in those books there's always some big street party, or accident, or something that distracts the police while the criminals are digging the tunnel under the bank."

"And it can't be anything like that here. The bank's vault is above ground, and most of what it currently contains are those counterfeit notes that we seized."

"Right, so what's the use of some big distraction?"

"That," Mitchell said, "is what I was asking you."

Thoughtful silence descended again, but didn't linger for long.

"What if they come back to destroy the evidence?" Ruth asked. "If they were going to do it, it would be now, first thing this morning."

"I left a guard there."

"You did?"

"Isaac."

It wasn't only Isaac. Gregory was standing close by.

"Ruth, how are you!" Isaac said, as effusively as ever. Gregory moved his head a fraction of an inch in what might have been a nod of greeting.

"Is it just the two of you?" Ruth asked.

"Kelly is around, somewhere," Isaac said. "You can tell by the fact you can't see her. This cottage is as secure as anywhere can be in these troubled times."

"No one's turned up, then?" Mitchell asked.

"People? No. Not within two miles. There have been five robins and a… what's the collective noun for a group of starlings?"

"A flock," Mitchell said.

"No, no, there's a specific word for them," Isaac said.

"So no one's come," Mitchell said. "Have you been inside?"

"No one has tampered with your evidence," Isaac said.

"You mean you did go inside," Mitchell said.

"Briefly," Isaac said. "During the dark watches of the night, when the beasts of the forest—"

"Keep watch while we look around," Mitchell cut in. "Warn us if anyone approaches."

"With gunfire, if nothing else," Isaac said.

Ruth couldn't tell if he was being serious. Certainly, he seemed to be enjoying himself.

"If no one has come back, then that means there's probably nothing of worth inside," she said, as she followed Mitchell through the broken wooden gate and up the cracked-paving path.

"Don't assume that," Mitchell said. "Perhaps Ludd's arrest has yet to reach Emmitt's ears. If I were a saboteur, I'd baulk before taking him that news. Even if Emmitt does know, and knows there's nothing here that will lead us to him, we can learn something about the groups that cut the other wires. Do you see the weeds? Someone attempted to create a garden but gave up five or six years ago. It's the same with the house." He walked off the path and rapped the wooden board covering the window. It gave a flat thud. "Rotten, and the gutters haven't been touched in months. What does that tell us?"

"That Ned Ludd wasn't here long?"

"Probably for no longer than a few nights," Mitchell said. "So where did he live last week?"

"It's a shame, really," Ruth said. "It's a nice spot for a cottage. I wonder why no one lives here."

"There's no well," Mitchell said. "And it's too far from the nearest stream. Go inside. Take a look around. Start upstairs and work your way down. I want to have a word with Isaac. Oh, and Deering?"

"Yes, sir?"

"Don't forget your gloves."

Upstairs had a small bathroom and three bedrooms that weren't much larger. One had a rusting metal bedstead that looked far less comfortable than the mattresses on the floors of the other rooms.

"Five mattresses, one bed. I wouldn't sleep in it," Ruth murmured. The thin sheet covering it suggested someone had. "But it doesn't mean six people were here yesterday."

There was a single wardrobe out on the landing, but its only contents were a few rotten strands of black cloth hanging from a brittle plastic hanger. The rough woollen tunics and trousers were discarded in a pile on the floor of one bedroom. Gingerly, she separated the garments. There were five sets.

"Five sets. So there were six of them. The three who ran came back here, changed, and left. They took their things away with them." As she said the words she knew she was missing something. "Ned Ludd. Where are his clothes?"

She checked under the bed and lifted the mattresses. There were no sign of them. "They took them away. Or…" Maybe they hadn't. They'd been able to run because they were wearing shoes. Presumably the same shoes they'd worn after they'd discarded the wool tunics. Whether those were old-world trainers, or newly made leather boots, they wouldn't be noticeable on the feet of someone walking down the high street in Twynham. Perhaps Ned Ludd wore clogs because they were his *only* pair of shoes, and the tunic and trousers were his *only* set of clothes. In which case, there was no sixth set of clothes to be taken away.

"It's a theory," she said, and looked around for the evidence to prove it. She went into the bathroom long enough to take in the cracked ceramic, the mould in the sink and the… she wasn't sure what was in the bath except that it was a silvery green, and at least an inch deep. She backed out onto the landing.

She went downstairs, ignored the two front rooms, and headed for the small kitchen. It was as sparsely furnished as the rest of the house. There was a cracked pine table, and a small cupboard attached to the wall. From the discolouration of the plaster she guessed there had once been more cupboards.

"Probably used as kindling for the open fire." The ashes had been raked, and a metal saucepan sat in the corner. It was empty, but clean.

In the one remaining cupboard was a mismatched collected of mugs and plates. She picked one up. It looked clean. On the top shelf was a half-filled kilo sack of coarse oats.

"What do you think?" Mitchell called, coming through the door.

"Firstly, that one bed and five mattresses doesn't mean that six people were here. The five sets of clothing might, but I can't find any other proof."

"There're six sets of footprints near the back door, all leading off into the trees," Mitchell said. "If you've seen the bathroom, I think you can guess why. As for confirmation, Kelly got close enough to count them before she went looking for Isaac."

"Oh. I see. Well, these footprints, does one set match Ludd's clogs?"

"I'd say so," Mitchell said.

"Then Ned Ludd's wearing his normal clothes," Ruth said, relieved she'd deduced something correctly.

"Yeah. You remember what he said about buttons and zips? That man is a true believer. What else?"

"They took away anything they thought would identify them. Either that or they didn't bring anything with them. No books, no entertainment. But assuming they left on foot, they can't have carried much, so that confirms they weren't here for very long."

"Have you seen the front room?" Mitchell asked.

It wasn't a large space, but it was full of wood. The floor was carpeted with sawdust. Thin, uncut sections of planking leaned against the boarded-up window. Against the far wall was a haphazard stack of placards. Some had slogans painted on them, others hadn't.

Mitchell picked up a sign. "Radio means AIs," he read aloud. "So I guess they don't approve of the transatlantic broadcast. Imagine a dozen of them holding these signs, with someone like Ned Ludd yelling out slogans." He picked up another sign. "Technology equals death." He let it fall to the ground. "Well, at least it's succinct." He gave her a look she was growing to know well. It was his way of prompting her that she'd failed to notice the obvious.

"There's too many placards?" she guessed, saying the first thing that came to mind.

"Close. You said these people left, taking anything that might identify them. I agree with you. But how did this wood and those mattresses get here? There's no sign of a horse being grazed outside. There are a few rutted wheel marks though they begin about fifty yards from the house. Someone dropped them off, with the mattresses, the wood, and the food."

"There are too many signs to carry, so they wouldn't have made them if they were planning on leaving here on foot," Ruth said.

"Right. So who was driving the cart? It's something to think about while you make a start on the placards. Write down the slogans, add a tag to each, and take them outside. I'll deal with the tools."

Ruth hadn't noticed those. There were two saws, four hammers, and a pair of very crude looking shears, similar to the kind with which Ned Ludd had wanted to cut the telegraph wire.

"The placards," Mitchell prompted.

Ruth took out her notepad. "Technology is Death," she read aloud as she wrote it down. "Progress means Poverty," she read on the next one. An idea struck her, and she quickly went through the signs. "It's not here," she said.

"What isn't?"

"The truth lies in the past."

"I don't suppose they've been so kind as to leave a map stating where they've gone, or a signed confession stating what their next target will be, either. Write down the slogans and take the placards out to the cart. I'd like to be done before lunchtime."

"At least we know none of them were carpenters," Ruth said, coming back inside after taking the last of the placards outside. "None of those nails were straight. They weren't tailors, either. That's obvious from the tunics."

"Which eliminates about twenty thousand people from our inquiries," Mitchell said. "Metal nails, metal saucepans, metal tools – they reject some trappings of technology, but not all of them. Except for Ned Ludd. Interesting, indeed. I'll take the cart back to Police House. You can start gathering evidence."

"Start? Haven't we finished?"

Mitchell grinned. "We haven't even begun. Start with the sawdust. Sweep it up, and as much of as it you can."

"Why?"

"Because there seems like a lot more of it than has come from the placards that are here. We'll get someone to make a few, and we'll weigh the sawdust and compare it to the amount you collect. That will confirm how many were made. From that we'll know whether someone came here to collect the ones that were finished. After that, check under the mattresses, behind the sinks, the backs of the cupboards. Look for scraps of paper, wrappers, anything else. Then start on the exterior. Look for soil that's been recently disturbed – oh, but do remember that there doesn't appear to be an outhouse."

"I have to do all of that?"

"I'll send someone to help."

Sweeping the sawdust into a pile didn't take long. Gathering it all into evidence bags did. Ruth tried to get Isaac to help.

"Wouldn't that be interfering with a crime scene?" he asked. "I wouldn't want to break the law."

When she'd finally finished, she began a slow, methodical search of the cottage. There were two jars of cheap paint, both of the blue-black colour used on doors and windowsills by people who couldn't afford any better – which was most of the population. It was in a glass jar rather than a recycled can, but it had to have come from the chemical works on the River Stour. Would Ned Ludd have known that?

She was steeling herself to attempt a search of the vile bathroom when there was a shout of greeting from outside. She didn't recognise the voice, but from the Welsh lilt, she guessed it was Sergeant Davis. Grateful for the excuse, she went downstairs, and outside. Davis had brought the horse and now-empty cart with him.

"Are you here alone?" he asked. "Captain Mitchell said he'd left some hunters here, guarding the place."

"Hunters? Oh, yes." Ruth looked around. There was no sign of Isaac or the far more easy to spot Gregory. "They must have left. I've bagged up the sawdust and was about to start searching the bathroom."

"Good," Davis said. "I'm to instruct you on processing a crime scene. We'll start with fingerprints. Bathrooms are good, since everyone needs to wash."

"Not in this bathroom they didn't," Ruth said. "It's pretty grim. I don't think they washed while they were here."

"After seeing the state of your man in the cells, that doesn't come as a surprise. We'll try the kitchen. People gravitate toward food, and criminals are no different from anyone else in that regard."

"You interviewed Ned Ludd?" Ruth asked.

"I did," Davis said. "Or I asked questions, and he responded with words. Calling them answers would be a stretch."

"Oh. So you didn't learn anything?"

"Do you know the lawyer trick?"

"No."

"It is a wonderful little loophole in our new legal system. Everyone is entitled to a lawyer," Davis said. "A lawyer asks for a name and an address. That goes into the court docket to which we have access. If a suspect isn't willing to give us a name, sometimes they don't realise they shouldn't tell it to their legal representative. You know what he told the man from the Home Office?"

"I'm guessing he said that his name is Ned Ludd?"

"That's right, and his address is Sherwood Forest."

"Oh. So not exactly helpful."

"Not exactly." Davis grabbed a small wooden box from the back of the cart and followed Ruth into the house. "But he does seem to believe what he says. Hmm. Smell that?"

"Damp?" Ruth said.

"And thankfully not the stench of ripe human bodies. Captain Mitchell likes to read a criminal by their clothing. I say follow your nose. It's the most overlooked instrument in a detective's arsenal. Where's the kitchen?"

Ruth pointed. "You're from Wales, aren't you?" she asked.

"Born and baptised, and except for a few jaunts here to the south coast, I've lived there all my life."

"As a police officer?" Ruth asked.

"That's right."

"And that's an old-world uniform, isn't it?"

"It is. I was police before the Blackout," he said. "I swore my oath to Queen Elizabeth and joined Her Majesty's Constabulary. I was a sergeant then, and I'm a sergeant now. No one can take that away, and I won't let them promote me out of it."

"Was there anything like this in Wales?" she asked.

"You mean a conspiracy hell-bent on bringing down civilisation? Not recently. There are a few outlandish cults, and many who believe in the literal truth of The Good Book. Of course, each group is referring to a different book when they say it. But I don't think Mr Ludd is religious. Not in the conventional sense."

"What about an anti-technological attitude?" Ruth asked. "Is there much of that?"

"A little, but the prevailing attitude swings the other way. Have you ever been to Wales?"

"No."

"Oh, you should. It's the most beautiful place on Earth," Davis said. "It's God's own country. They say He made it after He'd learned from His mistakes with England."

"You lived in a city there?" Ruth asked.

"In the mobile mining city currently ripping coal out of the verdant soil of Glamorgan," Davis said. "I will grant you that those aren't beautiful in the traditional sense, but there is a precise elegance to them that I find striking. I don't suppose you know much about mining?"

"You dig coal out and stick it on a train," Ruth said.

"I stand corrected!" Davis boomed. "When we were starting out, there weren't many who knew any more than that. We needed electricity, but the refineries were gone, as were the pipelines. There was so much ash in the sky that solar panels were next to useless. We had wind turbines, but they were in the wrong places. What we had was the strength of our arms, and what Britain had was coal, see? Not as much as it once did, but enough to get us through. We hacked it out of the ground, and it fed our locomotives and the power stations, and so we built the factories. But soon that first pit was mined out, so the city had to move. The miners went, as did their families, the traders, the cooks, and all the other hangers on. Then we started to dig again. The furnaces were fed for nearly two years before the pit was so deep it was taking as much energy to get the coal out as it was providing, see?"

"Um… no. Not really," she said.

"Miners have to be fed. They have to be watered. They have to be housed, their children schooled, and so the teachers need to be fed as well. That means farmers, and whether you want to call it food or energy, ultimately it comes down to the same thing. The mines moved, and so did the miners and everyone else. That's why they call them the mobile mining cities. It's that constant movement that causes friction in the local community. If a miner wants to settle in a place, to make a home they can call their own, they move to a deep pit in Scotland or northern England. They leave Wales, and there are enough of us who remember the stories of when this happened before that we won't let the mass exodus happen again. To stop it, we need to create something more permanent in Wales. It's not based on coal. It has to be something else, something new. So, in short, no you'd be unlikely to find much of this technophobic sentiment there, nor much sympathy for Mr Ludd and his friends. Have you done much fingerprinting?"

"In the academy, yes."

"That place? Ha!" he said with as much scorn as Mitchell used to describe it. "They asked me to teach there, you know. I'd have said yes if I could have stayed a sergeant. It's sergeants that run the world, always has been. Remember that. Now, I'll show you how it's done, and as we work, you can tell me about this assassination. Captain Mitchell told me you were the one who shot Emmitt."

"Well, it was nothing really," Ruth said. "I saw Jameson outside the apartment block. I went in. Emmitt was there with a gun in his hand. I fired. I hit his arm. He ran. I chased. I caught Jameson."

"Oh, come now, that isn't how you tell a story so it fills a long afternoon of tedious work. Try again, this time without missing any details."

So Ruth did.

Chapter 3
The Embassy
3rd October

Ruth was halfway through breakfast when there was a knock on the door. Expecting to see Mr Foster, their landlord, she threw it open and almost jumped in surprise at the sight of Captain Mitchell.

"Sir? What's happened?"

"Nothing. You and I have an appointment at the embassy."

"Henry? Is that you?" Maggie called as she came to see who was at the door. "Why don't you come in and have some tea?"

"I'd love a coffee, Maggie," Mitchell said, stepping inside.

Ruth knew that the captain had been to the house before, but it was supremely surreal to see her commanding officer sitting at the kitchen table.

"You can't have come all this way to tell Ruth that she has an appointment," Maggie said, as Ruth tried to work out the etiquette of the situation.

"I was in the area. It was because of something you said, actually," he said, speaking to Ruth. "I was trying to work out why the telegraph wires might have been cut. She told you about that?"

"She did," Maggie said. "Did you discover the answer?"

"No, though I thought I had," he said. "What do we have that's worth stealing? Not jewels, not money. There's food, but why not take that from a farm? Last night a shipment of rifle ammunition arrived from Loch Creigh, destined for the Naval training centre. I thought cutting the telegraph wires might have been practice, and they might try to rob the train."

"I take it they didn't?" Maggie asked.

"It arrived without incident, which means we're back to square one."

"You think there's a theft at the heart of all of this?" Maggie asked.

Mitchell took a sip of coffee. "At the heart of all crimes lies theft. Either of property, of life, or of land. It's sometimes that the land being stolen is an entire country."

"And I know that you got that from a book, Henry," Maggie said.

Mitchell grinned and suddenly looked twenty years younger. "We do have a meeting at the embassy," he said, speaking to Ruth. "So get yourself ready."

Ruth went upstairs to dress as the two old friends talked in voices too low for her to hear.

"Why *are* we going to the embassy?" Ruth asked, as they cycled toward the waking heart of the city.

"Yesterday, Riley spoke to Jameson," Mitchell said. "All she got from him was a claim that the ambassador was as much of a target as the Prime Minister. I don't know if we can believe him, nor do I know how it helps us. At the university, Kowalski learned that three students and two members of the janitorial staff disappeared during the early part of the year."

"They've gone missing?" Ruth asked.

"Missing, at least for us, is a technical term. The students withdrew, and the staff quit. They did it properly, handing in their written notice. The letters gave no reason behind their decision, but before they left, all of them were talking about injustice and the secret threat posed by technology."

"Five people. Plus Ned Ludd makes six," Ruth said.

"Don't forget the other telegraph lines that were cut," Mitchell said. "We're looking for more than five saboteurs, and there could be an entirely mundane explanation for the disappearance of these five individuals. Perhaps they got it into their heads that the Holy Grail was hidden in a crypt under the British Museum. Or that, before the Blackout, someone in Warwick had invented portable cold-fusion. It wouldn't be the first time. Besides, why quit when they could feign illness for a couple of days, commit the sabotage, and return as if nothing had happened. They did change back to their ordinary clothes, after all."

"But?" Ruth said. "I mean, there is a 'but', isn't there?"

Mitchell smiled. "Of course. I think that Emmitt was using the university as a recruiting ground in the same way that he used that pub, the Marquis, to recruit Josh Turnbull and Hailey Lyons. If so, it means that after they took off their tunics, the saboteurs no longer had an ordinary life to disappear back into. In the same way that Turnbull was kept at that house after he was recruited, these Luddites are being harboured somewhere."

Ruth mulled that over for a quarter of a mile. "So is that why we're going to see Fairmont?"

"No. Last night, I got a message from Agent Clarke saying that Fairmont wanted to speak to us."

"Why?"

"That is another good question."

The embassy occupied an old four-storey office block to the west of the main railway station. Next to it was a patch of mostly cleared rubble, and next to that was the central telegraph switching station.

"Where are the wires?" Ruth asked.

"For the telegraph? They come in underground, through the pipework that once carried the fibre-optic cables," Mitchell said.

Next to the telegraph, was the office of the newspaper. Opposite, the road was lined with two-storey terraced houses. It was easy to spot which belonged to the Americans by the Stars and Stripes flying from poles bolted to the brickwork. Those were nothing compared to the flag inside the compound's gate. The pole was taller than the four-storey embassy, and the flag was at least twenty feet wide at the top. The base was slightly narrower due to a missing corner where the fabric was scorched. Ruth wondered where the flag had come from – it was imposing in a way that the flags hanging outside Parliament weren't. It offered a stark contrast to the drab office building that didn't even bear a sign. Though, with that flag, they hardly needed one.

A pair of soldiers in immaculately pressed old-world uniforms snapped to attention as they approached.

"Mitchell and Deering, to see the ambassador," Mitchell said.

"Sir!" a sentry barked. Mitchell shrugged and opened the door. Inside was a hive of activity. Plastic boxes of every shape and colour were stacked on, and occasionally underneath, far sturdier wooden crates.

"Are we really going to see the ambassador?" Ruth said.

"Probably," Mitchell said. "There's a lot of guards. Have you noticed that?"

She had. There were another two inside the entrance, again dressed in that old uniform. As she and Mitchell navigated the maze of boxes to the reception desk against the atrium's far wall, they passed an open doorway. Inside were at least a dozen men and women, all in a mottled grey-yellow camouflage, with helmets on and rifles held at the ready.

"*They're* not ceremonial," she murmured.

"Mitchell and Deering. We're expected," Mitchell said to the woman behind the desk.

"Yes, of course," the receptionist said. She reached behind the counter, picked up a telephone, pressed a button, held it to her ear, and frowned. "They've already disconnected the switchboard. Please excuse me." She disappeared through a door behind the desk.

"They have phones!" Ruth hissed. "Working phones!"

"Not at the moment they don't," Mitchell replied. "I'd say it's an intercom system using the old telephone wires and a mechanical switchboard."

"We should get one for Police House," Ruth said.

"I hope not. Phone calls are one thing about the old world I don't miss. Now, remember that this is foreign soil. The ambassador is an ally, but he'll have an agenda of his own."

"So what should I say if he asks about the investigation?"

"Tell him the truth," Mitchell said. "He'll already know most of it. The Prime Minister will have told him. You know they play chess?"

Before Ruth could reply, the door opened and Agent Clarke stepped into the lobby. Ruth wasn't entirely sure to which government agency the woman belonged, but she wore her black suit as if it was the dress blues of the Marines standing sentry outside.

"Good morning, officers. Welcome to America. Come this way." She indicated a door in a corner of the atrium.

"I take it you're moving," Mitchell said.

Clarke seemed to consider that. "Yes," the agent finally said, having given the question far more deliberation than such a brief answer deserved.

"Where to?" Mitchell asked. Inside the door was a stairwell.

"Upstairs," Clarke said.

"You're moving all of this upstairs?" Mitchell replied.

"I mean you should go upstairs," Clarke said. Ruth reached the first landing before the agent continued. "We're moving to the apartment block opposite the radio antenna."

"The one Emmitt used as his sniper's nest?" Mitchell asked. "Isn't that a little ostentatious?"

Clarke gave a shrug as if to say that while she may have an opinion on that, she wasn't going to share it with these officers of a foreign power.

The ambassador's office was plainly furnished with a quintet of shabby armchairs in one corner, a utilitarian desk in the other, and a grey metal cabinet against a wall. The only decorations, if they could be called that, were five clocks. All showed different times, from four to nine hours behind.

"Cadet Deering, I wanted to thank you for saving my life," the ambassador said, as Clarke closed the door. "I understand Jameson informed you the assassination was planned so they could get two birds with one stone, if not one bullet. Personally, I don't believe that was the only motive. I doubt it mattered which of us died, as long as it was during the broadcast. But you stopped it, and as I'm alive to thank you, I will. Thank you."

"It... it was nothing, sir," Ruth said. "I was just doing my job. But how did you know what Jameson said?"

"I have my sources," Ambassador Perez said.

"He means the Prime Minister," Mitchell said. "You do, don't you, sir?"

"Indeed I do. Friends talk, detective, and what are Britain and America if not friends? And we repay our debts, so if there is anything I can ever do for you, cadet, please don't hesitate to ask."

"Um… thank you," Ruth said.

Perez flashed a smile that was gone in an instant. "Now to business," he said. "You want speak to Fairmont and he wants to speak to you. He asked for you personally, captain. Do you think it's connected with the telegraph lines being cut?"

"You heard about that?" Mitchell asked.

"The sudden absence of any telegrams is hard not to notice," the ambassador replied, waving at his window. "The street filled with idle staff from their office, and so did the pub at the end of the road. After half an hour, there was an impromptu street-party taking place outside. I would have been tempted to join them if the reason for their lack of work wasn't so troubling." He smiled, and Ruth dutifully did the same. "I ask because Fairmont has been under close guard. He's had no contact except with Agent Clarke and her trusted officers."

"And they *are* trusted," Clarke interjected. "Sorry, sir," she added. "But I do trust them." It sounded as if that was something the two had argued about.

"You're worried that his sudden request to talk to me is somehow connected to the telegraph being cut? I couldn't say until I speak to him," Mitchell said. "But if you say he's had no contact, I can't see how the two events could be connected."

"Have you discovered the reason for the sabotage?" Perez asked.

"The suspect we have in custody acted in protest against technology," Mitchell said. "A better question is why the sabotage occurred now, and I have no answer to that."

"What about you, cadet? Do you have any theories?"

"Um… no, not really," Ruth said. "If I had to guess, I'd say that Emmitt was using them as a distraction."

"A distraction from what?"

"I honestly don't know, sir," Ruth said.

"Captain?" Perez prompted.

"Nor do I, but Fairmont might. You say he wants to speak to me?"

"Yes, in your capacity as a representative of the British government. Clarke?"

"Up until now, he's appeared to co-operate," Clarke said. "He told us what information he sold and gave us the locations where he met his contacts. All were either outside or in abandoned properties. In short, they led us nowhere. Feeling that he was no longer of any use, we decided he should be sent back to the United States to stand trial for treason. That was when he requested to speak to you. He claims to have tangible information about a real and present threat, but he won't divulge it to us."

"And in exchange, he wants to be set free?" Mitchell asked.

"Surprisingly, no," Perez said. "He wants to serve his sentence in Britain."

"He hasn't asked for immunity?" Ruth asked.

"Intriguing, isn't it?" the ambassador replied. "Shall we go and see what he has to say?"

Agent Clarke opened the door. Ruth and Mitchell followed her down the stairs. The ambassador followed.

"You're coming with us?" Ruth asked. "Don't you have anything better to do, sir? I... I don't mean... I mean..." She stammered to a halt.

"You mean shouldn't a high-ranking politician have matters of state to attend to? Yes, but I trusted Fairmont, and he betrayed me. I want to know why."

They descended below the ground floor and paused outside a door guarded by a sentry. Clarke took out a key from a chain around her neck.

"There's one door and one key. This one," she said as if proving that Fairmont could have had no unauthorised contact. "There is a guard here." She unlocked the door and opened it. "And inside." Another sentry stood by the wall. Judging from the rapid blinking of her eyes, Ruth guessed she'd been dozing in the folding chair before the door had opened.

"The guard changes every six hours," Clarke continued. "I bring the prisoner his meals, and he doesn't get to speak to anyone else."

The corridor was lit by freestanding electric lamps, with unlit candles positioned next to each.

"Are these all cells?" Mitchell asked, indicating a closed door.

"No, they're used as storage," Clarke said.

"When we took over the building," Perez explained, "our mission was to encourage Britain to trade with America over anywhere else. I didn't think we'd need any cells. Fairmont himself was the one who suggested we might. The actions of a guilty conscience, perhaps?"

"What's inside these other rooms?" Mitchell asked.

"Papers," the ambassador said. "Files recovered from the old embassy in London."

"Anything valuable?" Ruth asked.

"Only to a historian," Perez said. "They're destined for the new Library of Congress, just as soon as we've built it."

"But is there something down here that one of your staff could want to read as a pretext for getting access to the man?" Mitchell asked.

"No," Clarke said. "Any request would have to go through me, and no one's made such a request. He's in here."

Unlike the other doors, this one was metal and appeared to have been recently installed.

"I'll need you to hand over your weapons," Clarke said.

"Of course. This is American soil, after all," Mitchell said. He took out his revolver and handed it to Agent Clarke. Ruth did the same. She noted, however, that the captain didn't remove the small pistol he kept in an ankle holster.

Fairmont was awake, sitting on a narrow cot in a room that was larger than the cells in Police House but just as sparsely furnished.

"Nice digs," Mitchell said. Aside from the bed, there was a bucket and a metal jug. The only other furniture was a row of fixed wooden cabinets that ran along the interior wall.

"Do you remember me?" the captain asked, as he opened a cabinet door. There was nothing inside.

"You're Sergeant Mitchell. You arrested me," Fairmont said.

"It's captain now," Mitchell said, opening another cabinet door. It too was empty.

"Congratulations," Fairmont said. "I assume you're here because of my offer?"

Mitchell turned to look at him. "What do you want, and what are you offering?"

"I'll tell you everything I know. What I want is to serve my sentence in Britain."

"That's all?" Mitchell asked.

"Not quite," Fairmont replied.

"I thought not. Stop playing games," Mitchell said. "Give me precise details, or I'll leave and no one will come back. Start with what you want and what you're offering, and I'll see if it's worth the price."

"I'll serve ten years," Fairmont said, "and be eligible for parole in five. I won't go to prison, and it won't be hard labour, but somewhere remote. Not Twynham. Not one of those mines in Wales or the dockyards in Scotland. Not a ship, either. It has to be somewhere that I can stand in the fresh air and see nothing but trees and grass. There'll be no other prisoners, just me and the guards, and they have to be British Marines. You arrange that, and when I'm there, I'll tell you everything you want to know."

"You've committed treason and you want to serve five years under house arrest with your meals provided. Presumably you want your guards to take care of the laundry as well."

"No, I don't mind doing that," Fairmont said. "It's my own safety I'm talking about. I want to know that I'll still be alive when this is all over."

"Do you have any other requests? Would you prefer a sea view, or somewhere up in the mountains, perhaps?"

"As long as it's remote, I don't care. I want to be safe."

"Safe from whom?" Mitchell asked.

Fairmont shuffled on the bed.

"Tell us," Ruth said gently.

Fairmont bit his lip. "I have to, don't I?" He swallowed, licked his lips, and took a shallow, ragged breath as if the words were fighting against being said. When he spoke, it came out in a rush. "There's an organised crime syndicate spreading throughout the United States. I took this job to get away from them, but they've come over here. That's who I'm giving up."

"Are they the people to whom you were selling details of those oil fields?" Mitchell asked.

"Yeah. Donal and Jameson were their agents. If I get sent back to the States, they'll kill me. It's the same if I go to prison here. The only way I'll stay alive is if I'm somewhere they can't reach me."

"And for five to ten years, which is how long you think it will take for us to dismantle this group?" Mitchell said.

"Pretty much," Fairmont answered.

Ruth had been expecting more guile. Perhaps the man truly believed this was his only chance.

"Tell me about them," Mitchell said.

"Then you agree to my terms?" Fairmont asked.

"No, not yet, and it's not me who'll make that decision. The ambassador will have to agree, and so will the Prime Minister. If you persuade me, I'll persuade them. Start with this organisation. Who are they?"

"Throughout the American Midwest, the towns that survived the Blackout were run by gangs. When the government came back, some of the gang-lords ran for political office. The rest were forced into exile. They formed The Syndicate. That's what they call themselves. It started as a protection and extortion racket. They graduated to blackmail, targeting former members who'd become politicians. That's how they came to run those towns again. They control the trade in them, and through them. Their influence now extends from Alaska to Maine."

"Corrupt politicians and ageing gangsters. It sounds like a matter for the local police," Mitchell said.

"No, because they have very international goals."

"Like what?"

"No, I won't tell you that, not until I'm somewhere safe."

"Unless you do," Mitchell said, "I can't see how we can agree to your terms."

Fairmont shrugged.

"How did you come to work for them?" Ruth asked.

"Originally? I was looking for employment. A guy said he'd get me a job as assistant to the mayor."

"Out of the kindness of his heart?" Mitchell asked.

"That's what I thought. It's not a sin to be naive. The mayor wasn't one of theirs, you see. After a few months they came asking for information on him. I couldn't refuse. I stole some documents, listened in on a few conversations, and a month after that, they owned the mayor."

"What mayor and which town?" Mitchell asked.

"I'll tell you when I'm safe."

Mitchell gave a frustrated sigh. "Fine. So they owned you. Did they get you the job in the embassy?"

"No. I left the state and took a job with the Federal Registration Office in Maine. They found me again. That's when I applied for the post with the embassy. I thought I'd be safe with the Atlantic between us. I wasn't, and this time I'd nowhere left to run."

"Well, I'm sure the details would interest the ambassador and the governments he represents. I don't see why Britain should care."

"I can give you the addresses of the places where I went to exchange information," Fairmont said.

"You already gave those to Agent Clarke," Mitchell said.

"I gave her some places that were outdoors, and others which were abandoned. There are six houses in Twynham, all within a few miles of here. They won't be empty."

"What's inside?" Ruth asked.

"Between six and ten armed men and women."

"What are they doing there?" Mitchell asked.

"Waiting. I don't know what for. But that's around fifty hired thugs right here in the city. That information has to be worth five years of safety.

I'll give you all six houses when I'm somewhere remote. No farmers, no towns, no fishers—"

"No," Mitchell said. "That's too vague. I need some names. Some details."

"When I've got my deal."

"You won't get it without giving me something here and now."

"I've already told you about Donal and Jameson," Fairmont said.

"Then tell me about someone else," Mitchell replied.

"There was a man called Carl and he—"

"He's already dead," Mitchell said.

"Oh. I didn't know."

"A name, Fairmont, or I walk out of here, and you'll have to take your chances in an American court." Mitchell took a step toward the door.

"Wait. Okay. There was this guy. I don't know his name, and he wasn't there to meet me, but he was in four of the houses when I went to give Jameson the information."

"And?" Mitchell prompted.

"Like I said, I don't have a name, but you can't miss him. He's got a scarred face, like someone carved lines into it."

Ruth's heart skipped a beat. That had to be Emmitt.

"And he was in charge?" Mitchell asked.

"I don't know. I was always meeting Donal or Jameson. But he was there in the room. Watching and listening. Look, I didn't have a choice. The ambassador's a good man. If I could do it over I'd—"

"I'm sure," Mitchell cut him off. "These houses, where are they?"

"Near here. That's all I'll say without a deal."

"I'll need more. Give me an address."

"Show me something in writing, then I'll tell you."

"There'll be no deal until we've searched at least one house and found something pertinent."

"Agreed," Fairmont said, "but you can put that it writing, too."

"Deering?"

Ruth followed Mitchell out into the corridor where the ambassador and Agent Clarke were waiting. Mitchell gestured they should move out of earshot of the cell.

"You heard what he said?" Mitchell asked.

"Yes," Clarke said. "The Syndicate is real, but it's not nearly as influential as he claims. It consists of the remnants of four gangs we pushed out of Boone. They've taken root around the Des Moines River in the old Brushy Creek State Park, but they're more of a biker gang without the wheels than an organised crime outfit."

"They're not into blackmail and extortion?" Mitchell asked.

"Bushwhacking travellers on the I-20 is about as complicated as they get," Clarke said.

"Then he's lying?" Ruth asked.

"Probably," Clarke said.

"You've got some doubts?" Mitchell asked.

"It's possible that he's been fed a story that he wants to believe," Clarke said, "but there could be someone, or some group, working behind the scenes, blackmailing politicians, and using gangs like this one to control the trade routes. In which case we need to crush them as soon as we can."

"Then we need to ask a different question. Do you think he believes he's telling the truth?" Mitchell asked.

"If he was genuinely contrite," Perez said, "he'd offer up everything he knows before asking for something in return. Not keep it back until he's threatened with deportation."

"Unless he's scared," Ruth said. "And he seems to be. I think he's more scared of someone else than he is of us."

"Does the fifth mean anything to you?" Mitchell asked.

"As in a date?" Perez asked. "Why?"

"We have reason to believe that the telegraph will be cut twice more, with the third time being on the fifth of November."

"Ah, I see. Well, I'll have to check my diary, but I can't think of anything," Perez said.

"What worries me is that it will happen once between now and then," Mitchell said. "Fairmont's our best lead."

"It was the threat of deportation that got him to talk," Perez said. "If that's what he's afraid of, then we have to make it work for us. However real this Syndicate is, our world is a fragile place now. Britain, America, those are just geographical distinctions. The reality is that we're talking about civilisation itself. We have to protect it. If that means I forego justice, so be it."

"Then I better have a word with my superiors," Mitchell said. "Deering, you might as well stay here."

"I'm sure we can entertain her," the ambassador said. "Do you play chess, cadet?"

Ruth stared at the board. She *did* know how to play chess, in theory. She moved a pawn. Perez tutted. Ruth didn't know if that was a good sign or not.

"Sir, are those clocks showing the time in America?" she asked, hoping to distract him.

"They are," the ambassador said. "Puerto Rico, Maine, Iowa, Washington, and Alaska. The five great population centres."

"But there are only three presidents?"

"The governors of Puerto Rico and Alaska never claimed their states were the natural successors to the old federal government. The others did. They weren't the only ones. Your move."

Ruth moved another pawn. "There were more presidents?" she asked.

"On finding themselves the sole occupants of a dung heap, some people will call themselves king. About half of the rulers of small towns called themselves president. Some tried to fight, or to seal themselves off, but most stood down when the troops came marching in. A few even arranged formal ceremonies that will make for an interesting footnote in history. Your move."

"So how come there are still three presidents?"

"Because a lot of officials in the chain of succession survived the nuclear holocaust, but lacked the ability to communicate the fact with the world. It was years before anyone in Fort Dodge knew that there was a president in Gray's Harbor. Your move. But the old vice president was in Fort Dodge. That's in Iowa. His plane crash-landed there after the EMP knocked out the electronics. That's how the town became the centre of government, and why the state of Iowa, rather than Nebraska or Missouri, became the hub for that part of our country. The President Pro Tempore and the five other senators were in Washington State, on their way back to DC from a Trans-Pacific conference. The Speaker of the House escaped to Maine along with myself and a few other members of the House of Representatives. Thus, on either side of our nation, and in its centre, there were three groups who knew nothing of the others' existence, but in each was someone who thought they were the legal and just successor to the dead president. Not only that, but they had the lawyers to back them up. You should understand that taking that oath wasn't about power. It was done in the hope that maintaining the familiar structures and institutions would offer comfort at a time when uncertainty was as rampant as disease. Checkmate."

Ruth stared at the board.

"You need to practice," Perez said. "It's a useful game to play."

"Useful? You mean you don't play for fun?"

"Ah, the perspicacious police officer. Yes, useful. It's a game played across the world, and as such it cuts across barriers that language often creates. You start."

Ruth moved a pawn. "But the vice president should have been the rightful president, right? So why didn't the others resign?"

"Because he died in the second year, before communication had been re-established. When it was, it was a matter of a few scouts travelling across the country seeing if anyone else was alive. The news they returned with was little better than rumour. In those days, a person's world consisted of where they could reach in a day's hike, or perhaps a day's ride. Who they called the president didn't matter. What mattered was that the president was elected. *They* were. The elections went ahead. Three presidents took their oaths, all on the same day, but thousands of miles apart. Your move."

"So it's taken this long to sort it all out?"

"Pretty much. It's been one long legal battle, but having seen the other kind, I'm more than happy that we've been fighting one of those. Take California. After the Blackout, but before the earthquake – do you know about the earthquake?"

Ruth shook her head.

"Some say it was long overdue, but it's a terrible tragedy nonetheless. But before it hit, the governor sent emergency delegates to find the capital. Now, the governor, being a woman who understood the perils of our new world, had ensured that, even if half the delegation succumbed to disease or worse, there would still be enough representatives to arrive in the capital."

"If they could find one."

"Precisely, but they found two. The group became lost. Half ended up in Gray's Harbor, the other half in Fort Dodge. Thus we now have senators for California in the United States Congresses of Washington *and* Iowa. There were dozens of cases like that."

"Gray's Harbor is in Washington?"

"Washington State. Fort Dodge is in Iowa. Pinebreak Ferry is the capital of Maine."

"What about the other two clocks? Puerto Rico and Alaska?"

"They're still run by governors. Juneau's one of the largest cities to have survived the Blackout. I couldn't say why it wasn't destroyed. Perhaps it was luck. Somewhere on this planet had to be blessed with that. It wasn't connected to the rest of America by road so wasn't swamped with refugees. Puerto Rico is an island. With no oil for ships or planes, it was in much the same situation as those in Alaska. No matter how hard things got, there was no escape. There's was a binary choice: survive or die."

"But why didn't they call themselves president? Or declare themselves a new country?"

"What does it matter what you call your home when the roof is on fire? Names are only important when you need to establish that you are different from someone else. It's hard to explain it now, but during those first years, we all felt the same, that we were all that was left. But when contact was re-established it was with steam ships from Britain that had come via Maine. There were other people out there, and they were trying to rebuild. If anything, that made worrying about sovereignty even less important. Ah." He smiled and moved his king. "You almost had me. Check."

Ruth stared at the board. She moved her bishop.

"Are you sure?" Perez asked.

Ruth hesitated, and moved the rook instead. "Are all those presidents running in this election?"

"None of them are. That was part of the deal, the final concession that enabled re-unification to take place. No current president, vice president, or governor can stand. Your move. In politics the trick is to avoid making too many concessions. You have to keep one eye on the present with another on the future. If President Peterson had been asked to stand down at the beginning of his term, he would have wanted some great concession for Iowa, perhaps that the new District of Columbia be built there. President Delaney of Washington wanted senators-at-large to be elected to represent those states that are still mostly ungoverned wasteland. By waiting until now, we've reached a time where both Peterson and Delaney have come to the end of their second terms. Be thankful for term limits as it means they gain nothing by trying to cling on to power, but instead have their eyes fixed on how they will be portrayed by the history books. President Brooker of Maine has only served one term. She is willing to step aside in the hope that her lawyers can find a way for her to serve a full eight years as president of the re-united nation."

Ruth looked over the flag secured behind a glass frame on the wall. "Fifty stars, yet only five states remain."

"There are seventeen who'll send delegates to the new capital. In four years it will be thirty. Four years after that, who knows? Puerto Rico never had a star on that flag. It will on the new one though I don't think we'll redesign the flag. It represents an idea, and though that idea may have been poorly executed at times, it is still better than any other than has ever existed on this planet."

"Even better than here?" Ruth asked.

"Of course."

"But then you'd have to say that, wouldn't you?" Ruth asked. "Because you're going to run for president."

"Checkmate."

Ruth flicked over her king. "You are, aren't you?"

"Only if it is in the best interests of my constituents."

"That's a politician's reply."

"It's your move," he said. "Now, tell me about the assassination. I am rather curious as to how you came to save my life."

Wistfully remembering the time when her life was so simple that she had no stories to recount, she began the now familiar tale.

"Those are the terms," Mitchell said. "Do you agree?"

Fairmont picked up the document, started to read, and then gave up. "What's the point? It's not like I have a choice."

"No, you don't," Mitchell said. "This is the only deal you'll get."

"Fine. One address now, the rest when I'm somewhere remote and safe, surrounded by mountains or fields. Is that what it says?"

"More or less. The rest is legalese, stating that the deal is off if you fail to share everything you know."

Fairmont took the pen from Mitchell and scrawled his name at the bottom.

"Now give us an address," Mitchell said.

"Windward Square," Fairmont said. "I don't know the number, but it's the house with the red door and iron railings on a low stone wall at the front. The railings have a shield worked into the design. There are columns either side of the door, and the ground-floor window on the right-hand side is cracked."

"And what did you see there?" Mitchell asked.

"Jameson was there. So was the man with the scarred face. They looked like they were only visiting."

"Visiting whom?"

"Two women and six men. I wasn't there long, and I didn't see much. I was ushered through a living room and into a… I'd say it was a library, except there weren't that many books, just lots of shelves."

"And what were these people doing?" Mitchell asked.

"Talking. Lounging around. A couple were lifting weights. Three of them were cleaning weapons. Basically, I think they were waiting."

"What kind of weapons?" Mitchell asked.

"Shotguns. There were some handguns as well."

"What about upstairs?" Mitchell asked.

"I don't know. I came in, handed over the papers, and left."

"Who let you in?"

"Jameson."

"There was no sentry on the door, anything like that?"

"No."

"When was this?"

"The beginning of September."

Mitchell picked up the agreement Fairmont had signed. "I'll go and have a look at this house, then I'll come back, and then we'll talk some more." He walked to the door, paused, and turned back to Fairmont. "This is your last chance," he said. "If this is a trap, you won't like what happens next."

"It's not a trap," Fairmont said. "It's the truth."

Chapter 4
Arrests

"Atten-SHUN!" Lieutenant Lewis of the Marines barked. Ruth's feet reflexively clicked together.

"Thank you," Assistant Commissioner Weaver said. "We've received information that a group of six men and two women, and possibly more, are hiding in a house in Windward Square. They are armed with shotguns and pistols, but we must assume they have more powerful weapons. We believe these people are connected with the sabotage of the telegraph wires. Captain Mitchell?"

"The suspects are waiting. We don't know what for, but they've been there for at least four weeks. We know of five other properties like this. There could be more. It's fair to assume that as soon as we raid this house, they'll bring their plans forward and mobilise the rest of their followers. We don't want a siege. We need arrests, and we need evidence. Can you all see the map? This is a residential area. Hopefully most people are at work, but we can't guarantee it. To avoid a siege, we're going to get them to run. You'll be deployed in the streets leading from the square. Your role will be to catch them as they escape. Arrest them," he added. "Don't kill them."

"Thank you, Captain Mitchell, I think you've made that point," Weaver said. "Assuming the wind holds, in thirty minutes a hot-air balloon, currently tethered near Highcliffe, will come loose and drift over the city. It will crash in the allotments to the west of Windward Square. The pilot has been directed to fly as low as possible over the house. This should get the suspects into the rear garden. Mitchell, Riley, and Davis will make a loud and forceful entry through the front door. That should get them to run. From the rear garden, they have two possible routes. Here, along Fenwick Road toward…"

Ruth tuned Weaver out and focused on finding a position where the bulletproof vest would be comfortable. She was coming to the slow realisation that there probably wasn't one.

It was two p.m., barely three hours since she and Mitchell had left the embassy. They'd returned to Police House to find Weaver had already mobilised half a regiment of Marines. When Mitchell had given her the address, Weaver had announced that they would storm the house immediately. Nevertheless, Ruth had thought the planning would take hours. Mitchell had disabused her of that by saying it was a decision between two bad choices. They could either contain the suspects in the house and storm it, or flush them out. The first carried the risk that they might have the supplies and weapons to withstand a long siege, the second that they might escape.

"As soon as we move in," Mitchell had said, "word will reach Emmitt. He could bring forward whatever this is all building toward. Having half the city's police tied up in a protracted siege can only help his cause. If Emmitt has at least five other properties with people like that inside, what does it matter if a few of these thugs escape? We need information, and this is the only way we're going to get it." It had taken barely ten seconds of deliberation for Weaver to agree with him.

Ruth looked at the faces of the sixty Marines in the hall. They seemed relaxed. Perhaps they didn't think a mere eight civilians in a residential street bore much of a threat. As for herself, she wasn't sure how she felt and knew it didn't matter. She wasn't part of the assault, but would be waiting with the rest of the Serious Crimes Unit in a pub to the east of the square. Only when the house was clear would she be allowed inside. That hadn't stopped Mitchell insisting she wear the bulletproof vest.

"Any questions?" Weaver asked, bringing the briefing to an end. "Then get to it, and make sure we catch them all."

"What are you doing?" Simon asked.

"Trying to see," Ruth said. She stood on a table in the pub's garden, but it only gave her a view of the house opposite. She jumped down, her eyes on the roofs, watching for sight of the balloon. There was a cheer from inside. Ruth sighed.

"We should be helping," she said.

"We're police. Not soldiers," Simon said.

"Nor are we," the corporal in charge of the platoon said. "We're Marines."

There were eight of them in the pub garden. The moment the balloon was sighted, they would seal the road to stop any gawkers from heading into the square. Only after the all clear was given would Ruth and the rest of the unit be allowed inside the house. She peered up at the sky. The waiting was interminable, and the noise from inside the pub was only making her agitation worse.

On being told that his establishment was being requisitioned, the landlord had been livid. When they were told that they couldn't leave, the early afternoon customers had been on the verge of rioting before Constable Kingsley had opened a tab on the police's behalf. That had quietened them down, at least initially. Now it sounded like they were on the brink of a very different type of riot.

"I meant we're not trained for this," Simon said, speaking quietly so the Marines couldn't hear. "We're police. We're not even that," he amended. "We're just two cadets."

Ruth waved that away. He was correct, but also very wrong. They were officers of the law. No matter how inexperienced they were, that meant something. Emmitt and his cronies wouldn't care that they'd only recently graduated from the academy. She was formulating how best to express that idea when there was another yell, not from the pub, but from a few streets further away. The shouting drew nearer. There were occasional words, but it was the tone of bemused surprise that gave a clue as to the commotion's cause. It was the balloon.

Ruth had seen them before, hovering around the lighthouse on the coast, and again near Southampton. Those had been seen from a distance and hadn't given her a true indication of the craft's size. The balloon was bigger than a house, with the basket underneath almost as large as a horse-drawn carriage.

A dangling rope brushed against the pub's roof. Only the calm and calculating expression of the woman peering over the side gave the clue that the balloon's excursion was no accident. All too quickly, it was over the pub and drifting in the direction of the square.

"That's our cue. Get to it!" the corporal of Marines barked at his troops. They grabbed the tables and ran out into the street, using the pub's furniture to create a crude barricade. It was a strangely disquieting sight.

"Get Kingsley," Ruth said to Simon. "There should be police standing out in the street." She followed the Marines out into the road.

"Sorry, it's for your own safety," the corporal said, raising a hand to stop a pair of pedestrians from trying to get past. The civilians hesitated, shrugged, and turned around. Ruth didn't know if they would continue about their day, or simply look for an unguarded street. It didn't matter. She turned to look toward the disappearing balloon. The curve of the street hid Windward Square from sight, and she found herself walking away from the Marines in the hope of getting a better view. Occasional faces peered down from upper-storey windows but, by the time she'd reached the end of the street, no one had come outside.

She edged around the corner of a pebble-dashed wall until she could see the square and the house with the red door. Mitchell and Riley were walking slowly toward it from the left. Davis was coming from the right. The curtains were closed. During daylight that was unusual, even in a house with electricity. No one pulled them back to see who was outside, not even when Riley opened the gate. The three officers ran up the path to the house. Riley pulled out a crowbar. There was a moment of quiet consultation before the sergeant stuck the crowbar between the lock and frame, and heaved. The lock splintered.

Mitchell squared his shoulders and kicked the door inward. "Police!" the captain's voice echoed across the square. "Police! Don't—" A gunshot drowned out the rest of the sentence. There was another shot. Mitchell charged through the doorway. Riley and Davis followed, close on his heels. There was a flurry of small arms fire, and then a roar from something far louder.

Ruth turned around, wanting to signal the corporal to bring his Marines to Mitchell's aid, but they were hidden by the curvature of the road. Without thinking, she ran toward the house.

When she was halfway across the square, there was another fusillade, this time accompanied by the sound of shattering glass as a first-storey window blew outwards. She reached the gate, and ran up the uneven drive, only remembering to draw her revolver when she was at the front porch. It was still pointing down when a man staggered out of the door. Surprised confusion was fixed on his face as he threw an arm out toward her. Ruth ducked, falling into a crouch as Riley had taught her, then swept her leg out. The man's own momentum did most of the work. He toppled down the steps, landing heavily on the drive. Ruth quickly cuffed the stunned man, and hoped that Simon, Kingsley, or someone would arrive before the man regained enough sense to stand and run away. She went inside.

Smoke. Noise. Dust. From somewhere upstairs, she heard a shout halfway between a prayer and a promise, bellowed in a Welsh lilt. There were other shouts, some sounded like pleas, others like orders. Ruth struggled to make sense of it.

Weird shadows coalesced into the shape of a woman holding a… Ruth ducked as the woman pulled the trigger. The rifle in the assailant's hands didn't fire. Ruth rolled to her feet, but whatever instinct had been driving her vanished. In front of her, the woman worked the mechanism of the gun, trying to clear some blockage. Ruth could feel the weight of the revolver in her own hand, yet she was frozen to the spot. The woman wasn't. She dropped the rifle, fumbling for a pistol at her belt.

Seemingly from nowhere, Riley appeared, swinging her truncheon in a massive overarm blow that ended at the woman's head with a dull crunch. The woman crumpled to the floor. Before Ruth could think, let alone thank her, Riley disappeared through a doorway.

Ruth swallowed, breathed, and bent to check whether the suspect was still alive. There was a shout from a room on the opposite side of the atrium.

"Drop it!" she heard Mitchell call. Ruth ducked though she knew the command wasn't directed at her. Captain Mitchell was on the ground with his back against an armchair, frantically reloading. Ruth couldn't see either

Davis or Riley. On the other side of the room, a man was loading a sawn-off shotgun.

"I surrender," the man yelled, closing the breach of his double-barrelled weapon. Before Ruth could warn him not to, Mitchell stood up, one hand holding his side, the other his gun, but it was pointing too far to the left.

Time slowed, and everything went quiet.

The man dived across the floor, bringing his shotgun to bear on Mitchell. The captain moved, twisting and crouching as he tried to bring his arm around. He was too slow, and the chair would offer little protection against the shotgun's blast. Ruth's arm was already up, her revolver pointed straight at the criminal. She pulled the trigger. Again. And again. The man dropped the gun and clutched at his legs. Ruth frowned. She'd been aiming at his chest. Sound returned, and only then did Ruth realise how silent everything had seemed. The man was crying in pain, his sobs interspersed with pleading and cursing. Ruth's hands began to shake, but she couldn't lower the wavering barrel. Almost as if it was coming through a thick fog, she heard footsteps behind her. The corporal of Marines pushed past, then another Marine, and another.

Time sped up. Ruth's arm dropped to her side. She slumped against the wall.

"You all right?" Mitchell asked.

"Yeah. I'm fine," Ruth murmured.

"Going to throw up?" he asked.

"Probably not."

"Then get up." He reached down, and she let him pull her to his feet. "You can put that away," he added.

"What? Oh. Yes." She holstered the gun.

"You sure you're okay?" he asked.

"Really, I'm fine," she said, more forcefully than she believed. "What happened," she continued, wanting to move the subject away from herself. "What went wrong?"

"They didn't run. They didn't even go into the garden. It says a lot that a balloon can scrape the rooftops and they stayed inside. They did move to the back of the house to watch it from the kitchen. That probably saved our lives."

"It did?"

"The automatic weapons were all in the front room," he said.

"Automatic… the rifles?" She looked across the atrium to the woman Riley had knocked out. "She tried to shoot me. The gun wouldn't fire."

Mitchell walked over to it, and picked it up. "Safety's on," he said. He ejected the magazine and removed the round in the chamber. "An SA80, the standard service weapon for the old British military, though this isn't the modified L85A2 our Marines use." He held up a cartridge. "5.56mm NATO rounds. Old-world weapon, old-world ammo. Interesting."

"I need some air," Ruth said.

As Mitchell bent down to check the pulse of the unconscious suspect, Ruth went outside. More Marines, some carrying stretchers, arrived along with the rest of the squad. She ignored them.

She might have shot the man in the legs, but she'd been aiming at his chest. What did that mean? And she'd frozen when that woman had aimed the rifle at her. What did *that* mean?

"Two dead," Mitchell said, coming outside to join her. "Both theirs. We arrested six, and I don't think any got away. Two of them, the two women, are people Riley discovered had gone missing from the Marquis."

"Oh. Good."

"Thank you," Mitchell said.

"What for?"

"For shooting that man. You saved my life."

"I… Yes. Right." She wasn't sure what else to say.

"The man will live," Mitchell said. "He'll probably limp for the rest of his life, but he'll be alive."

"Good. Great. So, where do we start?"

"You sure you're up for it?" he asked.

"Yeah, no, I'm fine."

Mitchell gave her a look filled with scepticism and, Ruth was embarrassed to realise, concern. She squared her jaw, stiffened her shoulders, walked up to the door, and then had to step aside as Constable Kowalski escorted a handcuffed prisoner outside.

"No sign of Emmitt," Riley said. She was in the atrium, watching a pair of Marines load the unconscious woman onto the stretcher.

"I suppose it was too much to hope we'd catch him here," Mitchell said. He dropped his hand to his side, wincing. "I must have torn the stitches again. Riley, start upstairs. Deering, take the kitchen. I'll see if anyone has a bandage to spare."

The kitchen was at the rear of the house, separated from the garden by a pair of sliding glass doors. They were locked. Ruth leaned her forehead against the door, revelling in the feel of cool glass against her hot skin. Her head was pounding as the last few minutes played over and over, though each time her imagination drew up an alternative, tragic ending. She took a step back, dug her nails into her palm, and spoke aloud in the hope of drowning out those nightmare visions.

"The garden's dug over," she said. "But covered in leaves. Nothing would grow in it. The locked door… where's the key?" It wasn't in the lock. She opened the nearest drawer. Cutlery. The next contained kitchen knives and three can openers. The third contained a few pencils and nothing else.

"No key. Were they locked in? Or just locked out of the garden?" It was a good question. Worried she might forget it, she reached for her notepad, but her hand was trembling too much to manage the button on the pocket.

"Were they locked in?" she repeated to herself. She slowly turned a full circle and looked out on the garden once more.

"Okay. What can you see?" she asked herself. "What can you see? Nothing but leafless trees and the walls of nearby houses. No overlooking windows. That makes sense. Neighbours would have noticed if no one had planted vegetables in a garden that size."

It was interesting, but it didn't help. She turned back to the kitchen. "Fitted cupboards. A wood-burning stove with a chimney built into the wall." She stared at it, knowing that her eyes were seeing something that her brain wasn't processing.

"Properly fitted," she realised. "And so are the cupboards. There's no discolouration on the walls from where old electric appliances once stood."

During the last twenty years, the kitchen had been properly converted. That would have been expensive, but then it was a large house near the centre of town. Property prices were strictly regulated, but this one would still have demanded a small fortune.

"I wonder if it was paid in twenty-pound notes."

She tried a tap. Water came out. She reached out to touch it. The sensation was marvellous. Suddenly, she realised she wasn't wearing her gloves. As she reached for them, she found her hands had stopped shaking. That was a good sign, wasn't it? Should she have recovered so quickly? And behind those questions, she could feel a hundred more queuing up to be asked.

She threw open the cupboard under the sink. "No bucket. Just pipes," she said, speaking loudly and quickly. "Some bleach. Dish soap. All neatly ordered." The cutlery drawers were the same. Everything was in its place.

"Twelve Plates. Fourteen cups. Eight bowls. Not matching," she said, staring at the contents of the next cupboard. That wasn't surprising. Matching crockery was expensive, but then so was running water. She tried the light switch. Nothing happened.

"Canned beef. Pork. Fish. Carrots. Peas." Was there a clue to be found in the selection? The next cupboard contained dry goods. "Pasta. Ersatz tea. Dehydrated potatoes." Now she saw it. The food was the type given in food aid to those overseas communities still struggling to become self-sufficient. That was significant, she thought, though she wasn't sure why. She found more dried food in the next cupboard, more cans in another. But what did that tell her? What did it mean?

She realised that she'd been staring at a cupboard door for the last few seconds. On it was pinned a piece of paper divided into a grid with names written into each square. Along the top were chores, along the y-axis were days of the week.

"Did you find anything," Mitchell asked. She hadn't noticed him approach.

"There's a rota." She heard the disbelief in her own voice. "They actually had a rota for the chores."

"Let me see." He peered at it. "Brilliant," he said as he pulled out the pins. "Now we have their names. Or their first names, but that's a start."

"But a rota, I mean…" Ruth wasn't sure how to frame the question.

"They've been here at least a month," Mitchell said. "It's a good way of ensuring they don't descend into violence."

And another cog fell into place. "There's no coffee," she said. "No sugar, either. Or alcohol, for that matter. Only bland, easy to prepare food."

"Makes sense," Mitchell said. "It's what I'd do. If you can't supervise them directly, you put procedures in place to manage their behaviour." He tried the sliding doors to the garden.

"They're locked. There's no key," Ruth said.

"Which explains why they didn't go outside," Mitchell said, "but not why it was locked in the first place. The front door could be opened from the inside, so they weren't prisoners here. Interesting. How many days of food do they have left?"

"I'm not sure." Ruth looked in the cupboard again. "A week. Eight days. Not much longer."

"We know that Emmitt was here a month ago. Hmm." Mitchell walked across to a closed door on the room's far side. Ruth had thought it led into the neighbouring room. It didn't. There were stairs, leading down. Mitchell took a stub of candle from a shelf by the door, lit it, and held it in front. He went down a few steps but quickly retreated. "I envy whoever has to sort though that," he muttered.

"What is it?"

"Their waste. Cans. Wrappers. Food. All decomposing unpleasantly. So," he said, blowing out the candle and closing the door. "They have food for eight days. Let's say a week. Is that a week until they were going to be resupplied, or is that when Emmitt's plan will be put in place?"

Ruth shrugged. "It's not enough to last them until the fifth," she said. "Maybe we were wrong about that."

"Possibly. But there's that second attack on the telegraph we're meant to expect."

"Unless Ned Ludd was wrong about that," Ruth said. "He's hardly a reliable source."

"You're forgetting the placards in that cottage, and there's something else I want to show you." Mitchell led her out of the kitchen. "The question we have to ask ourselves is whether Fairmont's information panned out."

"Well, it has, hasn't it?"

"We've found eight people here, all heavily armed," Mitchell said. "But what we're looking for is some connection to Emmitt, Wallace, or the conspiracy. These people could have been involved in anything. They could even have been working for Fairmont, and he threw them under the train in an attempt to save his own neck."

"Is that likely?"

"No, but it's always good to be distrustful of a person like Fairmont."

He led her into the room where she'd shot the man. The man was gone, presumably taken to the hospital while she'd been in the kitchen. She wondered how long ago that had been. It must have been far longer than the few minutes she'd thought. She turned away from the slowly congealing pool of blood and found herself looking at three wooden crates stacked one on top of another. The top most one was open. Mitchell reached in and pulled out an assault rifle.

"Ten in this crate," he said. "Let's assume the same in the others. Ammunition's in those boxes in the corner."

"Did you say they were British made?"

"Yes, standard issue for the old military, but these rifles?" He turned the weapon over in his hands. "They would have been withdrawn from service at least a decade before the Blackout."

"So where did they come from?"

"Probably some old government armoury. The barrels aren't modified to take the new calibre of ammunition, so we know they didn't come from our Navy or Marines. That's something. As for the ammunition, there're at least two thousand rounds here."

"Eight people, but thirty rifles," Ruth said. "Who are the other twenty-two for?"

"That's what I'm worried about. Were these people involved in sabotaging the telegraph, or were they destined for something else? These weapons are troubling. The only thing they could want with so much firepower is revolution. But, according to Riley, those two women were criminals, not insurrectionists."

"Always more questions," Ruth said.

"Quite. However we have found a concrete, if tangential, link to the Luddites."

He walked into the next room. Ruth followed. In the corner was a metal contraption Ruth didn't immediately recognise.

"It's a printing press," Mitchell said, passing her a sheet of paper.

The text was densely crammed on the page and slightly smudged. "Workers should control the means of production," she read.

"It's a modern twist on an old slogan," Mitchell said. "The rest of that page has an anti-technology slant, but there's no mention of Ludd or of sabotage. If you turn it over, the other side has a completely inaccurate explanation on how radio waves can be used to control machines, and so destroy the jobs of people."

"It can't, can it?"

"Not in the way they describe, but most people under the age of thirty would probably believe it. Why wouldn't they? It's a story that fits with their understanding of history. It would be very persuasive in our world with only one newspaper. The second paragraph from the end describes that paper as the mouthpiece of imperialist technocracy. Any rebuttal of the pamphlet could be dismissed as propaganda by anyone who wanted to believe this garbage."

"But surely—" Ruth began, but before she could finish the question, there was a shout from upstairs.

"Mister Mitchell," Riley called. "You'll want to see this."

Sergeant Riley stood outside a room at the top of the stairs. "Six bedrooms," Riley said. "Three over there." She pointed at a door on the other side of the landing. "The others are on this side. This is the smallest, and the least private."

Ruth looked inside. There was one bed, and a mattress on the floor.

"From the clothes," Riley said, "this is the women's room. Two of the men shared a room over there." She pointed across the landing. "The other four men had rooms of their own."

"Did the women share a room because there's safety in numbers?" Ruth asked.

"Possibly," Riley said. "But that's not the most interesting part. There are clothes in the cupboard. All old-world. Nothing like the rags Ned Ludd was wearing. There are some books, but no personal items except for this." She picked up a small black backpack. "There's one by each bed."

Riley pulled the items out, one by one, and placed them on the mattress. "It's a go-kit. Knife, towel, first aid-kit, matches, cord, ammunition, chlorine tablets, and so on. Then there's this." She looked first at Ruth, then at Mitchell, before she gave a theatrical grin, and pulled out a stack of banknotes.

"Are those twenty-pound notes?" Mitchell asked.

"Every one of them. The serial numbers are in the range for the counterfeit currency," Riley said.

"How much is there?" Ruth asked.

"Around four thousand pounds. Each bag contained the same amount."

"Do you think they know the money is forged?" Ruth asked.

"No," Mitchell said, "but I'll enjoy telling them."

He picked up the bag and bent over to refill the contents. He winced and reached for his side.

"Let me see that," Riley said, and was lifting up the side of Mitchell's shirt even as the captain stuttered a protest. "Go and get it stitched," she said. Mitchell opened his mouth to object. "Now." Riley said, and surprisingly, the captain did.

"He's like a father?" Ruth asked, after Mitchell had gone.

"I suppose. We've been through a lot together. Good and bad. Danger and joy. More danger than joy, now I think about it. How are you feeling?"

"Fine."

"Really?" Riley asked.

"Sure. I want to get on with the job, you know?"

"Were you finished in the kitchen?"

"I think so," Ruth said.

"Then you can help me up here. Start by putting those items back in the bag."

Ruth picked up the stack of bank notes. A sudden sweep of tiredness crashed over her.

"You all right?" Riley asked.

"Sorry, yes. I… It all happened so quickly."

"It's like that. You spend days searching for leads, and when they turn up, things spiral. Sit down if you need to. It's better than falling over."

"No, no. I'm fine," Ruth said.

"Okay," Riley said doubtfully. Silence had barely a chance to settle before she continued. "You shouldn't have come in on your own."

"I heard the shots. I knew something was wrong. You needed help," Ruth said.

"Yes," Riley said, "but you shouldn't have come in *alone*." She lifted the mattress, looking underneath it. There was nothing there. She moved over to the small dresser. "Acting the hero works in books. In real life it gets people killed. If that woman's gun had worked, you'd be dead. You can say your survival is down to luck, but if you trust to luck, you'll die. In this job, so will those around you." She closed the dresser drawer. "We have to rely on training, on experience, and on each other." She turned her head up, then down, looking slowly around the room. "No, there's nothing else here. We'll try the next room. We're looking for a journal, diary, or scrap of paper. You'd be surprised what people write down. About five years ago there was a murder where the killer wrote down a step-by-step plan of how to get away with it. He didn't include 'don't leave the instructions hidden in a box halfway up the chimney'. Do you enjoy policing?"

"What? Um… yes, I think so."

"You're not sure?" Riley walked out of the room. Ruth followed her along the landing to the next one. The sheets were balled up on the bed, the clothes pilled on the floor. There was a thin line of bare boards visible between the two beds, demarcating which slovenly mess belonged to which criminal. "That's good."

"It is?"

"You'd have to be weird to enjoy spending your time around so many thugs," Riley said.

"Um… yes." Ruth wasn't sure if that was a joke. "But you enjoy it, right?"

"Most of the time," Riley said. "But for me, it's about maintaining control of the world around me. It doesn't make for much of a social life."

"Oh." Ruth had no idea what to say to that. She kicked at the pile of clothes. She was in no mood to sort through them. "I went to the psychiatrist," she said. "You know, because of the man I killed."

"Yes. And?"

"And nothing. I sort of talked for an hour, and then he said I'd have to come back again. That it would take a lot of time."

"Hmm." Riley picked up a pair of trousers and turned them over. "No mud on the legs, so they haven't been worn outside, not recently." Gingerly, she checked the pockets, and found a folded sheet of paper. "See?" she said, unfolding it. "Ah." Her flash of vindication vanished.

"What is it?"

"A copy of the pamphlet they were printing," she said, turning it over. Her brow furrowed. She looked at it more closely.

"What?" Ruth asked again.

"I've read something like this before. No, I heard it," Riley said. "Where? At dinner, I think. I'm trying to remember… oh. Rupert." The name was said with heartfelt disappointment.

"Who?" Ruth asked.

"Rupert Pine. It doesn't matter." She folded the note and placed it in an evidence bag.

"Isn't he an MP?" Ruth asked. "How do you know him?"

"It's a long story," Riley said in a tone that suggested that it wasn't one she was going to share. She kicked at the pile of clothes. "So you saw the psychiatrist," she said, unsubtly returning to the previous topic. "In the last two weeks, you've seen a lot. You probably do need to talk about it with someone. If that guy doesn't suit you, go and see someone else. After today, I'd say you should. But what you need to understand is that this job isn't going to change. If you stay in the police, there will be more days like this. You need to decide if this is something you can do, year in, year out, for the rest of your life."

"What else is there?" Ruth asked. "I mean, I joined the police because I didn't get into university. I thought it would be a good career, but now? I don't know."

"It can be a good career, but it's a hard and lonely life. Only you can decide if it's the right one for you."

Though that question rang in her mind as they continued searching the house, Ruth couldn't decide on an answer.

Chapter 5
Interview

"Diane Frobisher," Riley said, walking into the interview room. "Remember me?"

The prisoner glanced warily between Riley and Mitchell as the two officers took a seat opposite her. Ruth, with Davis and Weaver, was on the other side of the one-way glass that partitioned the old schoolroom. Sergeant Davis lounged in a chair as if he was at some theatrical performance, Weaver stood, arms folded, eyes drinking in the prisoner's every shuffle and twitch. Ruth's own eyes felt heavy, and she had to keep blinking them open. The woman who'd tried to shoot Ruth –Jenny V according to the rota, but known as Jamie Vance to Riley – was in the hospital, unconscious with a fractured skull. The woman handcuffed to the desk was the other suspect Riley had discovered was missing from the pub by the docks.

"I remember you," Riley continued. "And I remember the scam you were running. You'd find a moderately wealthy mark and 'fall in love'." The inverted commas clanged into place as Frobisher looked from one officer to the other, and then to the door, seeking some way out. "You'd persuade him to finance an expedition to the wasteland in search of some great national treasure," Riley continued, "with the promise its recovery would bring you both fame, wealth, and a lifetime of marital bliss."

"What kind of treasures?" Mitchell asked.

"The crown jewels," Riley said. "The location of a missing nuclear submarine. Once it was the only extant copy of Shakespeare's lost play, Cardenio." She turned back to the prisoner. "And as soon as you'd milked him dry, your missing first husband would return, as if from the grave. You were left richer, and the poor sap was left broke. You did two years light labour, one clearing the roads from here to Folkestone, another digging drainage ditches around farms in northern Dorset. I remember you, Frobisher."

"Diane F, on the cleaning rota," Mitchell said, taking the piece of paper out of the folder he'd taken in with him. "There's no point denying it."

Frobisher took one final look at the door before turning to face Riley and Mitchell.

"I wasn't going to," she said. "And yes, I remember you."

Ruth hadn't expected that. From the way that Weaver was smiling, the assistant commissioner had. Ruth wanted to ask what verbal trap Frobisher had talked her way into, but couldn't. Though the mirrored glass prevented them from being seen, they all knew the room was nowhere close to soundproof.

"Good," Mitchell said. "Then tell us what you were doing in that house."

"Waiting and not breaking the law." The suspect spoke with a cultivated accent that sounded almost cultured. Almost. She was concentrating so hard on not dropping her 't's that she'd forgotten about her 'g's.

"You had a lot of illegal firearms for a law-abiding citizen," Riley said.

"You won't find my fingerprints on any of them," Frobisher said.

"That won't stop us from charging you with their possession," Mitchell said. "Perhaps I wasn't clear. You don't know how much trouble you're in. I'm going to set out your situation clearly and honestly. If you do the same with your replies, it's possible you might escape the death penalty."

Surprise knocked the mask from Frobisher's face. "Death penalty?"

"It's still on the books," Mitchell said. "A legitimate punishment for treason and insurrection. That's what you're involved in."

"I…" Frobisher began, but then the smile returned, pulling the mask back into place. "You're bluffing."

"I'm not. Longfield!" Mitchell yelled at the door.

Simon came into the room carrying one of the backpacks they'd found in the house's bedrooms. Frobisher watched him with suspicion.

"I'm going to tell you something, Frobisher," Mitchell said, taking the bag from Simon. "And then I'm going to show you something. After that you'll be given your chance to talk. Six of you are still alive. One of you will take this deal. That person will live. The rest of you will go to prison.

You'll be sentenced to death. There are some lawyers arguing that the death penalty is illegal. That it was established as part of the Emergency Powers Act after the Blackout by a government that wasn't properly constituted. So, your lawyer will stage an appeal. It doesn't matter. You'll be a dead woman walking from the moment you step into prison. Your boss won't let you live. He'll kill you so you won't talk."

Frobisher smiled. "Is that it? That's what you wanted to tell me? It's a variation on the same threat every police officer has used since the dawn of time."

"I hadn't finished," Mitchell said. "Whether or not you understand the danger you're in, *I* want to know that I've informed you as to the risks. You can ignore me, but my conscience will be clear." He opened the bag and pulled out the stack of banknotes. "There's four thousand pounds here, and the same in each of the backpacks we found in that house. That's telling. Specifically, it tells me that you were all terrified of the person who gave it to you. Otherwise you'd have stolen it." He paused. There was no response from the prisoner.

"It was payment wasn't it?" Riley asked.

Frobisher's eyes narrowed, but she said nothing.

"You have a cleaning rota," Mitchell said. "There's no alcohol in the house. No coffee. No sugar. Not even any sweetener. The garden door was locked, but we found a key around the neck of one of the men we killed." He moved his finger across the handwritten rota, but kept his eyes fixed on Frobisher. "Manuel G? No." His finger stopped. "Mark R? Ah. He didn't open the door when a hot-air balloon flew overhead so low that the rope dangling from the basket knocked against the windows of your house. That's telling me you were told not to go outside, and so you didn't. You were paid in advance, yet you didn't steal the money and run. There's only one thing that can do that. Fear. You are terrified of the man who paid you."

The woman smirked and leaned back. The chain clinked as she tried to move her handcuffed hands. The smirk briefly flashed into a scowl.

"Why were you there?" Mitchell asked. "That's my question."

"Six men, two women," Riley said. "Only a handful of books to read. Was that it? You and Jenny Vance were there for entertainment?"

"It wasn't like that," Frobisher said.

"No? What was it like?" Mitchell asked.

Frobisher shook her head.

"I said I would tell you something. Here it is," Mitchell said. "The money's fake. The serial numbers confirm it. We broke the counterfeiting ring two weeks ago and have been following their trail ever since. That's how we found you. Because of this, the Mint is going to withdraw all twenty-pound notes from circulation and replace them with a new design. In a few weeks, this money will be worthless. Four thousand pounds? It's nearly two years of my salary. How would you spend that in a week?"

Frobisher's eyes flicked between Mitchell, Riley, and the notes.

"She doesn't believe you," Riley said.

"No. Perhaps I should prove it to her. Longfield?"

Simon went out into the corridor and brought in a metal trolley. On the bottom shelf was a metal bin. The top shelf was covered by a thin sheet. Despite everything that had happened so far that day, or perhaps because of it, Ruth was looking forward to what was about to happen.

Mitchell removed the sheet, revealing row upon row of neatly stacked bank notes. "There's two hundred thousand pounds here," he said. "And that's not even a fraction of the amount waiting for disposal in the vault." He placed the bin on the floor, took a bundle of notes from the trolley, removed the string holding the stack together, and dropped them into the bin.

"Do you have a match, sergeant?"

Riley reached into her pocket, and with deliberate exaggeration, pulled out a book of matches. Mitchell took them, struck one, and dropped it in. They'd soaked the bin with accelerant, so when the flame hit the evaporating vapour, it caught with a soft whoosh. Flames licked upward for a second, bathing the room with a sinister orange glow. Mitchell picked up the stack of notes from the table and riffled through them.

"They're forged. Do you understand?" he said.

"It's... it's a trick," Frobisher said.

Mitchell pulled out a note and dropped it into the bin. "No, it's not. The money is forged. Either you were meant to be caught when you tried to spend it, or you were never going to get the chance to do so. You're disposable." He dropped another note into the bin. "Or perhaps the person behind this doesn't care. They set you up. Who hired you? What's his name?"

"It wasn't…" Frobisher began, blinked, and stopped. "I can't."

"You can't? I bet I can guess why. There was a demonstration. Something emphatic and violent that came with a promise that you'd face the same fate if you ever mentioned his name. Yes?"

Frobisher shook her head.

Mitchell dropped the rest of the banknotes into the bin. "We only need one of you to talk. This person you're afraid of will assume you all did. One of you will get the chance at a new life, the rest will go to prison, where you'll wait for the day he finally gets to you."

"Wait. You'll let me go free?" Frobisher asked.

"That depends on what you can tell us," Mitchell said.

"If you let me go, I'll tell you everything."

"That's not how it works. You know that," Riley said.

"I want a boat that will take me to Europe or Africa. I'll never come back, I promise."

"You're that scared of him?" Mitchell asked.

"It's not—" she began and again stopped. "Just let me go, please. I promise you'll never see me again."

"You know the game. You have to start by telling me something. So, let's begin with what you were doing in that house."

"Waiting," she said.

"Since when?"

"August."

"You were recruited at the Marquis?" Riley asked.

The woman looked startled for a moment, then her veil of composure returned. "That's right."

"What were you waiting for?" Mitchell asked.

"I…" She shook her head. "No. I can't."

"Then you force us to draw our own assumptions," Mitchell said. "Based on those assault rifles and that ammunition, there's only one reason for you to be in that house. Maybe you call it revolution, and maybe the court will call it terrorism, but I say it's mass murder."

"No, it wasn't that," she said. "I don't know why those guns were there. I really don't."

"Then what do you know?" Riley asked. "Why were you hired?"

"For a robbery," Frobisher said.

"A robbery? What were you going to steal?" Mitchell asked.

"I don't know. We were going to get the details closer to the time. There was a window of opportunity sometime between September and December, and we were waiting until it arrived."

"What about the printing press?" Riley asked. "Those pamphlets were revolutionary in nature."

"I don't know. I think they were to be part of the distraction."

"Distraction? During the robbery you mean?" Riley asked.

"I think so. That's what the men who brought the press said."

"When was this?" Mitchell asked.

"A week ago. We were to print out ten thousand of those leaflets."

"What else did he say?" Riley asked.

"He wasn't talking to me," Frobisher said. "He didn't even know I was listening. There were two of them. They brought the press along with the food. As they were bringing it into the house, he said that it would be a good distraction."

"Who was this man? What was his name?" Riley asked.

"I don't know. But I'd seen him before, and he had a face anyone would remember. It was all scarred, like someone had carved lines into it."

"A distraction," Mitchell said. He gave the still smoking metal bin a kick. "To distract who from what? And what could they possibly want to steal?"

"If they wanted to steal anything," Davis said.

Frobisher had stopped talking and had been returned to the cells. Weaver, Ruth, Davis, and Simon had joined Mitchell and Riley in the interrogation room.

"You shouldn't have destroyed evidence," Weaver said.

"I didn't," Mitchell replied. "The notes we found in the house are still down in the evidence locker. Those," he gave the bin another kick, "all came from the Mint. Since they're due to be incinerated, I can't see what harm there is in burning them here and now."

"There *are* procedures," Weaver said.

"Do they really matter?" Mitchell replied.

"She identified Emmitt, at least," Ruth quickly added, sensing that the truce currently existing between the two officers was about to break. "And she's not scared of him. I mean, she's scared of someone, but it's not him. In fact, I think it's a woman. You noticed how she automatically interrupted whenever the captain referred to the person as male?"

"Then there's the fact there were women there in the first place," Mitchell said. "If our mastermind isn't a woman, he's at least an equal opportunities criminal. What?" he added, addressing Weaver. "I can see you're thinking something. Do you have someone in mind?"

"Possibly. Wallace's wife. I have nothing on her, but there's no way she couldn't have known about her husband's plans. When I interviewed her, she didn't seem surprised. She's as much of a politician as him, and she was conveniently out of the city at the time. But I wouldn't have said she was intimidating."

"Could we get a picture of her, or a sketch?" Mitchell asked. "We could show it to Frobisher and see what her reaction is?"

"Certainly," Weaver said. "Do you think the others will be more responsive?"

"In time," Mitchell said. "The question is whether we have time. Cutting those telegraph wires, organising the Luddites for some kind of public demonstration, it's building up to something. Then there's this lot, waiting for a robbery with far more weapons than they need."

"She said it would be sometime between September and December," Weaver said. "Ned Ludd mentioned the fifth of November. That must be when it's going to happen."

"There was only a week's worth of food in that house," Mitchell said. "Fairmont said there were five others. What if Emmitt decides it's easier to bring his plans forward than to resupply them? But what are those plans?"

"Tell the newspaper," Ruth said.

"I'm sorry?" Weaver asked.

"Tell them to print the story about the counterfeiting. If Emmitt's hired people with forged currency, maybe they'll read the story and decide to quit."

"I didn't see any newspapers in the house," Mitchell said.

"But that doesn't mean all the houses are like that," Ruth said. "Someone, somewhere, who's working for Emmitt will read it."

"But they won't come forward," Simon said. "You saw how terrified Frobisher was."

"Maybe not," Ruth said. "Maybe they'll disappear, and if we can't catch them, that might be the best we can hope for. Besides, people have a right to know what's going on. How many people saw that balloon crash? How many Marines were involved today, or on duty when the Prime Minister was shot? They won't keep quiet forever. Rumours will start, and when the truth does get out, people won't trust the government. Wasn't that what Wallace wanted, for all faith to be lost in those running the country?"

"She has a point. The truth should be told," Mitchell said. "And," he added, "it will hurt Emmitt more than us."

"I can suggest it to the Prime Minister," Weaver said, "but the decision will be hers."

"That leaves Fairmont," Mitchell said. "What kind of deal can we offer him?"

"There's a lighthouse near Thurso," Weaver said. "It has two keepers who work the light, and twenty Marines who guard the facility. It's twenty miles from the Naval dockyard and is in constant contact by telegraph."

"The far north of Scotland? That would fit Fairmont's criteria of being remote," Mitchell said. "Double the Marines and arrange for a ship to sail within hailing distance at least once a day. Can they hold out if they're attacked?"

"For at least a week," Weaver said. "It's not an easy place to reach, especially at this time of year."

"I'll get him to give us another address before we leave, and the rest when we arrive in Scotland," Mitchell said. "If we send it back by telegraph we can have all properties searched within forty-eight hours. It's not as immediate as I'd like, but we can't lean on him too hard, not if we want to trust the information he gives us. It'll take me a few hours to arrange the train, which should give you enough time to get the Marines in place to raid another property."

"You?" Weaver asked. "You're taking him north?"

"My days of kicking doors down are over," Mitchell said, pointing at the bloody stain on his shirt. "The Marines can handle that. Riley and Davis can run the interviews of these suspects. *I* want to look Fairmont in the eyes when he tells us whatever he knows so I can be sure as I can that he's not lying. Deering, you're coming with me."

"To Scotland?" she asked.

"All the way."

Chapter 6
All Stations North
4th October

Maggie's loud snore brought Ruth back to consciousness. She tried blinking the room into focus. She realised she couldn't because it was almost pitch-black. There was a fading glow from the sitting-room fire, but the candles had long since gone out. She added another log to the grate, picked up the fallen blanket, and gently placed it back on her mother before going to the front door. There was no one outside. Moonlight caught the hands of the clock and told her it was three a.m.

Mitchell had told her to go home and pack, and that a carriage would be sent for her as soon as the arrangements for a train had been made. No one had arrived by midnight, and Ruth had said she'd stay in the front room to wait. Maggie had insisted on staying with her.

Two minutes past three.

She hated that time. No good thoughts came between one and five, only the demons of the past and the fears of the future. It was a time to sleep, yet she knew she wouldn't be able. She grabbed the kettle and went outside. An unseen downpour had doused the cracked paving. The air was cold and damp but, knowing that warmth was only a few feet away, it wasn't unpleasant. She pulled the lever and turned the tap, listening as the hiss of air in the pipes sent nocturnal visitors scurrying back into the hedgerow.

There were many things wrong with their home. In fact, there were so many it was easy to come up with a list of the things that were right. At the top of that short list was that it was the only home she knew, but it wouldn't be for much longer.

Another letter had arrived. The school would close before the end of this academic year. No exact date was given, but Maggie's job would go with it. Her mother's only response was that it was long past time for her to retire.

Ruth took the kettle back inside, hanging it on the hook over the fire. She stoked the embers until flames danced around its base.

The question Riley had asked came back to her. Did she want to stay in the police? The more she thought about it, the more certain she became that the answer was no. That left the bigger question of what she should do instead. Go to America, perhaps. The ambassador had said he owed her a favour. Presumably that could be stretched into the recommendation for a job doing… what? The water in the kettle came to a boil before she'd come up with an answer.

The carriage arrived just after four and was driven by a familiar hulking shape.

"Gregory?" Ruth asked, too tired to formulate a proper question.

"It's a matter of whom I can trust," Mitchell said, jumping down from the back. "Have you got everything you need?"

"Clothes for a couple of days," Ruth said, hefting a bag.

"And take this," Maggie said, holding out a bag. "Food for the journey. Did you pack your scarf?"

"Mum—" Ruth began.

"It's cold in Scotland," Maggie said, speaking over her daughter. "Go and fetch it. And your gloves. You'll keep her safe, Henry?"

"I will."

Maggie looked like she wanted to say something more. She didn't.

"Is Gregory coming with us?" Ruth asked as the horses' hooves broke the morning's silence.

"To Scotland? No. It's just you, me, and the Marines," Mitchell said. "Fairmont too, but I count him as baggage. I want as few people as possible knowing the specifics of what we're doing, that's why this has taken so long to organise. Realistically, and no matter what Clarke says to the contrary, there's no way of keeping Fairmont's removal secret from the people working in the embassy. Do you remember all of those crates in the lobby? I don't know who's doing the heavy lifting, but I'd bet it's casual labour hired because they were cheap. They'll talk, and Emmitt will be listening, so he'll know Fairmont's gone but not to where. The driver and stoker for the train will arrive at work thinking they've a normal day ahead of them. Rebecca Cavendish knows, of course, as she had to arrange for our train to disappear."

"Disappear?" Ruth asked.

"Of course," Mitchell said. "There's going to be a smoke-belching beast driving through dozens of country stations without taking on passengers or goods. People are going to ask why. There needs to be a plausible reason, one the station managers believe is the truth. It's the same for the depots where we'll stop for water. They'll want to know why a train full of Marines is driving through their peaceful neck of the woods. It took us a few hours of scheming, but we've got it all worked out. The only truly dangerous part will be moving Fairmont from the embassy to the station. That's why we've got Gregory."

"You're expecting trouble?" Ruth asked.

"Always," Mitchell said. "Up until now we've been playing Emmitt's game and were always two moves behind. Yesterday we did something that will force him to change his plans. A natural response would be to seek revenge. But if he acts in haste, we've a chance he'll make some catastrophic mistake. It's not much to pin his capture on, but it might be enough."

Ruth leaned back in her seat. The shadowy fields and dark warehouses took on a far more sinister appearance as those words sunk in.

There were more Marines on duty in the embassy than there had been the day before. It was just light enough to make out a new gun emplacement on the roof. She wondered how many other guards were deliberately hidden from view.

The gate was pulled back, and the carriage let into the courtyard. Agent Clarke was waiting for them.

"Do you have any more intel?" Clarke asked.

"Not since we last spoke," Mitchell said. "You really upped the security here."

"If they're planning to make us the target, they'll regret it," Clarke said.

"Is Fairmont ready?" Mitchell asked.

"I picked his clothes myself," Clarke said.

The comment baffled Ruth until Fairmont shuffled outside. A Marine was in front, another behind, with two more either side. The prisoner's hands and feet were manacled with a thin chain connecting ankles to wrists. It was the suit that was most striking. It was of a lurid, orange chequered pattern. Clearly of old-world make, Ruth marvelled for a moment that anyone had ever made such a hideous garment, let alone worn it voluntarily.

"We could have provided him with a convict's uniform," Mitchell said.

"He was paid for the information he sold," Clarke said. "And do you know what he spent the money on? Suits. I thought this was a fitting punishment." She handed Mitchell the key to the manacles. "Safe journey."

Mitchell prodded Fairmont up into the carriage.

"Easy!" Fairmont said.

"If you want it easy, give us the other addresses now," Mitchell said.

"And have you go back on your word?" Fairmont replied. "Not likely."

"Then get in," Mitchell said, pushing the man into a seat. He drew his revolver and sat opposite. "Eyes on the road outside," he said to Ruth, "But don't sit too close to the window."

It was a tense journey, made worse by a gnawing expectation of trouble, but after five minutes they arrived at the train station without incident.

Gregory brought the carriage to a halt outside the goods' entrance.

"Take a look," Mitchell said, grabbing Fairmont's shoulder and moving him toward the window, before pushing him back into his seat. "We're at the station. Now give me the address."

"Not until I'm on the train," Fairmont said.

"Understand this, you're not in charge. Tell me the address or I'll let you go here and now. How long do you think you'd last out on the streets, handcuffed, and wearing a suit like that? An hour? I doubt it would be anywhere near as long."

"You do that, and you'll never find the—" Fairmont began.

"You're not the only lead we have," Mitchell interrupted. "You're expendable, Fairmont. What's the address?"

Fairmont looked from Mitchell to Ruth. There was no fear in his eyes, just cold calculation.

"Greychurch Street," Fairmont said. "Number fourteen. It's a terrace."

"What will we find there?"

"Six people, all armed. Pretty much the same as Windward Square. I take it that was as I said it would be?"

Mitchell ignored the question, scrawled the address on a piece of paper, and passed it to Gregory. "You know what to do with that?"

The huge man nodded. Mitchell pushed Fairmont out of the carriage. Ruth grabbed their bags and followed.

The station was virtually deserted. The few people present all wore the livery of the Railway Company, and formed a rough ring guarding a platform. Each held a thick metal pole or gleaming shovel, and it was a reassuring sight until Ruth remembered the automatic rifles they'd found in Windward Square.

Mitchell led Fairmont toward a small crowd waiting on the nearest platform. Here, the weapons were a mixture of shotguns among the railway workers, and automatic rifles carried by the Marines standing guard over the train.

A woman in a wheelchair rolled herself ahead of the armed group.

"Is this the terrorist, Henry?" she asked.

"It is."

The woman gave Fairmont a scowl of absolute disgust. She made a show of wheeling her chair out of his line of sight. "And this is Officer Deering?" she asked.

"It is," Mitchell said.

"Rebecca Cavendish," the woman said, extending a hand. "A pleasure to meet you."

"And you," Ruth said, adding, "ma'am." She wasn't sure whether Cavendish had an official rank, but from the way that everyone in the cavernous station deferred to her, she was the one in charge.

"Lieutenant Lewis?" Mitchell said. "Take the prisoner on board."

"Corporal Lin," the young lieutenant barked. A woman stepped forward, barked her own orders at four Marines, and Fairmont was hustled onto the train.

"I've cleared the tracks," Rebecca said, her voice low. Ruth turned back to face her. "There's a Mail train ahead of you, and you're to stay thirty-four minutes behind it until you're past Leicester. If there's trouble on the tracks, it'll run into it first."

"How would we know?" Ruth asked.

"From the telegraph. Each time a Mail train arrives at a depot, a message is sent back to confirm its arrival. We don't do that for passenger services – they don't want the line clogged. Thirty-four minutes, that's your window. You've got Greg Higgins as a driver, and Hamish Boyd as your stoker. Good men, both. They have the schedule, and it's fixed until you get to Scotland. There's a bad storm being reported in the Highlands, so check the weather report when you get to the border. You may need to take the lowland route."

"And banditry?" Mitchell asked.

"Shouldn't be a problem," Rebecca said. "There's an assimilation deal being discussed with the tribes around Leicester, and docility was one of the pre-requisites for the talks to begin. Other than that, you're going through mostly civilised areas where the bandits have become farmers or hunters, relying on the train for trade. Good luck, Henry, and to you, Miss Deering. Travel safe and return the same way."

Ruth nodded politely and followed Mitchell toward the train. The lieutenant fell into step.

"Lieutenant Charles Lewis," he said, introducing himself to Ruth, though she recognised him from the raid on the house in Windward Square. "I'm in charge of this detachment, and will take over command of the detail when we arrive. Corporal Helen Lin is my second in command." There was a pause. "We, ah, we don't know if she'll still hold that position when we arrive."

Ruth sensed there was a question hidden in that last remark, but wasn't sure what it was. Before she could ask, Mitchell spoke.

"Lieutenant, you're with me," he said. "I want to check the train's entry and exit points."

"Yes, sir," Lewis said, falling into step with Mitchell, leaving Ruth alone.

Realising that there was nothing she was supposed to do, she climbed aboard. The corporal was waiting inside, by the door.

"Corporal Helen Lin," the woman said.

"Hi," Ruth said.

"I don't suppose you know where we're going?"

"You mean you don't?" Ruth asked.

"I was blissfully asleep in the barracks four hours ago," Lin said. "Ten minutes later I was hustling this lot down here. I gather we're going to Scotland?"

"I think so," Ruth said.

"Corporal!" the lieutenant called. Lin rolled her eyes and hurried away.

The train consisted of two carriages, a tender, and a locomotive. From the outside it had looked like a normal service. Inside was much the same. The windows were scratched, and the seats were shabbily re-upholstered in every shade of faded red. Light came from electric lamps above the doors at either end. Another hung from a temporary fixture above Fairmont's cell – the wire-and-bar cage usually reserved for transporting parcels and letters. He, Ruth was pleased to see, had no seat but instead lay on a thin mattress on the floor.

Ruth took the bags to a spot near the rear, but from where she could still see the prisoner. The Marines settled in around her. From the occasional overheard sentence, this assignment was a welcome relief from the monotony of their usual duties.

There was a jolt, a soft whistle, and the train began to move. As they pulled out of the lit station, the view beyond the window darkened. As they went by the homes owned by railway workers, there were occasional pinpricks of light. The train sped up. They entered the warehouse district where goods were stored before being shipped to the far-flung corners of Britain, and the lights disappeared.

Ruth tried to find a comfortable position, but the seats were too narrow to lie down on, and too far apart to set her feet on the seat opposite. She glanced at Fairmont. He seemed to be asleep.

There was a soft flick and then a flare behind her as a quintet of Marines lit candles and began a game of cards. Ruth was tempted to join them, but they were playing for money and she had none. Instead, she turned her eyes to the window, watching for the dawn.

It was another half an hour before Mitchell returned. He paused by Fairmont's cage for a long minute before continuing down, past Ruth, to the Marines. There was a conversation spoken too softly for Ruth to hear. Mitchell took the deck, shuffled it, and dealt a single card to each Marine. Corporal Lin threw hers down with disgust. The others laughed as the corporal went to take up a seat near Fairmont. Mitchell came to sit down opposite Ruth. His thoughtful expression was somewhat marred by the wind-swept, soot-smudged face of someone who'd been in the locomotive's cab.

"Is everything okay?" she asked.

"Yes," he said. "It's all going exactly as planned."

"That makes you worried?" Ruth asked.

Mitchell smiled. "No, it makes me realise that the best we'll get out of Fairmont is the arrest of a few more hired thugs. There's a saying: the criminal only has to get lucky once, but the copper has to be lucky thousands of times a day. Today I was unlucky. I was expecting Emmitt to try something as we moved the prisoner."

"Try something? You mean try to kill Fairmont?"

"Like he did with Lyons and Turnbull. The embassy was the weak link. Emmitt must have known Fairmont was there. I bet he had someone watching the embassy. Or, since he had Fairmont working for him, why not someone else on the inside? Certainly, he must have realised who told us about Windward Square. It's why I enlisted Isaac's help, and used that carriage for transporting our prisoner. It's heavily reinforced and far more secure than any police vehicle. Gregory wasn't the only person I... ah, but it doesn't matter now. I made an assumption and I was wrong. Emmitt didn't attack, and that suggests whatever Fairmont might tell us no longer poses a risk to the man's schemes. He probably spent his time destroying any evidence he thinks we might discover."

"Then is there any point continuing with Fairmont's deal?" Ruth asked.

"You tell me."

Ruth considered it. "We don't have any better leads," she said. "And there's the chance that Fairmont saw or heard about something that can't be moved or destroyed. And Emmitt might still come after Fairmont."

"No. Not now we're on the train. We're safe."

"How can you be sure?"

"Trains have many faults, but they can only be run along tracks. Emmitt can chase us, but he can't overtake us. He might be able to hijack a train, but he'd run out of water and coal, be diverted into a siding, or find the gates of a depot closed to him. No, he can't catch us, and he doesn't know where we're going. Right now, we're heading east, but we'll soon turn north, cross the Thames near Oxford and head toward the ruins of Leicester. We'll stop in Darlington for the night, possibly Cumbria if we make good time, and cross into Scotland tomorrow."

"We won't try to reach the lighthouse today?" Ruth asked.

"No. It's not safe to drive through the wasteland unless you can see the tracks ahead are clear. So, sit back, relax, and enjoy the journey. Didn't you say you always wanted to travel?"

"Yes," Ruth admitted. Outside the window, the distant clouds were slowly brightening. "I suppose I thought it would be more exciting than this."

Mitchell smiled, and Ruth suddenly didn't know what to say. He might be an old friend of her mother, but he was also her superior officer. Silence grew. Wanting to fill it with something other than awkwardness, she took out a small paper bag.

"Maggie spent all evening making these," Ruth said. "And she said I should share them with you."

"She did?"

"She kind of insisted," Ruth said.

Mitchell peered inside the bag, cautiously selected the smallest bun, and took a reluctant bite. His eyes widened in surprise. "I stand corrected," he said. "This is actually rather good."

"Why do you sound so shocked?"

"When I first met your mother, she didn't cook," Mitchell said. "In fact, I don't think she'd ever scrambled an egg before the Blackout." He took another bite. "I remember…. let's see, when was it? About a month after we left London, we were in a multi-storey parking complex on the edge of Bournemouth. There were twelve of us, syphoning gasoline from abandoned cars. It was a lot colder than it should have been for September, but the weather was erratic during those first years after the bombs fell. We started a fire to keep warm. Maggie was put on tea duty. I thought, since she was a scientist, that she'd understand the principles of boiling water. Well, she knew about fire and heat, but not about putting a lid on a saucepan. The water was full of ash and cinders, which didn't stop her from making the tea. It tasted foul." Mitchell smiled as his mind swam in years gone by.

"That's a happy memory?" Ruth asked.

"It is," Mitchell said. "It is. The walk from London…" His face dropped. "We only had what we could carry. For the most part we were carrying each other. We had few medical supplies, but it seemed like each house contained someone screaming for help. There was nothing we could do. No, that's not true. There was one thing, but…" He trailed off. That brief spark of happiness was now entirely gone from his face.

"When we retreated into the tunnels, London was a living city," he said. "When we pushed the rubble away and climbed back out into daylight, there was nothing but desolation. Fire, smoke, and a terrible, noxious stench, permeating air too thick to breathe. We staggered away from those tunnels, eyes streaming, gagging on those acrid fumes. We moved, and kept moving, just to get away from it. Only painful discomfort prevented us from giving into abject despair. We were surrounded by death. Mile after mile of ash, bone, and blood. Then came the screams. At first they were too inhuman to identify as that, belonging to those who were technically alive, but whose only wish was that they weren't. There was a girl, perhaps eight years old, in the lobby of an apartment block. It looked like the skin had been boiled from her face. I picked her up, and carried her for seven long miles. I knew, with each incoherent bubbling breath she took, all she wanted was for the pain to stop. There was only one way her story would end, but I couldn't give her that quick release." He was silent for a moment.

"When she died," he said, "there wasn't time to bury her. I wrapped her in my coat and kept walking. Those seven miles changed me. Not in some sudden epiphanic moment, but step-by-step my beliefs were worn away. By the time I pulled my jacket over her sightless eyes, everything I knew and believed was gone. I saw the world as it truly was, with the veneer of polite civilisation torn down. I understood how much a life was truly worth. I—" He stopped. "Compared to that," he said, taking another bun out of the bag, "the recollection of a cup of sour, sooty tea truly is a happy memory." He turned to face the window. So did Ruth.

Dawn swept down from the horizon, bathing the fields with a brittle autumnal glow. The train slowed as it approached a set of points, giving her a view of a group of farmers trying to wrestle an obstreperous horse into the yoke of a plough.

"Life goes on," she murmured.

"It almost didn't," Mitchell said. "But it did, and it still does. That's worth remembering." He took another bun.

"But you didn't see much of Maggie recently," Ruth said. "I mean, you never came around to the house."

"I visited quite frequently when Riley was younger, and always for advice. With the sudden acquisition of a teenage daughter, I needed a lot of that. Then Maggie adopted you and moved into The Acre. There were some summer evenings when I would continue my walk along the coast, and head inland to visit. As the years went by, we both got busier, and found we had little to say to one another. We'd grown to know each other during a painful, tragic time that neither of us wished to remember. Perhaps we were trying to pretend the past never happened." He shrugged. "Or perhaps knowing that the other was alive was all either of us needed. Either way, we have enough to worry about in the present without dwelling on the past. You won't have seen today's newspaper."

"No."

He reached into his bag and pulled out a copy. "This came straight from the press. Have a read." He glanced over his shoulder at Fairmont, settled into his chair, and closed his eyes.

Ruth took the paper, and looked at it, unseeing. A dozen questions came to mind, about Mitchell and Maggie, and those early years after the Blackout. Ruth decided to keep them to herself. She could guess the shape of his answers, and somehow the specific details didn't matter.

A beam of light curled through the clouds to land on the newspaper. She realised that she'd been staring at the headline without reading it. It was one word, 'Counterfeit'. The article that followed described how a massive counterfeiting ring had been broken. Dozens of arrests had been made and... she skipped ahead a few paragraphs.

The old currency was being withdrawn. From that morning, twenty-pound notes would only be honoured at banks. To avoid disruption to normal business, banks would open on Sundays, with special counters set up. Customers would be allowed to exchange their currency on certain days, based on surname and address. There was going to be a cap on withdrawals and... and more details that she wasn't interested in. A sidebar caught her attention. It was a recruitment ad dressed up as an article about how the banks were taking on additional staff in each branch.

She scanned the main article again. The details about the counterfeiting ring were mostly false. Weaver got all the credit for breaking it. There was no mention of Mitchell, Riley, herself, or Serious Crimes. The inside pages carried a thoroughly vivid and entirely fictitious account of a gun battle between unnamed police officers and the counterfeiters. Ruth had never heard of Ollie Hunter, the journalist who wrote it, but thought he would be better employed writing fiction than news. The lurid tale was illustrated with the sketches of Clipton and Emmitt that had graced previous editions. Under Clipton's face was the word 'Dead'. Under Emmitt's was 'Wanted'. She turned the page.

The headline 'What Faces Now?' stood at the top of a debate the editor, Diane Goldstein, was having with herself over who should replace that long dead monarch on the new banknotes. Ruth turned to the next page and the next, but they were filled with the usual good-news-on-bad-days stories. When she reached the back page, and its mixture of sporting defeats, she looked up. Mitchell was watching her.

"There's no mention of the assassination attempt," she said.

"No. That's being held for the end of the week. You see the line, second paragraph from the end on the front page."

Ruth looked for it. "Some details have been withheld for operational reasons, but are expected to be released over the coming days," she read aloud. "That's the assassination?"

"And Wallace's part in it," Mitchell said. "It was Hunter's idea."

"He's the journalist? He didn't mention you, or Serious Crimes."

"Because I told him not to. He has rooms in the same pub I lodge in. I more or less dictated the story to him."

"You mean you came up with that gun battle?" she asked.

"That," he said, "is an almost entirely accurate account of an incident in Guildford that Riley and I got into a few years back."

"And the bit with the collapsing skylight?"

"It actually happened."

"Oh." Ruth quickly skimmed through the account again and decided she didn't believe him. "But you gave Weaver all the credit."

"Sure. As an assistant commissioner, her rank makes her a public figure. The rest of us need to be able to lurk in the shadows. As for the assassination attempt, Hunter thinks it's best we lead up to it. Goldstein, the editor, thinks there's only one front page per issue, and doesn't want to waste a headline like 'Assassination' somewhere inside."

"That doesn't seem right. People should know the truth. All of it."

"Even if it's printed in the paper, it doesn't mean they'll read it. Even if they read it, it doesn't mean people will believe it, let alone *know* it. But I take your point. However, this is the compromise we have to accept."

"The job ad's a nice touch," Ruth said. "It makes it seem like things can't be too bad."

"We play down the danger our civilisation faces and thus is normality maintained. When people aren't discussing the gunfight, they'll talk about who should appear on the banknotes. The paper is going to announce a public competition to make the final decision."

"They are? How did you get The Mint to agree to that?"

"By not asking them. The Mint will have to go along with it. After all, it'll have been printed in the paper."

Half an hour later, the train began to slow.

"Is there a problem?" Ruth asked.

"No," Mitchell said. "We're taking on water. Stay on the train."

Ruth felt increasingly useless as the Marines took up positions by the doors and windows. Again she wondered why Mitchell had brought her. It clearly wasn't to help guard their prisoner – who was currently staring fixedly at her. Ruth returned the stare. Fairmont didn't look away. Frustrated, Ruth pulled out her notepad.

"What are you writing?" Mitchell asked, returning as the train began moving once more.

"A list of questions we want Fairmont to answer," she said. "Like when he first met Emmitt, who he saw at those houses, and what he heard them talk about. We need to work out what they're waiting for. If it *is* a robbery, maybe he heard something that will tell us what they're planning to steal, and maybe that will confirm whether it's going to take place on the fifth."

Mitchell placed a yellow slip of telegram paper on the table between them. "Read it," he said.

"Searched House. Empty. AR.," she read. "Is that from Riley?"

"Yes. You understand what it means?"

"Emmitt's already moved the people out of the house in Greychurch Street," Ruth said. "We shouldn't be wasting time going to Scotland and back."

"*We're* not," Mitchell said. "You're not coming back to Twynham."

"I'm not?"

He tapped her notepad. "As you deduced, someone needs to interview Fairmont, and it has to be someone who knows the case. That's you, me, Riley, and Weaver. You're the only choice. Sorry, *cadet*. That's seniority for you."

"Oh." She looked from the notepad, to the prisoner, and then to Mitchell. "But that's not the only reason it's me?"

"No. I promised Maggie I'd keep you safe. I haven't done a very good job so far. You've been through a lot more than most people do in a career, let alone a few weeks. You need a break from it."

"I... oh. But what if there's some kind of connection between all of this, and me?"

"You mean that coin? If there is, and if it isn't that near-mythical beast some call coincidence, then the connection isn't with you but with your parents. Perhaps they knew Emmitt. Maybe there was some old-world cabal that found a new lease of life after the Blackout. Or perhaps it's something else, but what could it mean now? That your parents are alive? If they are, they never looked for you and that tells you all you need to know. Forget the coin. Forget any connection. Ruminating on it won't do you any good."

"There's no point arguing, is there?" Ruth said.

"We're already on the train, aren't we?" Mitchell replied.

"I suppose, in a way, this is what I wanted," Ruth said. "I mean, I only joined the police because I thought it would get me out of Twynham."

"That's the spirit. Always look on the bright side, even if the far north is a pretty dark place this time of year."

Mitchell closed his eyes and gave every appearance of having gone to sleep. Ruth tried pacing up and down the carriage, but found Fairmont watched her every move. In search of somewhere to think, she retreated to the back of the rearmost carriage, and watched the scenery disappear behind them.

The sun rose higher. The landscape changed. Neat fields became a patchwork of new-growth forest, and that was replaced by wide grassland broken only by occasional ruins. After they'd crossed the Thames, the train depots grew larger, and their walls grew higher.

By half-past two, as Ruth was realising that one ruined house looked pretty much the same as any other, the brakes squealed, and the train came to a screeching halt. Ruth peered around, but there were no tilled fields suggesting that a depot was just ahead.

"Watch for movement!" Corporal Lin barked, running down the aisle. "Get those doors open, but hold your fire!"

After the Marine had passed, Ruth edged down the aisle and back into the first carriage. She saw Mitchell jump out of the open door, and run along the train in the direction of the locomotive. She followed. As she passed the tender, she looked around. They truly were in the middle of nowhere. Other than the train and the tracks, the only sign of humanity was a few felled trees, dragged into the undergrowth so they wouldn't be blown onto the tracks during a storm.

"Why did you stop?" she heard Mitchell ask the driver as she reached the locomotive's cab.

"That's Leicester," the driver said. "We've got to go through it."

Ruth looked ahead. Perhaps it was the shadows cast by a sun heading toward the horizon, but the hulking mass of the city looked ominously forbidding.

"Can't we go around?" she asked.

"Nope," Higgins, the driver, said. "Birmingham's to the west and that place is more dangerous than London. If we don't go forward, we'd have to go south, then cut east into Wales, or head back toward Bedford and across to Cambridge before we'd reach some tracks that would take us north. There's a coastal route that leads from the Wash toward Hull, but it's rarely used. We'd not be able to travel faster than eight miles an hour in case the rails were blocked. If you want to reach Scotland quickly, then you have to go through Leicester. It should be safe enough. We use this route to bring medicine to the tribes in the area. If they block the tracks, then they'll cut off their own supply. They won't do that, particularly not now these talks are being held. No, this is about a safe a time as any to travel through the city."

"Then why did you stop the train?" Ruth asked.

"Just because it's safer than any other time, doesn't actually make it safe," Higgins said.

Corporal Lin came running up. "Sir, the lieutenant wants to know what's going on," she said in a tone that suggested she was the one asking the question.

"We're going through Leicester. Pass the word, we're expecting trouble," Mitchell said.

"Yes, sir," Lin said, and ran back to the train.

"Might as well get moving, then," Mitchell said, climbing into the cab. Ruth followed. The driver muttered something under his breath about people getting in the way.

"Who are these tribes?" Ruth asked as the train set off once more.

"For one thing, it's tribe, singular," Mitchell said. "And that's where the problems start. They call themselves Albion. It was a sprawling mess of competing gangs that coalesced around a single leader, and in animosity toward the common enemy. Us."

"Why?"

"Sadly, because it's easier to maintain control of a populace if someone else can be blamed for all that goes wrong."

"Are there many of them?"

"Not really," Mitchell said "Somewhere between five and twenty thousand. That's counting infants and the old. Most of them are hunters and farmers of one sort or another. I doubt there's more than a hundred dedicated fighters in the group."

"Why don't we send the Marines in?" she asked.

"Because dead is dead, whether it's from an arrow or a bullet," Mitchell said. "Besides, if you kill their fighters, there would still be thousands of them left. People whose friends, spouses, siblings, and parents you've just killed. The children would grow up in hatred and there'd be an uprising a generation from now. Instead we send in negotiators, and hold talks between us and their king."

"King?" she asked.

"Yes, they have a king. That's the current sticking point. Since Britain is still a monarchy absent of any head on which to hang a crown, and Albion has a king in search of a realm, he has gracefully offered his services."

"Will we let him?"

"Of course not," Mitchell said. "But when we say no to that, it's harder to say no to something else, like ownership of Birmingham for instance. The upshot of all of this is that they've been known to delay trains and sometimes ambush them to take hostages."

"How does that help their cause?" she asked.

"Because the king isn't the one to kidnap them. It's always some unknown group of bandits. The king promises to send his people to effect the rescue, and in return we'll show our gratitude by giving in to one of his terms. Of course, we know he's the one who organised the kidnapping, and he knows we know, but since we can't prove it, what can we do?"

"That sounds… complicated."

"It's politics," Mitchell said, "but it's better than the alternative. Keep your eyes ahead."

The city was approaching fast. Somehow it looked different from the ruins on the English south coast with which Ruth was familiar. There were the same skeletal frames where stubby towers had burned down or been partially collapsed. Nearby were houses with fractured roofs, and others that seemed intact. Those were familiar sights, but it was the absence of smoke that was different. The smog bank from the coal power station, the factories, the railways, the hundreds of workshops and thousands of homes, was so ever-present in Twynham that's she'd grown to ignore it. The other noticeable difference was the rubbish littering the side of the railroad. There was no path running alongside the tracks. Behind and sometimes in the midst of the wall of vegetation were the rusting remains of old motor vehicles of every size and model.

"It's like a junkyard," she said.

"They did that," Higgins yelled over the now-roaring engine.

"What?"

"Walled off the tracks and blocked every siding," Higgins said. "We can only travel the route they want us to. It keeps us away from their homes. We're going to have to slow. The tracks curve too tight for us to risk more than twelve miles an hour. Watch out, they might try to jump on."

The buildings grew closer together. Weeds and small trees had taken root in walls and roofs. Most looked like they would collapse in a strong storm, and the increasingly frequent piles of rubble suggested that many had. Ahead, Ruth saw something. She stuck her head outside the cab, trying to get a better view.

"There's a light," she yelled. "No. It's a fire. On that five-storey ruin. The top floor. It's… oh. It's gone out."

"It's a signal," Mitchell yelled.

"For what?" Ruth asked.

"Nothing good," Mitchell said.

The detached houses turned into a compact terrace of buckled roofs and broken windows.

"A face. There. Did you see it?" she called.

"Speak up," the driver yelled over the hissing, roaring engine.

"I saw someone!"

"Of course," Higgins said. "From now on, only interrupt if you've something important to say."

The driver slowed the train again. The terrace was replaced by a swamp. A half-submerged climbing frame suggested it had once been a park. Higgins growled as the wheels lost traction on the wet rails. Ruth wondered whether the people of Albion had flooded the land deliberately. She didn't ask.

"Bridge coming up," the stoker yelled, stowing his shovel. He grabbed a shotgun from the rack and moved to a window. Mitchell drew his own weapon and took station by the other.

"What do I do?" Ruth asked.

"Watch out for flames," Higgins yelled.

"Flames?"

The driver didn't reply.

The bridge grew nearer. It wasn't wide, with room for only two lanes of traffic, but she could see movement on it. Figures scurried from west to east, occasionally ducking down out of sight.

The driver pulled on the whistle. A loud screech cut through the air. Ruth was nearly deafened, but at least it drowned out the sound of her pounding heart. The wide plough at the front of the locomotive reached the shadow cast by the bridge. Ruth held her breath. A moment later the plough was under the bridge itself. Something rattled against the locomotive. Then again. And again.

"They're throwing rocks!" Ruth said, though everyone surely realised.

Mitchell and the stoker pulled themselves back inside as rubble rained down on the engine. Almost as soon as it had begun, and before Ruth could ask why they didn't shoot back, the engine was through to the other side. Ruth turned around. A few rocks fell on the tender and the carriages, but either they'd used up their missiles, or they'd realised they weren't going to do any damage. As to who *they* were, Ruth saw them standing on the bridge, watching the train head away.

"Why didn't you fire?" Ruth asked, watching the figures on the bridge.

"To what end?" Mitchell replied.

"In the old days," the stoker said, stowing the shotgun, "they used the bridges to jump onto the trains. I thought they might try it. That was just a demonstration of—"

"Ahead," The driver yelled.

They all turned to look. In the sky in front, Ruth could make out the bright red canopy of a balloon. She couldn't see the depot underneath, and it wasn't what the driver had been calling to their attention. The tracks were blocked with an improvised barricade.

"Don't stop," Mitchell said.

"You want me to ram it?"

"Do it!" Mitchell yelled.

"We'll derail!" The driver replied.

"You won't," Mitchell said. "Trust me."

The driver shook his head, but the train began to accelerate. Ruth kept her eyes fixed on the barricade. Wood. Metal. Brick. It looked crudely made, but it was approaching fast and with each passing second it seemed to grow larger and increasingly sturdy.

"Hold on!" Mitchell bellowed.

Ruth gripped a handrail and closed her eyes. There was a jolt. She was thrown back, and almost lost her footing as the train rose from the tracks and then slammed back down. Rubble and debris sprayed from the barricade as they drove through it. A metal bar spun upward, slamming into the reinforced window of the cab. The glass fractured, but didn't break. The engine rocked. For a moment Ruth thought it would topple. It didn't.

"You can let go now," Mitchell said. "We're through."

Ruth looked around. The captain was right. The tracks ahead were clear.

"That was stupid," Higgins said. "You didn't know what was in that barricade."

"I knew that they'd only had thirty-four minutes to put it into place," Mitchell said. "Remember the Mail train ahead of us? The barricade had to be made of what could be easily and quickly carried."

"It was still a gamble," the driver said.

"And I won," Mitchell said. "You see the smoke? The balloon? That's the next depot, less than five miles away."

Chapter 7
The Real World

"Welcome to the real world," Mitchell said, as Ruth jumped down to the platform. The rough-hewn planks creaked in protest. "No mains water," Mitchell continued. "No electricity. What people in Twynham call bandits, here they call neighbours. A lot of scavengers call this place home. Or, to be more accurate, they call it the place they send their children to school as they scour through the ruins of Birmingham and beyond. The rest make their living from trapping, hunting, and farming, and selling the excess to us in the south. We don't need the food or furs, but they need the money to buy medicines, and the tax receipts to send their children to school. There, they're taught about the wonders of the old-world, and how they can have it all again, if only they grow up to pay those taxes themselves."

"That's kind of cynical, isn't it?" Ruth asked, looking around.

"Maybe. Give a man a fish and he'll be fed for a day. Sell a man a fish and he'll come up with a way to buy more. Set the price too high and he'll learn how to steal. It's a balancing act. Some people need to be pushed, and others need to be dragged as we walk the tightrope, but it's far better than slipping into the barbarism awaiting us either side. We're in the way," he added as a trio of railway workers swung a coal-hopper over the tender.

"Sir, are there any orders?" Lieutenant Lewis asked, coming up to join them.

"Go to the telegraph office, see if there are any messages," Mitchell said.

The lieutenant saluted and headed toward the small brick building with a yellow stripe below the eaves. A dozen cables snaked into it from the wires that ran along the railroad.

"He seems like a good officer," Mitchell said. "Technically you won't be under his command, and hopefully it won't matter, but if it comes to it, do what he says. Now, I better go and report that incident on the tracks. Keep an eye on the train. No one gets off. No one comes on board."

"You think anyone will try?"

Mitchell smiled. "I didn't mean anything sinister. I meant people like that." He gestured toward a man standing by a barrow that held a trio of steaming pots. "We want to keep what we're doing secret, remember?"

"Oh. Yes. Of course." Ruth's stomach growled as her nostrils registered the scent of broiled meat. Hoping that by not looking at him, she might be able to forget the food vendor was there, she began walking down the length of the train.

The depot was far larger than any of the others they'd been through that day. To the south, the tracks ran for five hundred yards before reaching the currently open gate, guarded either side by two uniformed Marines.

"We allowed off?" Corporal Lin called down from the door.

"Sorry, no," Ruth said.

"One minute?" Lin suggested, gesturing toward the vendor. "I can be there and back before the officers return."

"Could you eat the food, and get rid of the bowls, too?" Ruth asked. "Sorry, it's the captain's orders."

"Fair enough," Lin said, though the look in her eyes suggested she'd probably try for the cart as soon as Ruth's back was turned. "Do you know what happened back there?" the corporal asked. "Is it connected to the prisoner?"

"I'm not sure," Ruth said. "Captain Mitchell's gone to find out."

Ruth turned around. On the grounds that if she didn't see the Marine leaving the train to buy food she wouldn't have to do something about it, she kept her eyes studiously forward as she walked toward the locomotive. To the north, the depot stretched even further. A hundred yards beyond the engine, the tracks branched, with the easterly set leading to a loading yard, the westerly to a mountain of coal. Using the train's tender as a guide, she tried to estimate how much fuel was there, but soon gave up. It was a lot, yet the coal heap was dwarfed by the steel walls surrounding the depot.

Beyond the platform was an open-air market with a dozen stalls. A trapper was holding up a squirming piglet. Ruth was too far away to tell if he was buying or selling. Opposite him, two women held a dead deer, strung on a pole by its tied feet. A third woman was arguing over the price it should receive. Beyond the stalls was a row of old cottages converted into businesses. She identified the pub by the tables outside, and the blacksmith next door by the furnace visible through the open door. Next to that was the familiar green cross of the apothecary, and then a shop with no sign, but an ornate candlestick hanging outside. Above and behind those were rooftops with chimneys pouring smoke. Surrounding it all was a sea of noise. No, it wasn't a depot but a town.

"The Mail train got through here on schedule," Mitchell said, when he returned. "But about an hour before we reached that bridge in Leicester, the talks between Albion and our government broke down. They're being held in the hall behind St Mathew's." He waved a hand vaguely in the direction of a spire. "Albion threatened to cut off the railway unless they get to appoint their own tax collectors."

"Is that a real issue?"

"If their king gets to appoint them, you can be sure they won't collect much tax. But the timing is a little too coincidental for my taste. I wonder if Emmitt was behind it."

"You think he could be?" she asked.

"Theoretically? Perhaps. He would have had to send them a message by telegram. And it would mean he had some sway with Albion. Maybe he was originally from here, but…" He trailed off, the sentence unfinished, as Lieutenant Lewis came running onto the platform.

"The telegraph's been cut," Lewis said.

"Where?" Mitchell asked.

"Around Twynham. The city's cut off."

"It's the fifth of October tomorrow," Ruth said. "Maybe that's what Ned Ludd meant, that the attack would be in October, not November."

"Then wouldn't they cut the lines tomorrow?" Mitchell said. "Has Emmitt brought his plans forward, or changed them in the hope he can kill Fairmont? Or…" He took a pace away from the train, looking at the town. "Or capture him? Taking hostages for ransom is something the people of Albion are familiar with," he murmured. "Maybe," he said, speaking more normally. "Stay here, go back, or go on; those are our choices. Whether or not Emmitt bribed Albion, we can't go back. At least, we can't go through Leicester."

"And if he bribed them, is it safe to stay here?" Ruth asked, turning to look in the direction of the ruined city, currently hidden by the town's high walls.

"I say yes," Lieutenant Lewis said. "We can seal the town off, kick out anyone who doesn't live here, institute a curfew, and—"

"And that's the logical response, isn't it?" Mitchell said. "It's what he'd expect us to do. It's what he's planned for. If we stay, there is a high likelihood innocent people will die. If people come for Fairmont, it will be in the middle of the night. We'll fire back and there's no telling where the stray bullets will go. No, Fairmont's not worth that. Was there any news from north of here?"

"The Mail train left here safely," Lewis said. "But it'll be another hour before it arrives at the next depot."

"But the telegraph is working north of here?" Mitchell asked.

"Yes, sir."

"Then perhaps we're being paranoid. If we wait for the mail train to reach the next depot, it'll be too late for us to leave. So we'll go on, and we'll go now. First, though, I want a word with Fairmont."

"We want the other four addresses," Mitchell said.

"Not until I'm safe, and this place doesn't look that," Fairmont said. "The fact you're wanting to change our deal confirms it."

"Don't be smug, Fairmont. You're the one they're after."

He blanched. "You're serious? They're coming for me?"

"Didn't you hear the rocks rattling on the roof? They tried to stop us in Leicester. The telegraph has been cut. We can't get word back to Twynham."

"I... I see. Well, what are you going to do about it? You're meant to protect me. That was the deal!" His voice rose to an almost comical squeak.

"And the best way of doing that is if you tell me everything," Mitchell said.

"No. Because if the telegraph has been cut then you've no way of getting the information back to Twynham. It won't do you any good, and you'll use it as an excuse to leave me in the middle of nowhere."

"Don't tempt me. You said that you regretted what you've done. Prove it. Tell me what you know."

"I can't trust you," Fairmont said.

"You've got it the wrong way round," Mitchell said. "It's me who has to trust you. Right now I don't. In fact, you know what?" He reached into his coat, took out a set of keys, and opened the cage. "Stand up."

"What? Why?"

Mitchell hauled the man to his feet. "I'm going to let you go, here and now. Not in this depot, but outside of it."

"They'll kill me!"

"You know how to save your life," Mitchell said. He uncuffed the man's wrist.

"Number fifteen Marchemont Place. Forty-eight Harrington Street. Number nine Trafalgar Road. Seven Harbour Rise," Fairmont said.

"Thank you," Mitchell said. He re-cuffed the man and locked the cage. He turned to Ruth. "I'm going to see if I can find someone to whom I can entrust that information," Mitchell said. "Watch him."

It was twenty minutes before he returned.

"We're stopping," Ruth said, an hour later, speaking at the same time as Mitchell stood up. Ruth followed him out of the carriage, and up the narrow ladder that led to the roof of the tender. As Mitchell ran, using his hands as much as his feet, across the tender and down the other side, Ruth paused. She stared ahead. There was a train stalled on the tracks in front of them.

"Deering!"

Ruth hurried after the captain, reaching the locomotive just as a last whoosh of steam heralded its final halt.

"It's the Mail train," Mitchell said.

"Can we reverse?" Ruth asked.

"Not if we want to get to shelter before nightfall," the driver said.

"Where's the nearest branch line?" Mitchell asked.

"About four miles ahead, there's a line that runs east to west."

"And behind us?"

"We'd almost be back at Leicester," the driver said.

"What does he want us to do?" Mitchell muttered. "What does he expect?"

"Where are the people?" Ruth asked. "Why's no one coming to ask for our help?" The driver's expression gave her the answer. "Oh, sorry," she said. "They're dead, aren't they?"

"Or being held for ransom," Higgins said. "That's happened before, though not this far north." There was a desperately hopeful edge to the driver's voice. He would know the train's crew, she supposed.

"We can't worry about that now," Mitchell said. "The easiest thing, the logical thing, for us to do is retreat, so we won't. Can we push that train four miles?"

"If the track's intact," Higgins said.

"Then we need to check. After four miles where does the branch line lead?"

"Toward the west coast."

"Is that section of railway passable?" Mitchell asked.

"Maybe. I don't know the last time anyone used it."

"That's the way we'll go," Mitchell said. "We'll assume Emmitt has learned where we're heading. We'll go west and try to get forty miles from here. That will put us beyond riding distance, and safe until dawn, at least from whoever did this. Tomorrow… well, we'll worry about that tonight." He turned to the stoker. "Can you drive that train?"

"Of course."

"Then you're coming with me. You can check the engine and I'll check the track." He turned back to Higgins. "If anything happens, go back to the depot."

Mitchell jumped down from the cab and ran back to the passenger cars. Ruth thought of following, but changed her mind. Whatever danger they were now facing, she'd rather be out in the open where she could see it. She walked along the railroad until she was in front of the locomotive.

The stalled train was five hundred yards ahead. Either side of the tracks, ferns jutted up from thick bracken. Beyond that was a forest of pines, spaced eight feet or more apart. Decades of fallen needles had kept the undergrowth sparse. Ruth couldn't see any danger in the trees. There was no sign of life ahead of them. No birds either, she realised. The only sound came from the engine behind. She drew her revolver, but found little comfort in the weapon.

She heard footsteps. She turned around to see Mitchell with Hamish Boyd the stoker, Corporal Lin, and two Marines.

Mitchell looked at her uncertainly before reaching some internal decision. "If you're coming, stay with the stoker. Keep your gun out, but don't fire unless I signal."

"Right. Yes. Um… what's the signal?" she asked.

"When I start shooting," he said and jogged off along the tracks. The corporal went with him, the two privates fell in behind. A hundred yards from the rear of the stalled train, Mitchell stopped. From the way he clutched one hand to his side, Ruth thought he must be winded. Then she saw him point ahead and crouch down. She ran to catch up, the stoker following.

"You see the body?" Mitchell asked.

It was lying on the southbound set of tracks, ten yards from the rear-most carriage.

"Maybe this was just a robbery," the stoker said, a slight tremor in his voice. "They got what they came for and went."

"No," Mitchell said. "This is because of us. Slow and cautious from now on. When we reach the train, stay close to it. Only stop when you've got a wheel shielding your legs. Boyd, Deering, you stay ten yards behind Lin and I. Khan, Conner, you stay ten yards behind them. Be prepared for a trap. Get ready to run in whichever direction the bullets aren't coming from."

All of sudden, what they were doing seemed very real. Ruth waited until Mitchell had started moving and anxiously gauged the distance before following. As she got nearer to the train she saw the bullet holes. There were dozens of them in the rear door of the carriage. When she moved off the tracks and onto the verge, she saw the train's sides. There were more bullet holes. Hundreds of them. An image of those rifles they'd found in Windward Square came to her, and she stopped trying to estimate how many shots had been fired.

Bullets had torn through both walls of the train, breaking most of the windows. As to the fate of the passengers, the blood dripping from an open doorway down to the track spoke to that. Inside were bodies. One wore the uniform of the Railway Company, the others were dressed in ordinary clothes. They were local commuters, perhaps visiting family in the next town, or travelling for business, or— There was a tap on her arm.

"Don't stop," the stoker said. His face was pale, twisted with shock.

The next carriage was the same. The bulkier tender was scratched from where bullets had gouged lines through the paintwork. Ruth reached the locomotive. Mitchell pulled himself up to the cab. Ruth stood with her back against one of the wide wheels, staring at the pine forest. There was no sign of life. She looked to the Marines for reassurance, but they appeared as agitated as she felt.

"There's no driver. Some blood," Mitchell said. "Come up here and see if you can get it moving. Do it!" he barked when the stoker froze for a second too long.

"No. No. It's no good," the stoker said after less than ten seconds in the cab. "They've smashed the valve."

"Can you fix it?"

"No."

"Can you get the train moving?" Mitchell asked.

"By shunting it. But we need to check the tracks ahead."

"Fine. Do what you need so the train will move. Private Conner, stay here, protect the stoker. Corporal, I want—" He was interrupted by a sudden barrage of gunfire.

Private Khan pulled Ruth to the ground. The firing stopped for a heartbeat, then it began again, this time continuing without a pause.

"Too late!" Mitchell hissed, dragging the stoker out of the cab. "Did you pull the brake?"

"You don't pull it," the stoker babbled.

"Is it off? Can we push the train?" Mitchell yelled.

The gunfire suddenly got louder. No, she realised. It wasn't the gunfire, but the sound of bullets ricocheting off metal. The first shots had been aimed at the other train. Now, the shooters were firing at them.

"They're on the eastern side," Mitchell said. "Keep the train between us and them."

"And if they're in the woods to the west?" the stoker asked.

"We hope they aren't." Mitchell said. "Move. Back along the train. We need to signal to Higgins, and get him to move his train forward."

Ruth didn't need the explanation. One word would have summed it up: crawl, and that's what she did. That hellish cacophony faded as the shooters shifted their aim again. All she could see was grass and gravel, and beyond that Corporal Lin's boots. The boots were getting further ahead. She crawled faster.

The shooting abruptly stopped.

Boyd stood up. "Run. Now," he said, sprinting along the tracks.

"Get down!" Mitchell yelled.

The stoker didn't.

"Keep crawling," Mitchell hissed at Ruth.

She didn't. She stayed unmoving, watching the stoker. He reached the end of the Mail train and kept running, his head down, his arms pumping, sprinting toward their locomotive. He would make it, Ruth thought. Whoever was shooting at them had gone.

A single shot, somehow louder than the cacophony that had gone before, cut through the silence. The stoker collapsed.

"Sniper," Corporal Lin said.

"It must be Emmitt," Mitchell said.

"It can't be," Ruth said. "I broke his arm. I'm sure of it."

"It doesn't matter," Mitchell said. "Keep going."

Just before they reached the end of the first carriage, the gunfire started again. It changed pitch, slowed, and sounded more measured. Was that the Marines, returning fire?

They were at the rear of the last carriage. Ruth could see the locomotive, and figures on the tracks to either side. She straightened, about to wave when Mitchell dragged her back down.

"Don't," he said.

"But…" Then she saw it. The clothing. Those people weren't Marines.

"Sir, we've got to help them," Lin said.

"I know," Mitchell said. "I count four by the train."

"The same," the corporal said.

"What about the sniper?" Mitchell asked.

"I've got a bead on him," Private Conner said.

"You sure?" Mitchell asked.

"Yes, sir."

"Take him out," Mitchell said.

Time stretched. Ruth looked at the train. One of the four figures had already disappeared. A second vanished, going inside. She wanted to scream at the Marine, to yell at him to fire and be done with it. The man waited. The last two figures started running away from the train.

Conner fired. "Got 'im!" he hissed.

There was a roar of sound. The ground shook. Fire and smoke billowed up from the prisoner-transport train, hiding the ambushers from sight. Something tugged at Ruth's leg. Mitchell was pulling her under the carriage as burning shrapnel rained down around them.

"Can anyone see anything?" Mitchell asked.

"I've no clear target," Lin said.

"Then fire at the damned trees!" Mitchell barked.

The Marines fired short, controlled bursts. Three shots, then three, then three more. The ambushers returned fire, sending bullets back in endless barrage.

"Incoming!" the corporal barked.

Ruth saw something streak from the treeline toward the distant locomotive. Mitchell rolled on top of her. There was another explosion, and then there was silence.

It seemed an age before the pressure on her eased as Mitchell crawled off and pulled himself a little way along the tracks.

"See anything?" he asked, of everyone and no one.

"No, sir," the corporal said.

"Everyone all right?" Mitchell added, in what was clearly an afterthought.

There were grunts of affirmation from the Marines. Ruth added one of her own though she wasn't sure it was true.

"Was that an RPG?" Mitchell asked.

"I think so," the corporal said.

"What's...?" Ruth began and found it actually hurt to talk. She opened and closed her mouth, stretching her jaw. "What's an RPG?"

"A rocket-propelled grenade," Mitchell said. "Think of it as one-person artillery. They fired twice. The first must have hit the carriage Fairmont was in. The second hit the locomotive. Corporal, eyes on the treeline."

"Sir, what are—" Ruth began, but before she could finish the question, Mitchell had dragged himself out from under the carriage and was running toward the ruined locomotive. He zigged. He zagged. He tried to roll and came back to his feet limping. By the time he reached the train, he was jogging barely faster than a walk with his hand firmly clamped to his side, but no one had shot at him.

"I'd say it's safe," the corporal said.

"Or they know we'll think that, and they're waiting for us to move," Ruth said.

"No," Lin said. "They were after the prisoner, and I'd say they got him."

The corporal was right. After Ruth had forced herself to stand and sprint along the empty stretch of track, she'd followed Mitchell to the wrecked carriage. It was split open, almost forming a V pointing toward the woodland. Wreckage was strewn across both the north and southbound sets of rails. Not just wreckage. Ruth stared at an arm, unattached to a body.

"The grenade must have been on a timer, or… I don't know," Mitchell said, looking at the wreckage. "It didn't explode until after it had entered the carriage. Unless… maybe it wasn't a rocket, but some other explosive. I hope not. It's one thing to fire a grenade at a target, another to force their way onto the train, strap explosives to the cage, and then run for it."

"But that's probably what they did, right?" Ruth asked. She was unable to tear her eyes away from the arm still clad in that familiar orange chequered suit.

"I think so," Mitchell said. "They really wanted to make sure he was dead. Corporal, check for survivors. Khan, you're with her. Conner, you're with me. Corporal, give me your rifle."

Mitchell took the weapon, checked the mechanism, then the magazine. "Deering, I want—"

"I'm with you, sir," she said.

Mitchell shook his head, but didn't argue as he stalked into the woods. Conner took up a position ten feet to his left. Ruth followed, keeping her eyes on the trees and the growing shadows behind them.

As they moved away from the smouldering train, she thought she could make out another sound, coming from somewhere distant and to the east. It was a little like thunder but, at the same time, it was an entirely unnatural sound. She didn't think she'd ever heard it before.

Something shiny caught her eye. She stopped. It was a pile of metal casings. Dozens, hundreds, she wasn't sure how many. When she glanced up she saw that Mitchell and Conner were still moving, and realised that the sound, whatever it was, had gone.

The casings were piled around a shallow pit dug into the earth. Ruth turned to look back toward the train. She'd not realised it before, but from this angle she saw that the tracks were curved and that the locomotive had come to a halt on a slight incline rising into the woodland. She could see at least eight miles of rails visible to the south. Her heart sank further as she realised it was an ideal spot for an ambush.

Mitchell and Conner were a hundred feet away. Ruth didn't try to catch up. It was clear that Emmitt was gone.

Careful of each step, she walked through the woods, replaying the ambush, but this time from the attackers' perspective. A little beyond the firing position she came to a series of drag marks. Had they tried to obscure their footprints? No, because there was a clear heel print to the west. They must have been carrying something. Or someone, she realised when, a little further on, she noticed a cluster of blood drops on the fallen leaves.

The sniper? Perhaps. But was it Emmitt? She doubted they would be so lucky, and she was sure she'd broken his arm. If not him, then who? It could be anyone. She kept on through the forest, throwing occasional glances back at the train. After another dozen yards, she stopped. She knelt down. The train was still visible. They had dug the pits and must have laid camouflage over the top. Blankets, perhaps, with branches sewn to them. Whatever they were, they'd been taken away.

Fifty yards further on, Mitchell and Conner had stopped at what looked like a firebreak. The Marine was alert, rifle raised, the barrel tracking left and right. The captain was staring at the ground.

"Do you see the tracks?" Mitchell asked.

"Are they wheel marks?" Ruth asked. They were around eight feet apart. The ruts were wider than those left by any horse drawn carriage Ruth had ever seen, and they'd left a pattern of lines and diamonds in the thick mud.

Mitchell bent down, and picked something up from the mud. As he straightened, he winced.

"Sir, are you—"

"I'm fine." He held out the object he'd picked up. "Have you ever seen anything like this?"

"No, I don't…" And then she understood. "That's rubber. Tyre rubber. I thought I heard something. Was it an engine?"

"From a truck," Mitchell said. "Diesel, I suppose." He looked down at the piece of rubber in his hands. "It's badly perished, but there's some of the tread-mark still visible. I don't know if Isaac—" He stopped and glanced at Conner, but the Marine wasn't paying them any attention. "In the old-world, they had databases of all the different tyre patterns. If any of those survived, we can check this against them."

"And that will tell us what type of car they were driving?" Ruth asked

"No, the type of tyre will tell us from what vehicle the tyres originally came. From the wheelbase, and number of passengers – you see the footprints over here? From those we know it's a truck. Taken together that might..." He trailed off. "I'm jumping on a haystack hoping the needle might stick in my foot." He walked over to the remains of a dull metal barrier at the edge of the road and sat down. He looked more lost than Ruth had ever seen him before.

"They had time to prepare," Ruth said. "Did you see the firing positions?"

"They must have been camouflaged. So, yes, they had time to prepare the firing positions. They drove from Twynham, and that's the direction in which they've driven away. They must have left soon after we did. Which means they've cleared a stretch of road here, to this point, where they had those positions prepared."

"But how did they know we'd come this way?" she asked.

"Exactly," Mitchell said. He stood. "They drove away to the south. How do we find them? We can't catch them. Not on foot. So, we go back to the train."

"Aren't we going to gather evidence?" Ruth asked.

"Later. In this job you focus on the most pressing danger to life. That was the shooters. Now they've gone, the evidence will wait until we've tended to whatever wounded are left on the train."

"They're all dead?" Mitchell asked.

"Yes, sir," Corporal Lin said. "The driver, the lieutenant, everyone. Shot multiple times, or died in the explosion. It looks like at least two were executed." She shook her head. "All to kill that man. Who was he? You have to tell us. We've earned it. These are comrades. Our friends."

Mitchell nodded. "He was the assistant to the American ambassador. He sold information to a man named Emmitt. You might have seen his pictures in the paper."

"The assassin who tried to kill the Prime Minister?" Lin said. "We were there at the radio broadcast. On duty. We all were."

"I see. Well, Fairmont was selling information to Emmitt. After we caught him, he was trading what he knew with us in exchange for a cushy prison sentence. Essentially you were to be his bodyguards as we extracted all the information out of him that we could."

"So what did he know?" Lin asked.

"Something worth doing all this for," Mitchell said. "As to exactly what, I don't know. There's an hour before dark, and I gave instructions at Leicester that no more trains were to be allowed through until dawn. We're here for the night. Deering, Corporal, check the woods for evidence. Make sure we didn't miss anything. Conner, Khan, and I will take these two trains. In thirty minutes, or if you hear a shot, come back here. No later."

"Understood, sir," Lin said.

"Stay close," Lin said. "If I say run, you do it, understand?"

"Do you think they'll come back?" Ruth asked.

"Probably not," Lin said. "But it isn't people I'm worried about. There's lions and bears in these woods. They escaped from zoos soon after the Blackout. It's why there aren't many people living around here. Not anymore. Come winter, humans are just another form of food. They'll probably come for the bodies later." The corporal spat. "And there's nothing we can do about it. Where do you want to start?"

"Oh. Um… I suppose we should start by counting the firing positions," Ruth said. She started walking toward the woods. "You were on duty during the assassination?" she asked.

"I was," Lin said. "I remember you, on the beach. You looked ferocious."

"Did I?" Ruth tried to remember the faces of the Marines who'd come running down with Riley and Agent Clarke. "And were your... the Marines, they were all there?"

"They were. We guessed that this had to be connected when we saw you board the train this morning. Can you make a guess at what the man knew?"

"It has to be something big, doesn't it?" Ruth said. "Probably an address of where we'll find Emmitt. But whatever it is died with him."

She came to a halt by the first firing position.

"How long would it take to dig?" she asked.

"This?" Lin asked. "An hour. Less."

"So it could have been done this morning?"

"Sure. The time-consuming part would have been finding this spot. Do you see how there's a clear line of sight of any train coming from the south? They didn't find this location by luck."

There were around a hundred and fifty casings. Ruth pocketed a couple of them. "For fingerprints," she said.

"You have some suspects in mind?" Lin asked.

"Not really, but what else can we do?"

They found the drag marks and followed them back to a firing position near the woods' edge.

"This is where the sniper was," Lin said.

"You're sure?" Ruth asked.

"Positive."

There was a bloodstain against the tree. It was some consolation that one of the attackers had been wounded, if not killed, but not much.

"Twenty minutes," Lin said.

"We can count the fox holes in the morning," Ruth said. "I want to check the road." She'd had an idea, and confirmed it half a mile further south.

"Saw marks, you see?" she said, pointing at a severed tree stump. "They cleared the road of debris. That must have taken a long time. Longer than a couple of hours."

"So when did you decide to move the prisoner?" Lin asked.

"Last night."

There was a soft glow near the Mail train's locomotive. Mitchell was sitting on the steps of the engine's cab, watching the flames of a wood and coal fire, set by the tracks.

"They picked this site for an ambush," Ruth said. "And prepared it. They cleared a road from Twynham to here. That's got to be at least two hundred miles. That wasn't done in a day."

"No," Mitchell said, his eyes on the flames.

"So they were planning on ambushing a different train," Ruth said.

"Yes."

"But then Emmitt changed his plan because killing Fairmont was more important than… than what?"

"How did they know our train was coming this way?" Lin asked.

"The driver of this Mail train is missing," Mitchell said. "Two of your comrades are unaccounted for. I don't suspect them," he added. "I mean that it's impossible to identify them from the remains. But the missing driver must have brought the Mail train to a halt here on Emmitt's instructions. Rebecca Cavendish must have told her why keeping to the schedule and sending those telegrams back was important. Or maybe Emmitt deduced it." He picked up a lump of coal and threw it into the fire. "Too many assumptions! Too many gaps! Too many guesses! What do we *know*? They drove here from Twynham. That must have been early this morning after Rebecca Cavendish told the driver to come into work. Someone at the embassy must have told Emmitt that we were moving Fairmont. Then what?"

"That tribe in Leicester," Ruth said. "The Albion people. They must have been involved. Maybe he got them to delay our train so he could make sure he reached this spot before us."

"Albion." Mitchell stood, and began pacing around the fire, hands gripped behind his back. "Except they didn't delay our train, did they? But you're right, he probably did have them working for him. Someone cleared that road, and I can't imagine Emmitt swinging an axe. How did he get them to help him? I don't know. The Mail train came to a halt. Emmitt boarded it. Everyone stayed in their seats until the shooting began. When it did, the passengers tried to run. Some made it as far as the doors. One made it out of the train. In the end, they all died. The shooters returned to their positions in the woods and waited until we arrived. They knew we'd come to a stop."

"But why didn't they fire straight away?" Lin asked.

"Divide and conquer," Mitchell said. "We had two choices; reverse, or send people to investigate the stalled train. If we'd reversed, they would have used the RPG. As it was, they waited, thus reducing the opposition against them. That meant they were able to come onto the train and confirm Fairmont was killed. Emmitt needed to know that for certain. But why? What did the man know?" He sat down again. "I'll need the coroner to confirm it, but the sniper got most of the kills. The rest were shot when they went on board. I doubt we'll ever know whether they allowed Fairmont the mercy of a bullet, but that explosive was probably attached to the cage."

"Did any of them die?" Lin asked.

"Around the train? I don't think so."

"Because that was a train full of Marines. We're good, sir. Very good, and that means these people had to be better."

"I think they knew how many of us there were," Mitchell said. "They must have done. Perhaps from a spy in Leicester? I don't know, but you're right; there are parts to this that don't make sense. But we will get to the bottom of it."

"Why didn't they stay and kill us?" Conner asked.

"I suppose because we'd taken out their sniper," Mitchell said.

"They could have flanked us," Lin said. "There were at least six of them, probably eight, maybe more."

"Or used that grenade," Conner said.

"The RPG? Yes," Mitchell said. "I think, perhaps, they only had one grenade and it was more important to destroy the train than kill us."

"Why?" Ruth asked.

"To buy themselves time," Mitchell said. "If the locomotive hadn't been destroyed, we could have taken it back to the depot, and sent word across the country. Those surveillance balloons might have spotted a truck driving across the countryside if they'd been told what to look for. Perhaps it wouldn't have made any difference whatsoever, but whether we are alive or dead clearly doesn't matter to Emmitt."

"How are you going to find him?" Lin asked.

"We'll follow the tracks south, see where they begin, and see if we can find the truck. We'll look for the fuel. It will be bio-diesel, I'm sure of it. There aren't many places that could have come from. After that, I don't know."

Nor did anyone else.

Ruth moved closer to the fire. It was barely evening, and still many hours away from night, yet it was already getting cold. She supposed she could go and get some more clothes, but even if her bag hadn't been destroyed in the explosion, she wasn't sure she wanted to go into that wrecked carriage.

There were a few more desultory attempts at conversation, but no one had anything to add. They sat alone with their thoughts, listening to the sounds of the night. The caws. The snuffles. The occasional hoot. Then a whistle.

"You hear that?" Mitchell said, standing up. The Marines were on their feet, hands reaching for weapons. Before Ruth could do the same, another sharp whistle rent the air.

A train had arrived, this one from the north, investigating why the Mail train had never arrived.

Chapter 8
Away From Home
5th October

For the first time since she'd moved to The Acre, Ruth woke in an unfamiliar bed. She'd had a restless night on a mattress that managed simultaneously to be both too hard and too soft. She was glad to get up, dress, and get out of the room. It was dark outside the cobwebbed windows, and even worse in the narrow corridors above the inn. Initially, she tried walking quietly so as not to wake any of the other guests, but after she'd stubbed her toe for the eighth time she stopped caring.

The train had brought her and Mitchell to Northallerton, forty miles from the site of the ambush. Corporal Lin and the Marines had insisted on staying with their fallen comrades. The guards from the train had been left with them. Almost as soon as they'd arrived in Northallerton, Mitchell had returned with a second train, taking a detachment of the town's guards with him. He'd insisted Ruth stay behind, and she'd not protested too hard. She'd sat in the backroom of the pub for a few hours as a bowl of stew congealed on the table next to her. Whispered rumours had buzzed behind her. She'd ignored them, and the inn's customers had had the grace to leave her alone.

The inn was now empty. The landlord sat in the kitchen, reading a newspaper by the light from a roaring range-fire over which a dozen massive pots hung.

"Hot water for washing'll be ready in five minutes," he said, not looking up.

It was last week's paper, Ruth saw. She stood in the doorway, idly wondering whether the man was only just getting around to reading it. Did news really take that long to reach places like this?

"Did Captain Mitchell come back last night?" she asked.

The landlord looked up. "Oh, sorry. I didn't realise it was you. Hang on." He fished in his apron until he found a thin envelope.

The newspaper's cheap ink left a smudgy fingerprint on the equally cheap envelope. The note was brief. Mitchell had gone to the railway office.

"Sleep well, I hope?" the landlord asked.

"Very well, thank you," Ruth lied. She considered whether to ask the landlord to make some breakfast, or whether it would be better for her to make it herself. Looking around the grease-smeared kitchen, she decided no. She'd been through enough over the last twenty-four hours without adding dysentery to her problems.

"Excuse me." She left the pub.

She wondered what time it was. Then she wondered where the railway office was. Near the train station, she guessed, though she couldn't remember where that was, so she ambled randomly through the slowly waking town. Yawning figures trudged hither and thither, shrugging away sleep. Candlelight flickered from the windows of some houses, and under the doors of others, but not enough to do more than add shape to the muddy pavement that was as much gravel as it was old-world asphalt. In many ways it was no different from the suburbs around Twynham through which she cycled to work.

She stumbled across the railway tracks first, and into the platform second, and guessed the railway office was the building outside of which a small group was gathered.

"It's 'cos there was no Mail train yesterday, and there won't be any running today until those tracks are clear," a worker in railway green was trying to explain.

"I've got three hundred eggs on that train," a woman said.

"They're not going to hatch, are they?" the railway worker replied. "What do you want me to do about it? No, don't answer that. Look, you all heard what happened. The trains got ambushed. Until the line's clear, no traffic's coming in. We're doing all we can, and complaining ain't going to get it done faster."

"What about my eggs?" the woman asked.

"If there's no train, there's no train," the man said. "What do you want me to say?"

The group slowly began to disperse. Ruth waited in the shadows until they were gone before stepping forward.

"Good morning," she said, "I'm—"

"Officer Deering. It's a small town. We remember new faces. I'm Clive Akinweh. How can I help you?"

"I was looking for Captain Mitchell."

"He's down at the crash site. He said you should wait here."

"I'd rather not," Ruth said.

"There are plenty worse places to be."

"Oh, no, I didn't mean... I meant I want to help."

"Ah, right. Well, there's a train taking some lifting gear down at first light. You can catch a ride with that if you want."

"Thank you."

"If you wanted to wait in here, there's a kettle and a fire."

"Thank you," Ruth said gratefully.

She dumped a few spoonfuls of powdered coffee into a mug, and went to stand by the door, watching as the town emerged with the arrival of dawn. It had the same layout as the one near Leicester, except for the walls. If anything, those seemed higher. But the shops, the goods being loaded onto the market stalls, the clothing, it was all the same.

"The gates are closed," she said, as soon as there was enough light for her to realise.

"Of course," Akinweh said.

"In all the depots we went through, they were open," she said.

"At night?"

"Oh. I... I don't know."

"Around here, we keep them closed," Akinweh said.

"Because of bandits?" she asked.

"Bears. But there are worse places to be. Believe me."

"You're not from around here?" Ruth asked.

"We were visiting family in Birmingham during the Blackout. Sort of got this far and no further. Stayed here ever since."

"You don't ever think of leaving?"

"To go where?"

Ruth had no answer.

This was travelling, then. A blacksmith's forge, a train station, smoke from chimneys, and the same assortment of people working the same jobs as those hundreds of miles away. In the books she'd read, far away places were portrayed as exotic. Perhaps this wasn't far enough.

The train arrived. It consisted of a crane and two empty cargo wagons. Ruth found a perch on the crane's platform, and was grateful that the wind rushing through her ears meant that she didn't have to talk to anyone. The early morning fug had begun to clear, and the enormity of all that had happened the previous day was slowly sinking in.

There were a dozen Marines by the ambush site, along with another two-dozen railway workers and six people in oddly familiar dark suits.

She found Mitchell sitting on his own, twenty yards from the stalled locomotive. He looked thoughtful and unrested.

"Undertakers," he said.

She followed his gaze. "You mean the people in black?"

"There's no one else to deal with the bodies," he said. "There's no coroner here, just a local physician who signs the death certificates. To bring up a forensics team from Twynham would take at least two days. We can't leave the bodies on the train because the carriages need to be cleared from the tracks, and doing that will destroy any remaining evidence."

"Do you think there is any?"

"I gathered what I could," he said.

"You found something?"

"Not really." He pulled out a slim plastic square.

"That's a phone!" Ruth said, slightly scandalized.

"Yes. Keep an eye on the Marines. I don't want anyone to know I've got one."

"Why not?"

"Most people react a lot worse than you just did," he said. "They view them with suspicion, if not outright distrust. Without a cellular network it's not much more than a glorified paperweight, but it does have a camera. High fidelity photographs are most useful when no one knows that we can take them." He slid the phone back into his pocket. "It was a gift from Isaac. He's taken to collecting them."

"Does it do anything else?" Ruth asked curiously.

"Not that will help us solve this mess. But the photographs will help if I've missed something. Nor will it help us find Emmitt," he added, standing up. "Clearly he's abandoned his original plan. How are you?"

"Oh, I'm… actually I'm fine." And she realised it was true. Her head was clear, and except for being stiff, she felt better than she had in days.

"There are no flashing lights before your eyes? No buzzing drone in your ears?"

"No. Why, is that a symptom of something?"

"I was hoping it might have been." He sat down again and rubbed his forehead. "The Marines will help the undertakers collect the bodies. When they're finished, they'll use that crane to drag the locomotive and carriages off the tracks. Until then, I have to sit and watch. It seems like every time I move, I tear these damned stitches."

"Maybe I should go and help," she said.

"Definitely not. You'll see enough grim death in your life that you don't need to seek any more. Sit. Wait. Think."

"Where's Corporal Lin?"

"She set off at first light, following the tracks in the mud left by the truck." Mitchell said. "Took some Marines from the town's garrison with her, and she wasn't short of volunteers."

"Shouldn't one of us have gone with her?" Ruth asked.

"They won't catch them," Mitchell said. "Not now. But they might be able to confirm in what direction the vehicle went, whether it was south toward Leicester, or around it to Twynham, or east to the coast. It was the ammunition train, I think."

"What was?"

"That they were planning to ambush," Mitchell said.

"But they had plenty of ammunition."

"I don't mean small arms," Mitchell said. "I was speaking to some of the Railway Company signallers. It's no secret that munitions transit through here. The high explosive shells used by the Navy come from Loch Creigh, and travel along this route."

"You think that was what Emmitt was after?" she asked.

"Getting a truck to work, and finding the diesel for it, took a lot of effort. If they simply wanted to transport people, they could have used horses and saved themselves the effort of clearing hundreds of miles of road. No, the only reason you would use a truck is if you wanted to transport something heavy and get it away quickly. A hundred high explosive shells, for instance. We know they have ammunition for the rifles but few explosives, otherwise they would have used them during the ambush. Remember the fifth? If Parliament was his target, it isn't now."

There was a resounding crash as the ruined locomotive was toppled over.

"Frobisher thought that they were being employed for a robbery," Ruth said.

"Right. But were they? Was the munitions train the robbery she was talking about? Or was it to be part of whatever Emmitt wanted the explosives for? The only thing I'm certain of is that those Luddites are a distraction."

"It comes back to Fairmont," Ruth said. "He must have known something truly important. Something that he wasn't aware of, otherwise he'd have bragged about it when he was negotiating his deal."

"Right. But whatever it is, we won't discover it sitting here."

There was another clattering rattle as a carriage was levered off the tracks.

Chapter 9
Probable Targets
6th October

"This is busy work, isn't it?" Simon asked.

"I suppose," Ruth agreed.

They stood in the lee of a door behind the new theatre as rain hammered on the cobbles of Twynham.

"Find the target," Simon said, repeating Mitchell's instructions to them. "It could be anything. Even if we found what Emmitt had planned to blow up, he's not going to be able to now."

"No."

"I mean, how's he going to capture a munitions train? He can't, can he?" Simon asked.

"He can't," Ruth said. There had been a time, and it now seemed so long ago, that all she'd wanted was a job that would get her away from the city. Now she'd gone away and come back, she wasn't sure what attraction the wider world held.

"Did you see him?" Simon asked. He'd asked that question enough times that she knew he meant Emmitt.

"I told you, no. I didn't really see anything. Just some distant figures." None of whom she could identify. As she and Mitchell had left the ambush site, Ruth had felt confident about the case. As the train took them south, and she'd gone over the events, that confidence evaporated. The faces of the dead Marines swam at the forefront of her mind. They'd been there when she'd slept and there when she woke. That morning, she'd run down to the coast and back, and the murdered Marines had been her companions for every single step.

No, she hadn't seen anything, she didn't know anything, and after her run she'd had to go through that with Assistant Commissioner Weaver. That interview had taken three hours and at the end of it, Ruth had felt like a child, sent away so as not to get in the adults' way. Giving her the assignment in Scotland and then sending her and Simon to patrol the streets in search of Emmitt's possible target, that was how Mitchell saw her, too.

The rain pulsed harder, drilling down onto streets swept clean of leaves and mud.

"But there were eight of them?" Simon asked.

"Between six and ten, probably eight," Ruth said. That had been Mitchell's final assessment of the woodland. The captain hadn't even asked her how many she'd thought there were. No, he was the policeman and she was the favour to her mother.

"Maybe Emmitt was driving the truck," Simon said. "Do you think you can do that with a broken arm?"

"Maybe."

"And you don't know who that Marine shot?"

Ruth bit down a reply. Simon was so far up her nerves she wanted to scream, but if their situation had been reversed, she'd have been curious, too.

"I have to give a statement to the Naval Office later," she said, trying to think of some piece of news she'd not told him.

"You do? Why?"

"Because of the dead Marines," she said.

"Do you know what they're going to ask?"

"Probably the same questions as you. Do you know what answer I'll give? I don't know anything! None of us do. We're grasping at straws, doing something so that we're not just waiting for the next attack."

No one involved in cutting the telegraph wires had been caught, and other than the ambush, no crimes had been committed. That bothered Ruth. She couldn't see how cutting the telegraph had helped Emmitt ambush the train.

Mitchell had gone to search the house of the Mail train's missing driver. Kowalski had gone back to the university with another barrage of questions. Davis was interviewing Ned Ludd, and Weaver had been called to Parliament to answer questions. Riley had gone to interview the MP, Rupert Pine. Reading between the lines of a stilted conversation between the sergeant and Mitchell, Ruth gathered that Riley had gone on a date with the politician at some point in the recent past. There was something that the man had said which made the sergeant suspicious. Ruth wasn't sure if that counted as a lead, bitterness, or desperation.

"The rain's slowing," she said, and marched out from under the awning.

"Wait!" Simon called, running to keep up.

Ruth kept marching, away from the theatre, and down the next alley. The rain wasn't refreshing. Like the air itself, it felt thick and cloying, almost oily. She'd been back in the city less than a day and wanted to leave again, yet knew there was nowhere to go.

"Stop," Simon said, grabbing her arm. "At least until the rain stops."

She shook him off, but the caustic retort died on her lips when she saw his face. He looked anxious, nervous, almost scared. She stepped into the doorway of a closed dressmaker's.

"I think you need to—" Simon began, but Ruth cut him off.

"Captain Mitchell sent us out to find the potential targets," she said. "Maybe it *is* busywork, but we still have to do it."

Simon's eyes flickered as he wrestled with his own internal debate.

"Parliament?" he suggested. "If the attack is on the fifth of November, that's the obvious target."

"Right, and now it's got extra protection. Besides, what would be the point? This is a democracy, right? Emmitt kills one politician and we'll elect another."

"But if they were all dead—"

"Nothing would change," Ruth interrupted again. "People would still go to work, farmers would plough their fields, the trains would run, the water would flow, and the electricity would… do whatever it is that electricity does. At least for as long as it takes for us to elect more."

"Then what about the power station?" he said.

"That was what I was thinking. Or the radio antenna? But those are all being guarded, too. So what's left?"

"Ships?" Simon said. "The Mint?"

"No," Ruth said. She raised a hand, testing the rain. It truly was easing now. She set off again, this time more slowly.

"Where are you going?" Simon asked.

"The grain silos," Ruth said. "What's money if it's not a representation of food?"

"But..." Simon had to run a few steps to catch up. "But we'd just grow more."

"Not overnight," Ruth said, not slowing her pace. They were heading away from the centre of Twynham. The shops they passed were increasingly empty. Many had been converted into homes. Optimistic 'For Let' signs hung from boards outside of others. That was a new thing, Ruth thought. Rents and property prices were strictly controlled, but private ownership was increasing. Though, since the signs all bore one of five different names, ownership was increasing among a very small group.

"What's the point of going to the grain silos," Simon said. "We know where they are. Maybe we're asking the wrong question. Instead of looking for the target, we should be trying to work out who benefits. I say it's the Americans."

"What?" And this time, Ruth did stop.

"The Americans. Fairmont worked for the ambassador, didn't he? So maybe that's who's behind all this."

"But the ambassador let us take Fairmont away. He could have shipped the man back to the U.S. and we'd have never known."

"Governments were at war in the old-world, sabotage and insurrection are the kind of things they used to organise."

Ruth thought about that. "No," she said. "Emmitt wants power."

"Does he? How do you know?" Simon asked. "And who's to say he's the one behind all of this. I mean, if it was me, I'd send other people out to do all the work."

"You mean this woman that Frobisher is terrified of?" Ruth said. "Then why haven't we seen her? Maybe she doesn't exist." But Simon was right in that there was no point trekking the four miles out to the grain depot. She started walking again, this time letting Simon lead the way.

She didn't know this part of the city. Before she'd joined the academy she'd seldom ventured far from The Acre. Like most of the south coast, the area they walked through had once been a residential district, but here the homes had been turned into workshops. Ramshackle extensions had been thrown up in back gardens, and then over the earlier extensions themselves. Chimneys erupted from walls and roofs. Weird scents filled an air already crowded with the sound of hammering, sawing, and occasional swearing.

"Okay, so who benefits? You're right, that's the key," she said. "Isaac said something about politicians and about how this was about control."

"He did?"

"A while ago," Ruth said.

"You've seen him recently?" Simon asked.

"Not really," Ruth said. "He's not important." She'd told Simon about Isaac, though in general terms. She'd not said that Isaac had facilitated the escape of Mrs Standage and her family. Standage had supplied the counterfeiters with the designs of the banknotes because her husband and child had been taken hostage. Suspecting someone in the police department couldn't be trusted, Mitchell had arranged for Isaac to find somewhere safe for them. Precisely where that was, Ruth wasn't sure. She decided to move the conversation along. "A politician *could* be behind it. But politicians aren't..." She trailed off.

She'd reached an alley. At the far end was a figure, and there was something striking about him. He was dressed almost identically to Ned Ludd. Ruth froze, but only for a second, and then she ran. The man turned toward her. His expression twisted from self-satisfied glee to shock.

"Stop!" Ruth yelled. The man dropped something he'd been holding in his left hand. He still had something in his right.

"Don't!" she yelled, fumbling with the button on her holster. She vaguely heard the sound of shattering glass. The man was turning toward her, his hand swivelling with him. Before he could bring it to bear, she slammed into him, grabbed a fistful of dank wool, and shoved him against the wall. She drew her revolver and pressed the barrel against his forehead.

"Who are you?" she hissed. "Who are you!" This time she screamed the words into the man's face.

"Please!" he whimpered, his voice high pitched and shrill.

"Who are you?"

"Ruth! Ruth!" It was Simon. He had a hand on her arm. "Let him go. Please. Let him go!"

Ruth blinked. She saw the man's face, and saw that it wasn't a man, but a boy not much younger than she was. Slowly, she lowered the gun. She stepped back, and she saw the wall. She raised her gun again. "Cuff him," she said.

"What?" Simon said.

"Look at the wall."

The object in the man's hand had been a paintbrush. A jar of cheap paint lay smashed on the cobbles. On the wall were four letters, 'Ned L' with the 'L' painted backward.

"Did you get all that?" Mitchell asked as he came into the observation room. On the other side of the one-way glass, the suspect shivered.

"Yes, sir," Ruth said. She'd been transcribing the boy's statement as Mitchell had conducted the interview.

"He's terrified," Mitchell said. "But he's talking, and so far he seems to know about as much as anyone else we've spoken to. Is there anything you want to tell me about the arrest?"

"No, sir," she said. There was, or at least there was something that she wanted to talk to someone about. There had been a brief moment where she'd wanted to pull the trigger. Resisting that impulse had been the hardest thing she'd ever done. "What's going to happen to him?"

"We'll hold him until we've raided those addresses he's given us, and then let him go."

"But..." She looked at the boy on the other side of the glass. He looked scared, lost, and alone. "Emmitt will kill him," Ruth said. "And if he doesn't that gang boss of his will."

"What would you do instead?" Mitchell asked.

"I... I don't know. Keep him here?"

"You don't have the authority to do that. Nor do I, unfortunately. But I'll speak to Weaver and see if something can be arranged." Mitchell picked up the transcript. "You could do with some handwriting lessons," he said, peering at the page. "Let's see. Here, his name. There's only one 'I' in Ibn. So, he's Sadiq Ibn Faraud, a member of The Spade Boys, a fledgling gang based on the east side of the docks. He was given the paint, the brush, and a pound note with the instruction to paint that message up on walls across the city."

"He wasn't paid with a twenty-pound note," Ruth said.

"No. Let's hope it doesn't mean the man has started printing banknotes in other denominations." He looked at the account. "Sadiq was told not to return until the jar was empty. You missed the bit about how the clothing was given to him by the same man who gave them paint, brush, slogan, and money. Marshal Johnson. He doesn't know if that's a first name or a title, but the man is running that gang."

"No, here." Ruth pointed. "He said that Johnson ran the entire docks."

"He doesn't, but I'm sure that's what Johnson told Sadiq."

"Is that where we go now?" Ruth asked. "To the docks, to arrest this man?"

"No. Not yet. I doubt anyone will notice that Sadiq hasn't returned, not today. I doubt this Johnson will know any more than Frobisher or Turnbull. Johnson… Johnson… Riley was looking for a man by that name who'd gone missing from the Marquis. It's a common name, but maybe it's the same guy. Either way, I think he'll have been paid to get the slogans painted without knowing why. You heard the kid, he's only wearing those clothes because they were better than the rags he had before."

"So why paint the slogans?" Ruth asked.

"To have the name 'Ned Ludd' fixed in people's minds. You remember those placards we found in that house. If a public demonstration by the Luddites is part of Emmitt's plan, then it will work a lot better if people are familiar with Ned Ludd's name. Of course that means Emmitt's still going ahead, but we don't know with what."

"If we're not going to arrest Johnson, what are we doing?" she asked.

"What was the other address he gave? The one where he said the meeting would be held?"

"The Pokesdown Processing Plant," Ruth said, pointing at the transcript. "Do you know it?"

"I know it was shut down in July. They lost too much fish during the heat wave, so they moved to a location closer to the quays. You could fit a hundred people in there. Twice the number if the equipment's been removed. That's where we go. But not as a raid, initially we'll go in undercover. If they had to pay this kid to paint the signs, maybe they're paying the rest of the demonstrators, and maybe this, tonight, is when they tell them where to go. We'll have the Marines on standby, in case they guess who we are."

"Undercover? I should go and change."

"You should, but I've a different assignment for you."

"You have?"

"Riley's got some suspicions about Rupert Pine. He's holding a public meeting for his constituents. Riley's going. Davis is backup. I want you to go, too."

"But—"

"Those are your orders," Mitchell said. "Go and get Riley, let's see if Sadiq's description of Johnson matches the man she was looking for."

Chapter 10
Public Meeting

"Emma-Louise Tallincourt. Nothing incriminating found," Ruth read aloud from the summary Captain Mitchell had written on the search of the home of the missing train driver. "It's not very detailed."

"But it sums it up," Sergeant Davis said. For once he wasn't wearing his black old-world uniform, but a pair of shinny-at-the-knees trousers and a tweed jacket trimmed with almost matching leather. "And it's what we'd expect. These are professionals. They've been told not to leave clues behind, but what clues would we expect to find?"

A coin stamped with a backward 'L', Ruth thought, but if the driver had one, no doubt it would be on her person.

Like Davis, she was in civilian clothes, though hers were distinctly more ragged, and made even more so in comparison to Sergeant Riley.

"Turn around," Riley said. Ruth did. "No. That gun's too obvious. Here." She opened a drawer in her desk and took out a compact pistol, a third of the size of Ruth's service revolver. "Eight rounds in the magazine. Safety is here. Two spare clips."

Ruth took the weapon. Riley was wearing a short coat, medium height heels, and high-waisted trousers topped off with more jewellery than Ruth had seen anyone wear before in real-life.

"You're staring," Riley said.

"It's... you look nice," Ruth said diplomatically.

"No, I don't, but I'll stand out," Riley said. "That's the point. When I went to see Rupert Pine, he got defensive. He claimed not to know about the Luddites. I'm certain he was lying. He said I should come to this meeting so he could prove he was a friend of the working woman." Riley grinned. "And the moment he said it, I could see he wanted to take the words back. That's when I asked about Ned Ludd, and that was when he insisted I should come tonight. He was evading the question."

"And how big a place is the White Hart?" Davis asked.

"Two bars downstairs, one meeting room upstairs that can seat about forty," Riley said. "Pine told me he was the least radical scheduled to speak, but that he was the voice of reason. A moderating influence between the forces of labour and economy that drive our nation. To put it another way, he'll say anything to anyone if it'll help him get elected." She opened her purse, took out a snub-nosed pistol, and checked it was loaded. "He'll notice me. So will everyone else. They'll watch me, or the speakers. Deering, you keep an eye on anyone who doesn't. He'll have told them I'm coming. They'll know I'm a cop, so they'll try not to be noticed."

"But won't they recognise me?" Ruth asked. "I mean, won't Emmitt have given them a description?"

"Probably. Which should make them easier to spot. Davis, you're—"

"Downstairs, making occasionally dissatisfied comments about working conditions. If I hear a shot, I'll come upstairs. If I don't, I'll keep an eye on the people watching the people watching her watch you."

"And then what?" Ruth asked. "I mean, what's the signal going to be for us to arrest them?"

"We won't be making any arrests," Riley said. "Not tonight. We know these people aren't afraid to kill, and there will be too many innocent civilians in the pub. We want leverage on Pine. If Emmitt was planning on using the politician in his plans, then our presence tonight should make him a liability."

"And you think he'll crack?" Davis asked.

"Easily."

What Ruth thought was that Riley was being kept away from the real action as much as she was.

The moment Ruth opened the door to the pub, a wall of sound hit here. Partially deafened, she shouldered her way through the densely packed crowd. She caught sight of Davis, a pint glass in one hand, a dart in the other, seemingly engrossed in some half-shouted, half-laughed argument with a group by the dartboard.

"Excuse me, excuse me," Ruth muttered, more to herself than to the people she nudged, pushed, and in one case, kicked, as she tried to find her way to the staircase near the door to the rear bar. A man stood in front of it.

"You lost?" he asked.

"I'm here for the meeting," Ruth said.

He eyed her suspiciously. "You sure?"

"Like I'd come to a place like this for any other reason," she replied tartly.

The man grunted, but stepped out of the way. Ruth went upstairs. The meeting room was as crowded as the pub downstairs. Ruth elbowed her way to a spot behind the rearmost row of seats from where she could make out the back of Riley's head.

As casually as she could, she surveyed the room. There were seven rows of chairs, with people standing in the aisle either side. At the front was a lectern with five more chairs behind it. To one side was a door, with another man standing guard by it. Next to him was a young man, more a boy, Ruth thought, in clothing with too many pockets. It was almost like the style that Isaac and his followers wore, except the colours were far more vibrant. A flat piece of card stuck out of the brim of his hat, and in his hand was a notepad. He looked more out of place than Ruth felt, yet the man seemed more relaxed than anyone else in the room. They were a mix of men and women. Most looked like they'd come straight from work. A few were staring fixedly at Riley, but the rest were talking quietly, or simply waiting with varying degrees of patience. The atmosphere was expectant.

Hoping to eavesdrop on one of those muted conversations, she inched forward a step, but her foot kicked against the leg of the chair in front. Its occupant, an old man, turned around and saw her.

"Here you go, love," he said, standing up. "You take my chair." His accent was thick from one of those northern towns now lost to time.

"Oh, no, I couldn't," Ruth said.

"Not at all, lass. It's not right for a healthy man to sit when a woman is standing." This last was said in a far louder voice, and was clearly directed at the young men sitting near him. They kept their eyes studiously ahead as the old man shuffled into the aisle, but a lot of others in the room turned to look.

"Thank you," Ruth said, quickly taking the man's seat, and keeping her eyes down in the hope she might evade the sudden and unwanted attention. Before she dared looked up again, she heard a noise from the front. The door by the stage had opened. A tall man entered the room first. He had broad shoulders, and wide arms barely hidden by a thin shirt. A man in a suit followed. By the way he paused to smile at Riley, Ruth took him to be Rupert Pine. A woman in an austere black dress followed. There was a second woman in the doorway. She had golden-white hair pinned close to her head and an apron strapped around her waist. She surveyed the room before pulling the door closed with her on the other side. Someone who worked in the pub, Ruth thought, trying to remember if she'd been behind the bar earlier.

"Brothers. Sisters. Welcome," the man in shirtsleeves said. "For those of you who don't know me, my name is Lucian Fredericks. Tonight we're joined by the Member of Parliament for Milford, Rupert Pine, and by Grace Jollie from the League of Tomorrow. They'll be giving their own views about the future that awaits us after the next election, and as you can imagine those views are very different."

There was soft laughter from half of the room. Ruth ignored it, trying to find a position from which she could see Riley, but the people in the row in front were too tall for her to see over.

"Rationing is coming to an end," Fredericks said. "And when it does, the real struggle will begin. Our estimates are that we produce fifty percent more food than we consume."

Pine harrumphed in disagreement.

"Fifty percent," Fredericks repeated. "Without food being shipped to America, should our farmers and fishers still meet these absurd quotas? Where will they find employment? And what will that do to the wages in the workshops and factories? Britain was a nation built on inequality. For twenty years we have struggled together, but the economic divide has only deepened. The haves have everything, and the have-nots have next to nothing. It will get worse unless we act." Ruth leaned forward. "When you get to the ballot box, you will have a choice. Let this inequality grow, or vote for real change." Ruth leaned back.

She wondered who the man was. He'd given himself no real introduction, and from the atmosphere in the room he didn't need one. Everyone knew him and knew what he would say. The only exception, other than the young man in his bright, many-pocketed jacket, was a slovenly man in a green woollen cap, standing with his back to the wall, eight feet from the stage. He had his eyes fixed on the front row. Was he watching Riley?

There was a muted roar of agreement from the room, and Ruth realised she'd missed some key part of Fredericks' speech.

"And that is the truth of it," Fredericks continued. "It may seem like the struggle is coming to an end, that life is going to get easier, but the real fight has only just begun. I would like you to bear that in mind as I welcome tonight's first speaker, Mr Rupert Pine, MP for Milford and Christchurch South."

Pine stood up.

"Thank you," he said, shaking the man's hand, before taking a position behind the podium. "Thank you," he said again, and paused as if waiting for applause. It didn't come. "Your figures are wrong." There was a hiss of disapproval from the crowd. "I'm sorry, but they are. Not all food aid gets shipped to the Americas. In fact, when you consider the size of the planet and how few settlements we're in contact with, our efforts amount to very little. Last year we shipped supplies to forty-eight communities around the Mediterranean and West African coast. This year it was to forty-six. Two of those communities disappeared. They are gone. The inhabitants murdered or fled. That is the true reality of our situation. Yes, we are at a time of change, a moment that will decide the future, but it is not the future of us, or this country, or even our children, but the fate of the world itself. I have some figures for you…"

Ruth relaxed a little as Pine began reading from a list. She'd been right. Whatever Riley may have thought, this meeting was a way for Mitchell to get them both out of the way. She tuned back into the speech, but there was no mention of technology, or of Ned Ludd, or anything that might connect him to Emmitt.

"That then," Pine said, bringing his speech to an end, "is the decision ahead of us. Comfort today, or a future for the planet itself."

There was no applause.

"Thank you, Mr Pine," Fredericks said, taking the podium again. "Some interesting points. For an alternative perspective, I would like to introduce Miss Grace Jollie."

The woman took the stage.

"Waste!" she said. "Waste!" she said again. Ruth wondered if the woman would go for a third. "It is the bane of our species," Jollie said, and began an impassioned speech that Ruth struggled to follow. It was only when the woman launched into a point-by-point attack on Pine's parliamentary voting record that she understood. The woman was announcing herself as a candidate in opposition to Pine. Ruth couldn't work out what her policies exactly were beyond that it had something to do with abolishing rationing and overseas food-aid, while increasing wages for farmers and cutting prices for everyone else. From the audience's reaction, they'd known this woman was going to speak. From their perfectly timed cheers of agreement and hisses of disapproval, they knew exactly what she was going to say.

After twenty minutes, Fredericks did the merciful thing and closed the meeting. Pine rushed from the stage without another glance at Riley.

Ruth stayed in her seat as people filed out of the room. She wanted to see who else might linger rather than hurry down to the bar. The man to her left stood, and Ruth was forced to do the same, joining the slow shuffle as people headed downstairs. She found she was standing next to the old man who'd given her his seat.

"Was that what you were expecting?" he asked.

"I'm not really sure what I was expecting," Ruth said, finding herself answering truthfully. "Perhaps more about ordinary people. It was all a lot of words to say very little."

"That's politicians for you," the old man said. The queue for the door shuffled a few paces forward. Ruth looked around and saw Riley disappear through the door at the front. There were too many people in the line behind her for Ruth to follow.

"Looking for someone?" the old man asked.

"For Pine," Ruth said. "He's my MP, but this was the first time I'd ever seen him."

"It was better in the old-world," the man said. "Even if they didn't go door-to-door, at least you had posters so you could recognise them in the supermarket." He gave a low chuckle. "That's what I used to do – ambush them when they were shopping. They couldn't get away then, you see. Can't abandon your trolley in the middle of an— ah." He gave that sigh of someone who had temporarily forgotten how the world had changed. "But we can't have the old world back," the man said. "As much as we might want it. It's too dangerous."

Ruth's ears pricked up as she shuffled another few feet closer to the door.

"What do you mean?" she asked. "The AIs?"

"For a start. But then there's the inequality of wealth. Fredericks is right about that. It takes everyone's labour to pull in a harvest, so is it right that the landowner gets more than a fair share? Particularly when the only requirement to own land was to file a claim a decade ago?"

"You have a point," Ruth said, thinking of how her own landlord had been foisted on them.

"Did you notice the journalist?" the old man asked.

"The young man with the notepad?"

"That's him. Tomorrow they'll print an article saying that there was a small meeting at which Pine spoke, and that there was a spirited debate. That's all they'll say. Tonight's meeting won't make a blind bit of difference. It's not how a democracy should be run."

"Is there an alternative?" Ruth asked. She glanced down, but the man was wearing distinctly old-world clothing, complete with metal eyelets on his mirror-polished shoes.

"Jollie is good and honest, but far too opinionated to win an election. There are other candidates. A few of them will speak tomorrow. Do you know the old supermarket near the roundabout at the end of Spencer

Avenue? Tomorrow night, at eight p.m. Come and hear them speak if for no other reason than one of them will be representing you in government."

They'd reached the stairs. Another meeting? It was the thinnest of leads, like attending this one had been.

"Maybe," Ruth said.

"Think about it," the old man said. "And would you be a dear and help me down these stairs? They're a bit steep."

Ruth helped the man down to the pub. He asked if she was staying for a drink. She looked around and saw Davis. The sergeant downed the last of his pint, laid the glass down, and headed toward the door. Ruth did the same.

"It wasn't anything important," Ruth said when she met Davis in an alley two streets away. "It was just an attack on the MP. There was only one person not really paying attention, a man in a green woollen cap. About thirty, unshaven, beige shirt—"

"Droop to the left eyelid, walked with his right foot turned slightly inwards, wearing a belt on which he's had to punch out two new holes," Davis finished. "He was serving behind the bar when I entered the pub and disappeared into the back before you arrived."

"So he wasn't interested in what was being said because he works there? Then I really didn't learn anything tonight. Oh, except that there's going to be another meeting tomorrow. It's going to be some more candidates who are standing against Pine."

"In an old supermarket?" Davis asked.

"That's right. You heard of that?"

"You hear a lot more in a busy pub than a quiet meeting," Davis said.

"It's probably not worth going," Ruth said. "We're not likely to find anything there."

"That depends on how hard we look, but as to whether it's worth us turning up, that's up to the captain."

"Hmm." Ruth turned around, looking back at the now distant pub. "We should wait for Riley."

"She's already gone home."

"She has?"

"And you might as well do the same. Maybe tomorrow we'll turn up some better leads."

There were always more leads, Ruth thought as she walked through the dark streets. What good did following them do? The investigation was going nowhere.

She splashed into a puddle. Water seeped through the cracked leather, enveloping her foot in a damp cocoon. Perfect, she thought. A light drizzle had started while she was in the pub. It wasn't heavy, but it had a persistence that suggested it wouldn't stop before dawn. She'd be soaked by the time she got home.

Pulling her collar up, she squelched down the road, turning her eyes to the occasional pools of light ahead of her. She wasn't alone on the street. Others hurried along with more haste than she. One, about fifty feet ahead of her, stepped into a pool of light cast from an un-shuttered window. On his head was a green woollen cap. It was the barman. He'd probably finished his shift and was heading home. Probably. Ruth slowed her pace to match his. It wasn't as if he was being furtive. When he took the next road to the right, Ruth followed.

It was a narrow road with cream-coloured houses on either side. He didn't go inside, he kept walking. He took a left. She followed. He took a right. She followed. He took another left, and when Ruth turned the corner, he'd disappeared.

This road was completely dark. She took a step forward. Then another. There was a vague shape at the far end that might have been the next junction. But then again, it might not.

He must have gone into a building. Which? She looked up, hoping to spot some errant wisp of smoke from a chimney, but the rain was falling too hard to tell.

She took another step down the alley.

There was a splash in a puddle behind her.

She spun around.

A pair of figures loomed in the road's mouth. One massive, one of regular height, both male. Her fingers caught in her coat as she reached for the concealed gun. A square of light appeared in one of the figure's hands.

"A dark night," Isaac said, shining the light first on his own face, and then on Gregory's, standing next to him.

"What are you doing?" Ruth asked.

"When we first met, didn't Henry say that I had you followed? He was right."

"You were following me? Why?" she asked.

"Because it's a miserable night, and if I wasn't following you, I'd have no reason to leave my warm home," Isaac said. Which, like most of the replies he gave, was no real answer.

"I was following a man in a green hat," she said.

"Yes?"

"He disappeared down this road."

"Evidently."

"Can you help me find him?" she asked.

"By knocking on each door in turn? And what would you do if he answered? What would you ask him?"

Ruth stared at Isaac, then turned away to look down the dark street. There really was no sign of the man. What *would* she do if the man opened the door? What would she do if someone else did? She could picture herself storming a house, capturing Emmitt and all the others, but knew reality was far from that fantasy. Even if the man did open the door and allowed himself to be taken in for questioning, what precisely did she want to ask him?

She pulled her collar up higher, marched past Isaac and Gregory, and headed back toward The Acre. She didn't even bother checking whether the two men were still following her.

Chapter 11
Suspects
7th October

"Name?" Ruth asked.

"Edward Roberts," the man said.

"Occupation?"

"Carpenter. I've a shop on Prentice Lane, and I should be there now. What crime have I committed?"

That was a good question. Like the other one hundred and forty men and women in the hall, Roberts had been arrested at the previous night's meeting in the processing plant. Weaver had ordered the Marines in, the building sealed, and everyone there brought into custody. Mitchell had been furious, and that had provided Ruth with some relief until the captain told her she would be processing the suspects.

"Home address?" she asked.

"Above my shop."

"On Prentice Lane?"

"Yeah, so since when is it a crime to go to a political meeting?"

"That's why you went there, is it?" she asked.

"To hear people speak. Are you saying free-speech doesn't mean anything anymore?"

"I'm saying that I have to ask you these questions," Ruth said, holding up the piece of paper on which they were written. "Once I've taken your fingerprints and we've confirmed your address, you'll be free to go."

"You haven't said why."

"Why? Because it's what I've been told to do!" Ruth snapped.

"Just following orders, is it?"

Ruth gritted her teeth. "And how did you hear about the meeting?" she asked, returning to the questions on her list.

An hour but only four more citizens later, Ruth took a break and went searching for tea. She found Mitchell sipping a cup of coffee in a small room with wide windows that looked out onto the hall.

"This isn't getting us anywhere," she said.

"No," Mitchell replied. "Weaver insisted on rounding everyone up. Her argument is that it can't hurt."

"Unless part of Emmitt's plan is having us too busy scrabbling around that we don't have time to look for any *real* clues," Ruth said.

"It's a possibility," Mitchell said, "but it's out of my hands. Out of Weaver's too. The PM took a turn for the worse yesterday morning. The wound in her shoulder is infected. She'll live, but Deputy Prime Minister Atherton's running the country now. The only thing stopping him from being sworn in is that it would require the full sitting of Parliament."

"Which would have happened if the assassination had gone ahead," Ruth said.

"Yep."

"And that would be the perfect time to use an explosive to kill all the politicians?"

"Precisely."

"But that would have happened long before the fifth of November," Ruth said. "Wouldn't it?

"Which makes me even more worried. The Speaker suggested that the House sits in secret one evening to approve him. The Leader of the Opposition proposed appointing a monarch and returning to the old system where a politician was invited to form a government. Atherton's plan of waiting is the more palatable solution, but if there was any room left in my soul, I'd be worrying about that as well." He took a sip from his mug. "But I don't. Atherton went north this morning. He's going to take over the negotiations with Albion. Actually, from what Rebecca Cavendish told me, he's going to end the negotiations with an ultimatum. Either they agree to all terms, or he's going to send the Marines in to destroy them."

"Because they were colluding with Emmitt?"

"Because they might have been. He'll promise thunder and war, and we'll probably get it."

"That's not good," Ruth said.

"No."

"You got that from Rebecca?" Ruth asked. "How did she know?"

"Because people at train stations don't think the railway workers are listening," Mitchell said. "Anyway, Atherton's last orders to the Home Secretary were that everyone connected to this crime in any way, no matter how small, should be arrested. Hence this madhouse." He waved a hand at the hall.

"Were there any real suspects at the meeting?" Ruth asked.

"Not really. The man organising it was Silas Greenbaum. He's anti-government regardless of their policies, but he wouldn't do anything to harm anyone."

"You know him?"

"I do. His is a sad tale. His wife died in the Blackout, but his six kids survived. They've all died in the years since. Disease. Accidents. The last, the second from oldest, joined the Marines. He was killed by pirates during a survey mission around the Mediterranean eight years ago. Silas was making the rough woollen tunics and trousers, and selling them at the meetings."

"Who to?"

"Anyone who'd buy them. He says it's a symbolic rejection of the old-world, not to be worn as actual clothing. It started off as his version of sackcloth and ashes. Six months ago, someone asked to buy a set. He's been making them ever since."

"Did he sell any to a man with a scarred face?"

"No. Silas has sold a few dozen sets. Whether he sold them to Ned Ludd's friends, or whether Emmitt got the idea from him and had them make their own, I don't know. Davis is interviewing him now, trying to get some more details, but I'm not sure there will be any. I think Greenbaum is just another tool, someone for Emmitt to use, yet I'm still unclear as to what purpose. The only truly interesting point is that a year ago he was giving his speeches on empty street corners, and now he's speaking to hundreds. But is that thanks to Emmitt, or because there's a genuine interest in the ideas he's expressing? In short, we're no closer to catching Emmitt. Rupert Pine might be our best lead."

"He is? I didn't think he said anything at the meeting."

"Riley followed him home last night. She said he was uncharacteristically brusque as he tried to get rid of her. She suspects he's up to something."

"Can we interview him?"

"Officially? No. Atherton won't allow it. Unofficially, there's going to be a fundraiser at the Longfields tonight. Pine is one of the politicians who'll be there. Simon's spoken to his mother, and arranged for us to attend, and for a room to be found where we can talk to him in private."

"And if he is involved, and he does talk, what can he possibly tell us? He won't know where Emmitt is, will he?"

"Probably not, but it's what we do. We follow every lead. We'll take these people's fingerprints and compare them to the ones you and Davis collected in the house used by the saboteurs. The Marines will do double duty guarding the city, and the ones that aren't will scour the countryside looking for vehicle tracks. The Navy are conducting their own investigation in the armoury at Loch Creigh. If Emmitt was planning on stealing explosives, then it's probable that someone there is on the take. Tomorrow, we'll go through what we've found, and start all over again. As for you, I want you and Davis going to this meeting at the supermarket tonight."

"Why?"

"Because I was thinking about Fairmont and what he told us about The Syndicate. Their modus operandi was blackmail and extortion. So what if Pine is being coerced? Perhaps there's a rumour or two floating around as to what his secret is. The people most likely to know it are those standing against him."

Ruth thought about that. There was logic to it, but more importantly it didn't sound as if Mitchell was fobbing her off.

"Okay," she said.

"Good. Now, these people aren't going to interview themselves. Ah, but imagine a world where they would."

"I did a bit of work like this before the Blackout," Davis said as he and Ruth picked their way through the crowds of evening commuters. "The trick is to say as little as you can, but not to come across as ignorant or prying. Your best chance is to appear interested in the person, so I'd say stick with the young men or the very old. Don't ask 'why?' Not outright. Feign interested ignorance."

"Interested in the person, right," Ruth said, only half listening.

"Our story is that you're my niece. I've come to the city looking for work that's more secure than the mines. I didn't work a seam, anyone with half an eye could tell that, but worked in administration. That's all you know, and you don't care about the details. You've been working on smallholdings, mucking out pigs and the like, and are looking for something better. I'm with you tonight because a girl of your age shouldn't be wandering the streets alone. Got it?"

"Sure. Protective uncle. Awful jobs."

"Meetings like this aren't dangerous," Davis said. "The worse that'll happen is that they discover who we are and kick us out. Any real danger will be with the people waiting outside. If it happens, we're going to run. Not fight, see? And we're not going to make any arrests. We're after information, remember?"

"About Pine, and what someone might want to blackmail him with. Yes."

There were a couple of women by the door to the supermarket.

"They haven't started," one said, before returning to an animated conversation about what someone's boyfriend had said about someone else's wife. Ruth pulled the door open, more convinced than ever that whatever this night would bring, it wasn't going to bring them closer to Emmitt.

The old man was sitting at a small table just inside the door. A candle-lamp hung above his head, positioned to illuminate a sheet of paper.

"Good. You came, and who's this?"

"I'm her uncle," Davis said. "An old man invites her to an abandoned supermarket, and I'm not likely to let her come alone."

"We're all friends here, brother," the old man said.

"Brother, is it?"

"On whom can we rely but each other?" the old man asked.

"A very good question," Davis said. "When's the meeting start?"

"In about five minutes. If you could add your name and address to the list."

"What for?" Ruth asked.

"So we can make sure you vote come election time," the old man said. "It doesn't matter to us for whom you cast your ballot, just that you do."

Davis shrugged and wrote down a name. Ruth did the same, copying the sergeant's surname. The page was only half full.

"It's a smaller turnout than we were expecting," the old man said. "It's the weather, I suppose. You might as well go in." He pointed toward a set of doors, both of which had wooden panels covering the broken glass.

"After you," Davis said, pulling the door open.

Ruth stepped through it and into a corridor. At the end was a single candle. Something was— There was a sudden deafening bang. A gunshot. She turned around. She saw Davis. He was lying on the ground. Blood gushed from a massive wound in his head. The old man stood by the doors, a pistol in his hand, a calculating look in his eye.

Ruth reached for the weapon holstered at her back. There was an arm on her shoulder, a stinging sensation on her neck. Everything went dark.

Chapter 12
The Crypt

Ruth forced her eyes open. Everything was bright. Her mouth was dry and her brain thudded against her skull. Slowly, her vision cleared. She was in a long cavernous room filled with brick pillars and dark shadows.

She tried to raise a hand to her throbbing temples, but couldn't move her arms. It took a moment to remember how to do it, but she tilted her head and looked down. She was sitting in a chair. Tied to a chair, her brain corrected. She tried kicking her feet, but they too were bound. Everything came back. Davis had been shot by the old man. He'd seemed so nice, so — No! She shook her head in an attempt to dispel the wave of self-pity. Breathe in, breathe out, she told herself. In. Out. In. Out. Focus. She was a prisoner. They'd killed Davis. They would kill her. She had to escape.

She stretched and strained, first her arms, and then her legs, and then both together. There was a little give in the ropes, but not enough. She tried pushing down with her feet and pulling with her arms at the same time. The chair creaked, but it didn't break.

Relax. Count to ten.

Who had done this? Emmitt, presumably. But who else? The old man. What about the two women who'd been outside the supermarket? Probably. No. No more assumptions. From now on she only wanted facts. Ten seconds were up. She strained against her ropes, gritting her teeth as the cord bit into flesh. Five seconds. Ten. Twenty. Pain finally forced her to stop.

Try again, she told herself. In a moment, came the silent reply. The old man, the two women. Who else? There had been someone else. Someone behind her, someone who'd... what? Drugged her? She vaguely recalled a stinging sensation in the back of her neck. A syringe? Almost certainly. So there were four of them, and Emmitt had had between six and ten at the ambush site. Good, she was getting somewhere. Or was she?

She stretched the ropes again, this time trying to hold out for thirty seconds. It was slowly dawning that any deductions she might make, no matter how accurate they were, wouldn't save her. They'd killed Davis. They'd kill her. A wave of despair gripped her. She tried kicking her feet, but they were bound too tight. She yelled. She screamed. She stopped, listening as the unanswered echoes faded away. Echoes. Where was she? She grappled with the question to drown out the siren song of fear.

It wasn't a supermarket. At least she didn't think so. The room was large. Really it was too large to be called a room. Brick pillars were spaced ten feet apart, and she could count twelve of them. Two feet wide at the base, tapering upwards to a vaulted ceiling made of similar crumbling red masonry. No, it was a crypt, or maybe the wine cellar of some remote country house. Did it matter? Yes, she told herself, as she gave the ropes another experimental tug. Even if all she could do was process what lay before her eyes, it was better than meekly waiting for her fate. Eyes? And then she saw the thing that you never notice because without it you can't. Light. It was coming from the base of the pillars. Not candles, but electric lights, with cables snaking across the floor toward... but she couldn't see where they went. But electricity meant they were near the city. Or near a power station. Could she have been unconscious long enough for them to take her to somewhere in Wales or Scotland? No. Her mouth was dry, but she wasn't overcome with thirst. She couldn't have been unconscious for more than a few hours. Not much longer than it must have taken for them to bring her from the supermarket to here. But where was that?

She turned her head left and right, searching for some window hidden in a dark recess. There wasn't one. As she moved her head, the sharp pain retreated into a dull ache, and her mind cleared. No, there wasn't a window, but against one wall were a stack of metal containers, the kind she'd seen used for storing water. Was that important? Probably not. She turned her head again, and this time saw what had been almost in front of her all the time.

The chair was next to a table. Around it were four chairs made of the same polished wood. In the middle of the table was a carving of a blocky 'r'. She strained again, this time alternating left and right, left and right, trying to rock the chair over. As she shifted her shoulders, she looked down. The chair was bolted to the floor. From the dust around the metal bracket, it looked like it had been done very recently. Then she realised. The chair matched those four other seats around the table. Five chairs. She craned her head, looking at the table once more. There was no inscription, but if the chair had been on the other side, the carving would look like a backward 'L'.

Five chairs. Five stars separating each word in that hated inscription. Did that mean there were five conspirators? Emmitt, Wallace, Donal, and two others. Who? She had a feeling that she'd soon find out.

She heard the footsteps first. They came from behind. Ruth forced herself to stare straight ahead. The footsteps stopped. Ruth gritted her teeth, waiting.

"You're awake. Good." It was a woman's voice. Ruth played the three words over and over, trying to think if she'd heard them before. She was sure she hadn't.

"Good," the woman said again. She stepped into view. She was an inch above average height, with cropped white-gold hair and an expressionless, unlined face. It reminded Ruth of those pictures she'd seen in old-world magazines, of the models holding up a bottle of perfume or wearing some absurdly impractical fashions. Those faces were chosen because they wouldn't distract from what was being sold. It was a face that people wouldn't notice.

"I've seen you before," Ruth said.

"Indeed," the woman said. A carefully plucked eyebrow rose a fraction of an inch. "Where?"

"At the meeting in the pub. You were in the doorway when Rupert Pine came onto the stage."

The woman's lips curled into a smile absent of any kindness. "Ah, yes. Dear Rupert." The smile vanished. "My name is Eve. Of course that isn't really my name, but in the hours to come I will find it easier if you have a name to call me." In her hands was a thick leather case. She laid it on the table. Slowly, she unzipped it. "Please pay attention. You are in the crypt of a church two miles from the nearest dwelling. No matter how loudly you scream, the only people who can hear you will not come to your aid. There is one exit from this crypt. It is locked. Beyond it are my people. I have some questions. You will answer them. You won't lie. Ah, I can see you don't believe me. You will."

The woman opened the case. It was filled with metal instruments. Some long. Some thin. Most looked sharp.

"Do you have a coin in there?" Ruth asked.

"A coin?" she asked, running a hand along the steel tools.

"Five chairs. Five stars. Where's the truth?" Ruth asked.

"Ah, you mean like this?" Eve reached into her pocket and pulled out a small silver disc. "Where indeed is the truth? I think we will find it today."

"So there are five of you?" Ruth asked, her eyes watching the woman's hand as it played across the tools.

"It's a nice number, don't you think?" the woman replied.

"You, Emmitt, Donal, Wallace. Who's the fifth?"

The woman smiled. "I think it's time I asked you some of *my* questions." She pulled out a long slender needle.

"I won't tell you anything," Ruth said.

"Everyone says that. They are always wrong," the woman said. She held the needle up in front of Ruth's eyes. It was ten inches long, barely a centimetre wide, tapering to a fine point at one end and a bulbous tip at the other.

"This will hurt," she said and walked behind Ruth.

There was a tug, then the sound of material tearing as Ruth felt the shirt ripped from her back.

"I am fascinated by the human body," the woman said. Ruth shivered as she felt the woman run a finger down, then up her spine, and then along her shoulder blade. "A person can be beaten for days and yet hold onto that spark of self. Yet with the smallest of pressures, they can experience pain beyond their worst fears."

There was a brief stinging sensation, a moment absent of all feeling, and then a sea of agony unlike anything Ruth had ever known. She screamed. The pain didn't stop. It went on for eternity. And then it was over.

"That was ten seconds," Eve said, "of one, small, precise pressure. So much easier than beating you, and far tidier than extracting your fingernails. Now, listen."

Ruth gasped for breath, and then gritted her teeth, trying to prevent those gasps from turning into sobs. Her body was slick with sweat and shivering with the memory of that agonising pain.

"Listen," the woman said again. "Do you hear it? There is nothing. No footsteps. No calls of concerned passers-by. Do you understand? You are alone. Perhaps you don't understand."

There was the touch of metal against skin, and the pain began again. Ruth tried not to scream. She gritted her teeth, counting slowly in her head. She reached eight before it became too much, and a tormented wail erupted from her throat.

"There," the woman said, as the pain ceased. "If I want you to scream, you will. If I want you to stop, you will. You are here to answer questions. I already know some of the answers. How much you suffer depends entirely on how truthful you are. What is your name?"

Ruth shook her head. If she answered the easy questions, then she'd answer all of them.

The pain began again.

"That was ten seconds," the woman said. "What is your name?"

"Ruth. Ruth Deering," Ruth sobbed.

There was more pain.

"What is your name?"

"Ruth—"

More pain.

"It is a simple question. Answer truthfully and it will stop. What is your name?"

"Ru—"

Pain.

"Your name?"

"I... I've always been called Ruth Deering," she said.

"That is closer to the truth, but it is not entirely accurate, is it?" Eve said. The needle ran along her back, then up and down her spine. "A nerve bundle beneath your shoulder blades is one thing. Imagine what I could do with your spine."

"I've been called Ruth Deering for as long as I can remember," Ruth said.

"Good. Better. How old are you?"

"Eighteen," Ruth replied automatically. The needle plunged into her back. Ruth screamed.

"How old are you?" the woman asked.

"Not eighteen. I don't know. I lied about my age to get into the police. Seventeen probably. Somewhere between sixteen and eighteen. Maybe older. I don't know!"

The torturer walked in front of the chair and looked at Ruth more closely. "Interesting," she said. "Where do you live?"

Strike a match, Ruth thought, remembering what Mitchell had said. Try to fix something good in your mind so that when you're surrounded by darkness, you can remember the light. If this wasn't the darkest of moments, she didn't know what was. She tried to focus on the day she and Mitchell picked apples, on Maggie's face at Christmas, of anything other than the agonising present. She couldn't. The pain cut through it all. The only thing she could see were the flagstones in front of her.

The questions went on. Ruth answered them all, and as truthfully as she could. That didn't stop the torture. During the brief moments between, she wondered why the woman was asking them. They had nothing to do with the investigation.

"That is enough for now," the woman said. "I think I have proved my point. You will answer whatever I ask, and no one will come to your aid. Think on that."

Eve left the chamber.

Ruth forced her muscles to relax. As they did, she realised her entire body ached. She tried to think, not of herself, nor of the pain, but in the abstract, and of what she could learn from the torture. Not much, except that she could guess at the identity of the woman who'd terrified Frobisher into silence. Other than that... she searched around, replaying the questions, trying to find something, anything that would give her a sliver of hope. There was nothing. It was as the woman had said. There was no escape.

She slumped in the chair and noticed there was a little more give to the ropes. She stretched, tensed. With sweat as a lubricant, she was almost able to pull her left hand free. She pulled. Stretched. Pulled again. Almost, but not quite. Finally, she gave up. What did it matter? Even if she were to get free, what could she do?

Voices woke her. Three of them. The torturer's and two others'. They sounded familiar. She tried to make out the words. She thought she heard 'soon', and then a soft laugh. There were footsteps behind her, and they were getting closer. Please, no, she thought. Not again.

A man stepped into view. "Do you remember me?" he asked.

Even though she hadn't immediately recognised his voice, she would never have forgotten that scarred face.

"Emmitt," she said. Her throat was sore. It hurt even saying those two syllables. "I'm glad to see your arm's in a sling," she spat. "I hope it hurts."

The man tapped the arm in its discoloured cast. "Not really. I've had a lot worse. I am truly sorry that the first time we properly meet is like this. It is often the way."

Ruth was tired of riddles, and she wasn't going to play the man's game by asking the first question that came to mind. "When you shot Hailey Lyons, why didn't you kill me?" she asked instead.

"Those were my orders. Not to kill the police," he said.

"From Wallace?" Ruth asked. "He gave you those orders?"

"Orders are orders. Either you obey them all, or you obey none. Then I learned who you were. I could have killed you many times. In that apartment block by the radio antenna, by that stalled train. I didn't."

"Why not?" she asked, uncertain whether she believed him.

He smiled.

"There are five conspirators," she said. "Do you have a coin?"

"I don't need one," he said.

"Then you're the ring leader?"

He smiled again.

"No," Ruth said. "You can't be, not if you're obeying someone else's orders."

"Very good," he said.

"Wallace? It can't be him, he's dead."

"Very astute of you."

"Were you going to let him run the country?"

Emmitt's smile widened. "No."

"You would have killed him, like you killed Turnbull?"

"We would, simply because he could not be trusted to do it himself. He was an unreliable member of our organisation. An essential one, but no, he would have died before our plans came to fruition."

"What plans?" Ruth asked, not expecting the man to answer, just wanting to keep him talking so the woman didn't come back.

Emmitt pulled out a chair and sat down.

"I've wanted to talk to you for some time," he said. "I spared your life because I knew that our lives are interlinked. We were destined to meet."

"What are you talking about?"

"Do you read much history? There is an inevitability to events that can only be seen with the distance of time. The rise of Rome and fall of Egypt. The fall of Rome and rise of Europe. Empires, doctrines, religions; they come, they go. A battle won or an election lost may stave off collapse for a decade or three, but that collapse will still come. That is the truth of our past. Yet there are moments where a simple action could change the entire course of our species. A bullet fired in a theatre, a cannon not fired on the battlefield. A line drawn on a map, or the flip of a switch that turned a line of code into a sentient being. Those events are rare, yet they mark a crossroads. We are at one now. Britain is a paradise compared to the rest of the world. Your bandits and gangs are capitulating under the promise of electricity and old-world comforts. The rest of the world is tearing itself apart. Warlords, despots, zealots, and prophets hold sway over countries that used to think themselves the bastions of civilisation. We are approaching the moment when they can be stopped. All of them, and with a single act."

"What's that?"

He smiled. "Forgive me, but that is not something I am willing to share with you. Not yet, at least. What you must understand is that, though it may not seem like it now, what we do is for the betterment of all."

"Isn't that what all traitors say?"

"And if they succeed in toppling the government, they write the history books and call themselves the founding fathers of the nation."

"I can't see the Luddites writing many history books," she said.

"Ah, yes. Our technophobic friends serve their purpose, as I serve mine."

"Don't you have any remorse for all the people you've killed?" she asked.

"Remorse? Hailey Lyons was a criminal. She would have died sooner or later, leaving no contribution to our species save the nutrients her decaying body would have returned to the soil. I merely brought forward the date on which that contribution was to be made."

"What about the Marines?"

"Death is a risk of those who don a uniform."

"And the passengers on the Mail train?"

"Collateral damage," he said. "A few may die now, but their deaths mean that millions won't die in the years to come."

"And that's it? That's your justification? You have no right to decide who lives and dies!"

"And you do? Your government gave you a badge and sanctioned you to kill others. How many ethics classes did you take in the academy? How much did they teach you about good, evil, and the rule of law? Nothing. Some must die so that others can live. That is the law of our civilisation. All is done for the greater good."

"Why did you kill Fairmont?" she asked, not truly caring about the answer, but knowing that as long as he was talking the pain wouldn't begin again.

He took a deep, thoughtful breath. "That is something you will learn in time, but not before the information is no longer of any use to you. I would like to offer you an exchange."

"Like a prisoner exchange?" Ruth asked.

"No, I said I'm offering *you* an exchange. I want information about Isaac. Tell me everything you know, and I will tell you who you really are."

"Isaac?" Ruth asked, confused. The rest of Emmitt's words sank in. "What do you mean who I really am?"

"You weren't called Ruth when you were born," he said. "I know your name."

"How?"

"I can tell you the story of your past, but in return you must tell me about Isaac."

"No," she said, with barely any hesitation.

"Your name is Sameen," Emmitt said. "And you were named after your maternal grandmother.

Ruth stared at him. Was he telling the truth? It was the wrong question. Was there anyway that she could know he wasn't lying?

"Strike a match, Sameen," Emmitt said. "You've heard the expression before."

She shook her head.

"You're not very good at lying," he said. "It's something Isaac said. I know him, you see. Strike a match and remember something good. You know why he says it? Because *he* was the moment in history. He was the one who let all of this evil loose on the world. Whatever you think you know about him is wrong, and now *you* are on the wrong side of history. Tell me what you know."

Ruth considered it, right up until she remembered Sergeant Davis.

"No," she said.

"You'll change your mind. We have plenty of time. Weeks, in fact."

"Until the fifth?" she asked.

Emmitt smiled. "I will return in the morning. We'll talk then. Understand, however, that I do need those answers. If necessary, I will ask Eve to return."

Emmitt left, leaving Ruth feeling more alone than ever before.

Chapter 13
Strike a Match

"The fifth. That's when he's waiting for. It is, isn't it?" Ruth asked the empty room, wondering whether she was right, or just trying to convince herself. "What's going to happen then, and why can't it happen sooner." No answers came back to her.

What did it matter? What point was there in solving the case when she was trapped? She'd learned it was night. Or probably night. Maybe it wasn't. Perhaps that was why the electric lights had been left on, so they would mask any stray beams of sunlight creeping down the stairs. Morning or night, the time truly didn't matter. Emmitt would return, and then…

She began to shiver. In an attempt to stop it she slammed her palms up and down against the chair's wooden arms. She wanted to cry, not with the memory of the pain but out of the hopelessness of her situation. This was where she would die. Alone, and in pain, but not until she'd told Emmitt everything he wanted to know.

A sob escaped her lips. Despair flashed into anger. She pushed down with her feet, raising the chair the full inch the bolts would allow. She slammed it down with all the force her torn muscles could manage. There was a crack. Not a loud one, but the sound brought a ray of light to her soul. She braced her feet again, pushed, and slammed them down. Another crack. She tried moving her arms. The left had some give. Pushing and tugging, scraping off skin, she managed to pull the chair's left arm free from its support. Her hand trembled as she picked at the rope, freeing her other hand, and then her feet.

She was barely able to stand. Blood ran freely down her hand. She was trapped. She was alone. The best she could hope for was a quick death. No. Quick or slow didn't matter, and as long as she was alive she'd fight. She looked for a weapon. The leather case was on the table. There were some blades among the tools, but they were small, almost delicate instruments. She picked up the chair's broken arm. It wasn't the most formidable weapon, but the weight was reassuring. She listened. There were no footsteps, no sound of anyone coming down the stairs. Was the crypt soundproof? Was that why no one had heard her cries? No. No more questions, suppositions, or assumptions. Someone would return. The chair leg would be a feeble weapon when they did.

On unsteady feet, she made her way across to the metal canisters. A long-handled steel wrench lay next to them. The heft was comforting until she remembered the automatic rifles. Partly curious, and partly to put off the inevitable fate waiting at the top of the stairs, she pulled the cap off a metal can. She gave it a sniff. It wasn't water, but something oily. Could it be diesel? She hadn't a clue what that smelled like, but they had to store it somewhere. Was diesel flammable? She didn't know though supposed it must be. Whatever happened to her, she could at least destroy the building, and perhaps Emmitt's fuel store. Perhaps she'd even kill the man himself.

She laid the fuel can on its side. Oily liquid spilled out onto the floor. She reached for another, then a third. With the fourth, she trailed a line of fuel to the staircase. Almost as a reflex, she began searching her pockets for a light. A crooked smile crept across her face.

"Strike a match," she murmured, but she didn't have one. Would breaking an electric bulb provide enough of a spark to ignite the vapour? She had no idea, but the thought of burning alive in the cellar was even less appealing than being shot or stabbed to death. Perhaps she could find some stub of candle on the stairs.

Fear grew with each step she climbed. The staircase began to curve, and the light from the lamps was replaced by hideous shadows. After thirteen steps, she reached an iron gate. Paint flecks fell like snow as she brushed her hand against the metal, searching for the lock. She found it, but there was no key.

She backed away a step, and then another. Maybe, just maybe, she could hear distant voices. What to do? She retreated another step. Sit in the chair, with one of those long thin knives in her hand, wait until that woman got close and then… but the chair had its back to the stairs. Before anyone got close they would see the ropes were untied. She could smash the lights and make the cellar dark. When they came downstairs, they wouldn't be able to see her. Perhaps she could sneak past them. Perhaps even lock them in the cellar. Except what if smashing a bulb ignited the vapour? Even if it didn't, then surely, on seeing that the lights were out, one of them would come down with a naked flame. Either way, the fumes would ignite, and she would burn to death.

Despair returned. She retreated back into the crypt. There had to be some other way out. There had to! Her eyes roamed the room, searching for an escape. There wasn't one. Perhaps she could pick the lock. She crossed to the metal case and pulled out a long needle. Reason returned. She had no idea how to pick a lock, and wouldn't learn in the next few minutes. Despair turned to desperation as she paced the room, searching for a window, a door, or even a loose brick that might reveal some secret tunnel.

Her foot kicked against something. It rattled across the floor. She looked down. Her first thought was scrap metal, but no, they were cartridge casings. She bent and picked one up. Had Emmitt executed people down here? Except next to the casing was an unspent bullet. She held the cartridge close to the nearest light. The markings around the casing looked like they'd been made by pliers. She looked down at the floor. There were more cartridges. Perhaps forty or fifty of them. How much explosive propellant did that add up to? Was this Emmitt's solution to not being able to rob a munitions train? It didn't matter. She looked at the casing in her hand. The percussion cap looked undamaged. There was only one way to tell. She breathed out, then in, and her lungs filled with those oily fumes. Her hand trembled as she laid the needle against the indentation in the casing. Do it. Do it.

"Do it," she said aloud. But she couldn't. Not yet. The fumes were getting stronger. She retreated back to the gate. Perhaps they would ignite from the heat of the lamps. Perhaps. And perhaps the sound of the flames would cause someone to come down the stairs, unlock the door, and investigate. Perhaps she could get outside and slip away into the night. Perhaps. But more likely not. They'd come to the gate, smell the fumes, and guess something was wrong. In which case she had the needle, and the percussion cap.

"Strike a match," she murmured, sitting down on the step to listen. "Strike a match and end it all."

Time passed.

She heard voices. They got nearer. She braced herself. They went further away. They came back. She fixed the image of Maggie's face in her mind and remembered a Christmas of years' past. The voices faded. A tear rolled down her cheek. The sense of loss, of isolation, of utter abandonment was almost overwhelming. The voice telling her to just end it grew louder and louder and louder and—

The ground shook. A dull rumble echoed through the church above her. Dust danced down from the ceiling, and for a moment she thought it would collapse. The sound faded, to be replaced by a crackling. Was that fire? Flames? A wave of horror swept over her, but no, it was something else. Gunfire? Yes. People were shooting. That could mean only one thing. A rescue. Captain Mitchell had found her!

She stepped away from the gate, retreated down into the room, and leaned her back against the wall. A stab of pain ran across her shoulders as they touched brick. She ignored it. She would wait. Mitchell would call out for her, but Emmitt or that woman might come down to kill her. If they did… She gripped the metal wrench firmly. The gunfire got nearer, growing in volume, resolving into individual shots.

"Ruth?" A voice called. It wasn't Mitchell.

"Isaac?" She ran up the steps. "What are you doing here? How did you find me?"

"I told you I was following you," he said, running his hands across the lock. "I could probably pick it." He sniffed. "What's that smell?"

"Diesel. I've been spilling it on the floor. I was going to burn it."

Isaac sniffed again. "That's not diesel. That's gasoline." He disappeared before Ruth could ask him where he was going.

"Gregory!" she heard him bellow a moment later. There was no reply from the man, just a renewed crescendo of gunfire. The little light coming from the top of the stairwell vanished as Gregory pushed his way down the narrow tunnel. He had to bend over, with his shoulder blades brushing the bricks. He looked her square in the eyes, and she saw a furious anger burning deep within his. He growled softly, as he pulled out a crowbar, stabbed it between the lock and gate. His muscles stiffened. His veins bulged. Above, the gunfire grew louder, and nearer.

"Don't bother," Ruth began. "Get out. Both of you, before—"

There was a creak, a crack, and the lock broke. Gregory pushed the gate open, grabbed Ruth's arm, and hauled her up the stairs. The bare stone changed to shredded carpet, the stairs to a corridor, and then to a more modern wooden staircase. That led to a vestry with moss on the walls and two ropes hanging down from a shattered roof. Ruth stared upwards at stars she hadn't thought she'd ever see again.

"Get down!" Isaac yelled. Gregory pushed her to the ground. Isaac was in a ruined doorway, firing a pistol blindly around the corner. He rolled back into cover. "Here," he said, and threw her a pistol.

She caught it clumsily, crawled to the doorway, swung around the corner, and fired off two quick shots.

Beyond the door was a ruined church. Part of the roof was missing. She guessed the crypt ran under the altar and underneath a pile of rubble that had once been a side chapel. She ducked around the doorway, firing off another two shots. This time, she paid more attention to the dim figures lurking behind the fallen masonry. The ruin was filled with smoke from burning pews, but she could see shadows moving from one patch of cover to the next.

"Four or five of them," she said, as Isaac dragged her behind the stone archway.

"It would be a shame if you were to get your head blown off," he said.

Bullets chipped at the stonework surrounding the door. The fusillade seemed to go on forever.

"Sorry we took so long," Isaac said. The firing stopped. She braced herself.

"No," Isaac said, grabbing her arm before she could roll around the corner again. A moment later, the firing recommenced.

"How *did* you find me?" she asked again.

"The short answer is as I said, I've been tracking you for a long time. The long answer will have to wait. Are you okay? Can you run?"

"Probably. Where are we? And who's here? Are Captain Mitchell and Riley with you."

"No," Isaac said. "They're ripping the city apart. I didn't have time to get them. It's me and Gregory, and Kelly's outside with her rifle. I suggest we make sure that we're gone before they realise that we're outnumbered."

There was a ragged burst from somewhere outside of the church, and then another muffled explosion.

"Timed charges," Isaac said, firing off another two shots. "Nothing more than smoke and noise. There are three more."

"We can't leave," Ruth said. "Not yet. Emmitt is here."

"Look behind you," Isaac said.

Ruth turned. There was a body lying in the corner of the room. A rush of joy flushed through her, then anger that she'd not been able to kill the man herself. Then she saw it wasn't Emmitt, but a man dressed like Isaac and Gregory.

"That's Liam Greene," Isaac said. "He died as we came in through the broken roof. Nice lad. Wanted to be a shepherd, but he's allergic to dogs. Was allergic. He died so you could be rescued, Ruth. It's time to leave."

She opened her mouth to protest, but there was another distant explosion.

"Fine," she said. "But we can destroy this place, set fire to the gasoline, and at least stop Emmitt from using it."

"Here." Isaac pulled a small package from his pocket. "I kept one in reserve. You can set the time, anything up to five minutes."

Ruth looked at the ropes, and the hole in the roof.

"Is that how we're getting out? A minute should do it."

"It's counting down," he said, handing it to her. "Throw it down the hole."

"Strike a match," Ruth murmured, and threw the small device down into the dark, fume-filled stairwell. "And let the place burn."

"Not how I'd have put it," Isaac said, "but apposite. The rope. Gregory?"

Gregory grabbed Ruth by the waist and heaved her up. She caught hold of the rope and pulled herself up to the hole in the roof, and then outside. There was another muffled explosion from somewhere near the far side of the church, and then another barrage of gunfire. Ruth rolled over, checked her footing, then swivelled around to offer Gregory a hand, but the man had already reached the top. He pulled himself outside, braced his feet either side of a cracked roof beam, and hauled on the rope. A moment later, Isaac was on the roof.

"Go!" Isaac hissed. "Go."

Ruth looked for a ladder, or rope, or way to climb down. Something ricocheted off stone to her left. Before she could return fire, there was a whoosh from behind her, a sudden burst of hot air, and she was blown from the roof. She landed hard, jarring her elbow on broken brick. Hands pulled her forward, away from the ruined church, and into the relative anonymity of the woods.

"This way," Isaac hissed. Ruth couldn't see a thing, but the man seemed to know where he was going. She looked back at the building. Flames leaped from every broken window and gap in the stone. Ruth pushed herself away from Gregory, raising her pistol, looking for a target. She saw none, but pulled the trigger anyway, firing into the burning ruin and feeling no better for it. Her gun clicked empty.

"Strike a match," Isaac said quietly, as if he was speaking to himself, "and hope the world doesn't burn. That's what I said, once. A long time ago."

Ruth lowered her gun.

"You did?" Ruth asked. "Because Emmitt said—"

A window shattered as a figure leaped through it. Her jacket was smouldering, and hair was on fire, but Ruth recognised her torturer.

"Eve!" she hissed, raising the gun, pulling the trigger over and over, but the magazine was empty. A large hand pushed her aside. Gregory lumbered past.

"No!" Ruth hissed, raising the useless gun again. "She's mine!"

Gregory didn't stop his pendulous run. The woman didn't turn away. She patted at her smouldering clothing before taking a step toward the hulking man. Her hands disappeared under her coat and came out with two of those long needles. Gregory didn't halt. He didn't reach for the gun on his back. He stretched out his arms, as if he was intending to grapple with her.

The woman ducked under his reach and stabbed a needle into his side. Gregory bellowed a terrible, inhuman wail as he grabbed her wrist. The woman's left hand came around, stabbing into Gregory's shoulder. This time, he gave nothing but a short hiss as he grabbed her left arm and lifted her off the ground. The woman kicked her feet toward the needles embedded in the man's side. Gregory growled again, and this time Ruth thought there was almost a word in it. Then he twisted his hands. There was snap of bone, as the woman's arms broke. She shrieked in pain. Gregory let go of her right wrist and reached for her throat.

It was wrong. This wasn't what Ruth wanted. Revenge in self-defence was one thing, but this was murder.

"Stop!" she yelled.

Gregory didn't.

Ruth took a step forward. "Stop!"

There was an arm on her shoulder. Isaac.

"Make him stop," she said.

"No."

"You have to try," Ruth said.

"I don't, and I won't."

"But this isn't what I want," she said.

"This isn't about you," Isaac said.

"It's murder," Ruth yelled.

"No," Isaac said quietly. "It's revenge."

Gregory squeezed, tighter and tighter. The woman kicked and squirmed and then, abruptly, stopped. Gregory gave one last animalistic bellow before throwing her lifeless corpse against the church's wall. Finally he turned back toward them, staggered a pace, and collapsed to his knees.

Isaac ran toward the fallen man, lifting him back to his feet.

"Help me! Please, Ruth."

She ran to Gregory. Her own back screamed with the effort as she helped lift him.

The forest seemed strangely silent as they staggered through it. After fifty yards, they came to a clearing. Kelly was there, a rifle in her hands, a carriage and pair of horses a few paces behind. Isaac pushed Gregory into the back, Ruth followed. A moment later, the carriage began to move.

Ruth breathed out. Her heart didn't slow.

Then there was light, not from a flashlight or candle, but from a flat square Isaac had pulled from his pocket. Was that a phone? Ruth didn't care. She pulled herself up from the floor of the carriage, and into a seat. She leaned back, and winced with the sudden burst of pain.

"Are you okay?" Isaac asked, as he slotted the phone into a bracket on the ceiling. A bracket, Ruth thought, designed for an object that size.

"One more question that needs an answer," she murmured.

"I'm sorry?" Isaac asked.

"I'm fine," she said.

"Good. There's a green bag under the seat. It's a first-aid kit."

Ruth reached down, wincing with the effort, and passed it over.

"He shouldn't have killed her," she said as Isaac pressed a bandage against Gregory's side.

"Put pressure here," Isaac said. "He had the right to kill her."

"It was murder," Ruth said.

"No. It was revenge," Isaac said. "There's a difference." He raised a hand to the light. It was coated in blood. "There's another wound."

He tore open Gregory's shirt. Blood pulsed from a hole, high up on the man's chest.

Isaac hissed, leaning forward, and clamped a bandage against the wound. Ruth stared at Gregory's chest. It was a mass of white scars, carved with intricate precision deep into his skin.

"Did she do that?" Ruth asked.

"She did," Isaac said. "She called it practice. Gregory is a baker. A very good one. He was a peaceful man with a wife and two children. She came to their home one night. Drugged them and chained them up. She tortured them. First the children, then his wife. Gregory's screaming became too much of a distraction, so she removed his tongue. She left him for dead, but he survived. Now he's had his revenge, but you know what he really wanted? He wanted to know why she did it."

"And you found him?" she asked.

"I did. I didn't think anyone, no matter how power-hungry would choose to employ her. It seems I miscalculated."

"Emmitt," Ruth murmured. "Or was it?" The conversation they'd had started to come back to her. "He asked about you. It was all he seemed interested in."

"Me?" Isaac said.

"You. He said he'd trade me information about my past if I'd tell him everything I knew about you. Strike a match, he knew you said that."

Isaac stared at her for a heartbeat.

"Not the hospital!" he yelled.

"What?" Kelly called back. The horses slowed. Her face appeared in the window at the front of the carriage.

"We can't take Gregory to the hospital," Isaac said.

"We have to," Ruth said. "He's dying."

"If Emmitt was after me, and if he's still alive, that's where he'll go next," Isaac said. "It won't be safe."

"Where to?" Kelly asked.

"I'm sorry," Isaac said, speaking softly. "I didn't want you to find out this way, but we've no choice." His voice rose. "To the professor's!" he called to Kelly. The carriage jolted forward.

"Find out what? What's going on? Why was Emmitt interested in you?" Ruth asked.

"It's a long story," Isaac replied. "It begins with the Blackout, but this isn't the place to tell you."

Gregory groaned.

"Who's the professor?" Ruth asked.

"At one time, she was a skilled surgeon," Isaac said. "Not this type of surgery, I'll admit, and she hasn't practiced medicine for years, but she can fish out a bullet. She'll have to. We've got no choice."

"You're going to tell me everything," Ruth said.

"Of course. Believe me, I've got just as many questions for you."

Ruth doubted it.

She wasn't sure how long the journey took. It was longer than minutes but shorter than hours, and it was still dark when the carriage came to a halt. There was something hauntingly familiar about the tree next to the carriage's door.

"This is The Acre," she said. "My home. This is my home!"

Isaac didn't reply. He ran to the door.

"Maggie!" he called, as he hammered on it.

Upstairs, a curtain was drawn back. A match flared, a candle was lit. The light moved from window to window until it reached the ground floor. The door opened. Maggie didn't look like she'd slept.

"Isaac? What's— Ruth? You're alive. Henry said you'd been kidnapped. What's happened to you?"

"I'm fine," Ruth said. "I—"

"Time for that later," Isaac said. "There's a man hurt. I can't take him to the hospital. He's lost a lot of blood. Please." Then, with a pleading formality, he added, "Professor, please."

Maggie looked at Isaac, then at Ruth.

"He's in there?" Maggie asked, walking across the path to the carriage. "Why can't you take him to the hospital?"

"It isn't safe for him, or anyone who knows me."

Maggie paused. "What have you done now, Isaac?"

"I…" Isaac sighed. "I don't know. We can find out, but first there's Gregory."

"Let me see him," Maggie said brusquely. She opened the carriage door. "You, what's your name?"

"Kelly, professor."

"My name's Maggie, and we need to get him inside. Ruth, light the candles, and clear the kitchen table. We'll lay him on that."

"We need to get him away from here," Isaac said. "You, too."

"If the bleeding isn't stopped, he'll be dead in ten minutes," Maggie said. "Whatever trouble is following you, deal with it. Inside, Ruth, I need light."

Ruth went inside.

Nothing made sense. Her mother was a teacher, not a doctor. Ruth lit the candles and dragged the cloth off the table. Why did Emmitt want Isaac? The questions built up and up, one on top of another, a giant teetering wall that she knew couldn't stand.

Isaac and Kelly carried Gregory inside. Ruth thought of staying, of listening to the muttered conversation in the hope that it might give some explanation, but found she couldn't. She went outside, sat down on the cracked wooden bench underneath the apricot tree, and she cried.

"Here," Kelly said, after not nearly long enough.

Ruth looked up and almost laughed. It wasn't the handkerchief she'd been expecting, but the automatic pistol Isaac had given her back in the church.

"It's loaded. There's three spare magazines. If trouble comes, get your mother and run. It doesn't matter which direction. I'll hold them off."

Ruth looked blankly at Kelly and then shook her head. Kelly went back to the carriage, came out a moment later with a long, thin bag, and proceeded to climb up to the roof of their house.

Everything had changed so quickly. Yesterday, or she assumed it was yesterday, she'd been idly wondering where she would live after the school closed. Now, somehow, the house had become a trap. A sniper sat on their roof, a man was being operated on inside by her *mother*. Her mother the *teacher*, not the surgeon. Then there was Isaac. Without understanding why, she knew that everything she'd known was gone. Her childhood, her home, even, somehow, the woman who had raised her. All because of Emmitt. Her hand curled around the gun. He had to be stopped, not for revenge, nor even for justice, but because she couldn't have a future as long as he roamed free. She went inside.

"Can we move him?" she asked.

"In a few minutes," Maggie said. "He may die if we do, but he might die anyway."

She was bent over Gregory's chest, probing at the wound.

"Isaac, do you know of somewhere safe?" Ruth asked.

"There's a place, yes. Four miles from here."

"Is it clean?" Maggie asked.

"Spotless," Isaac said.

"But he *will* need a hospital," Maggie said. She looked up and finally seemed to notice her daughter. "What did they do to you?"

Ruth looked down. Her clothes were tattered from where the torturer had ripped them. Where they weren't, they were covered in blood.

"It's Gregory's blood," she said. "I'll change. Then we'll go."

She went upstairs. Her room seemed smaller than it ever had before. She wondered if she would come back. Even if she did, it wouldn't be the same. From now on, it would be a place she might sleep, but it wasn't a sanctuary. That was a childish notion, that a weak lock on a closed door created a refuge, but it had finally been ripped from her.

Quietly cursing Emmitt for all he'd done, she grabbed some clothes and thrust them into the bag. After a moment's hesitation, she took the ribbon from around the bear's neck. She left the bear on the shelf. She had no need for toys, but the ribbon was evidence.

Chapter 14
Answers
8th October

"This is where you live? It's not what I was expecting," Ruth said, looking at the coffins displayed around the room.

"A funeral home is anonymous," Isaac said. "They're a part of civilisation that no one wants to think of, yet for which there's always a need. Most coffins were built to survive a century, and they are exempt from the scavenger's tax. No one questions when a cartload are brought into the city, nor do they search inside."

"So you only live here when you're in Twynham? It's not your home?" Ruth asked, reading between the lines.

"It's good to see that your inquisitiveness survived the ordeal," Isaac said, flashing his crooked, knowing smile.

Ruth took a breath, but before she could let fly, the door to the basement opened.

"Gregory's unconscious, but alive," Maggie said, coming into the room. "I've stopped the bleeding, and he's stable, but he needs proper care. Are you sure that boy will know what to do with a living person?"

"Johnny can be trusted," Isaac said. "As can Mrs Zhang. Kelly, go and find Captain Mitchell. Bring him here."

Kelly headed to the door.

"Wait," Ruth said.

"What?" Kelly and Isaac asked simultaneously.

"Your rifle," Ruth said. "You can't wander the streets carrying that."

Kelly looked blank, seemingly having forgotten the weapon slung across her back. She leaned it against the wall, and left.

"She's got a surname?" Ruth asked, looking through the door to where Mrs Zhang sat at the small desk in the waiting area at the front of the funeral home. The shotgun under the desk was visible to Ruth though not to anyone who might come through the door.

"It's a necessity of running this business," Isaac said.

"Do you have a surname?" Ruth asked.

"I do, but it's not important," Isaac said.

"I think I'll be the one to judge that," Ruth said.

"Why don't we sit down," Maggie said. "Ruth's right, she deserves some answers. But not in here." She waved a hand to take in the rows of empty coffins. "Is there somewhere not filled with so much expectation of death?"

Isaac led them through to a small room behind the showroom. He sat. Maggie took a chair almost, but not quite, as far away from him as she could. Ruth stayed standing.

"Who are you, Isaac? Who are these people who follow you? Why don't you have surnames? And why are you more important to Emmitt than details about the investigation into his crimes?"

"Everyone who joins me is seeking a new life," Isaac said. "There are many reasons people do that, and often it is associated with the person who gave them their name. So, for the most part, surnames are a hindrance. As to who we are? Waifs and strays, dedicated to preserving the ways and ideas of the old world that might otherwise get lost during these tumultuous years. We like to think of ourselves as guardians of the technology and knowledge that, twenty years ago, they called civilisation."

"Like the people who work at the chemical works, going through old research papers?" Ruth asked.

"Yes and no," Isaac said. "They focus on scientific discoveries with a commercial application. We tend toward the more esoteric."

Ruth weighed up the answer, decided it was thoroughly lacking, and changed tack. "Why do you bother?" she asked.

"Because civilisation doesn't exist anymore," he said. "What we call civilised, and which might one day become something more, is a fragile thing. Canada is less of a nation, and more of an idea preserved by a handful of farmers. The United States is one wrong word away from outright civil war. Britain is one bad leader away from monarchic despotism. Ireland has already fragmented into its ancient kingdoms, even if the rulers there call themselves elected. Europe and Africa are geographical distinctions, not collections of nation states. Those coastal communities are two aid-shipments away from starvation. The Eurasian interior is a swarming mass of warlords and dictators who won't be stopped in our lifetime. All that prevents them from sweeping down on this island is disease and distance. But it may happen. If it does, then we can't lose everything that once was learned. We can't let this become the beginning of a new Dark Age."

"Emmitt said something similar," Ruth said. "Something about how we're at a turning point. Where one small action can change the outcome of the future."

"That's interesting," Isaac said. "But the world has always been on the brink of some tectonic shift. Every action is a product of all the events that went before. Every discovery has required dozens before then. Every political movement requires the right combination of social and economic factors."

"That's one theory," Maggie said, "I'm not sure I agree with it."

"And it's utterly irrelevant," Ruth said.

"And I agree with that," Isaac said. "Would you like some tea?"

"No."

Isaac walked over to a cupboard. "I am not trying to influence anyone. I want to keep the ideas safe against the time they're needed again. There's some soup here," he said, picking up a can. "Summer vegetables, whatever they are."

Ruth's stomach growled. She wasn't sure what time it was, or even what day it was, except that it had been a long time since she'd eaten. "Are you telling me that you're not trying to nudge things along?" she asked. "Because I know that would be a lie, and you promised the truth."

"A lie?" Isaac opened another cupboard and took down a long rectangle with two raised metal circles, and a long cable.

"You're here, aren't you?" Ruth said. "If you just wanted to preserve knowledge, you'd stay far away and avoid contact with everyone. No, you want to control events just as much as Emmitt."

"I suppose that's debatable," Isaac said. He removed a tile from the wall, exposing an electrical plug, and plugged in the hot plate. "Perhaps I would best express my goals by saying I hope to hasten civilisation's return. A world with fridges, air conditioning, microwaves, and soft toilet paper is one worth striving for." He gave her a smile. She didn't return it.

"And phones, computers, and networks," she said. "I've gathered that much. All of those require electricity, and more than we have here. So where do you live, Isaac? Where do you go when you aren't here?"

"You said Emmitt wanted information on me," Isaac said.

"So? Answer the question."

"And in return," Isaac said, "he'd tell you about your real parents?"

Ruth saw Maggie flinch. She didn't care. "Yes," she said.

"Then I won't tell you where we live. That piece of knowledge isn't safe to share."

"You said you'd tell me everything."

"I'll take you there, if you want," Isaac said. "But I can't risk—"

The door opened. Ruth spun around, drawing her gun.

"Easy!" It was Captain Mitchell with Kelly right behind him.

"Henry!"

"Maggie. Isaac." He nodded at both. "Some reunion. Ruth, you look.... alive."

Ruth looked at the captain. Mitchell looked exhausted. Then she looked at him properly. His shirt was flecked with blood, and his knuckles were bruised.

"What have you been doing?" she asked.

"Looking for you," he said. "What happened?"

Ruth told him, beginning with Davis. Halfway through the story, Kelly left to go and stand watch upstairs. When Ruth got to the part about the torture, Maggie tried to insist that the Ruth needed to be examined, or at least rest. She brushed her mother away, and kept on, until she reached their arrival at the funeral home.

"It was about half past ten that I went looking for you," Mitchell said. "I found Davis' body. After that..." He rubbed at his hands. "We'll go back to this church at first light."

"How long will that be?" Ruth asked. She'd completely lost track of time.

"Another hour," Mitchell said.

"Then there's time for some answers," Ruth said. "Could Emmitt have known my parents?"

"Possibly," Maggie said. "If he was a refugee in that camp, then he might have. His face is scarred, isn't it? So he's now unrecognisable from how he appeared before? There were some survivors. It's possible he could be one of them."

"Possible, but is it likely?" Mitchell asked. "Did he give you any proof as to what he was saying?"

"He said my name was Sameen, and that I was named after my maternal grandmother," Ruth said.

"Which is something he could have made up if he knew you were adopted," Isaac said.

"But how would he have known that?" Ruth replied. "No. Don't answer that. We could go around in circles trying to guess what he knows. But he said something else. Something about you, Isaac, and how you were responsible for the world being the way it was."

"He did?" Isaac asked.

"What did he mean?" Ruth replied.

Isaac looked at Maggie. So did Mitchell.

"In a way, he's right," Maggie said.

"But in another way," Mitchell added, with a noticeable air of reluctance. "He's completely wrong."

"What do you mean?" Ruth asked. "What do any of you mean?"

Again there was silence as the three exchanged looks.

"Tell her," Mitchell finally said. "It's not my place to do so, but if you don't, I will."

Maggie sighed. "I…"

"We created the AI," Isaac said. "The first AI. The only true artificial intelligence that was ever brought into existence."

"You?" Ruth asked her mother.

"I… I was a neurosurgeon but there were so many patients for whom I could do nothing," Maggie said. "I began my research into artificial consciousness as a way of understanding how the human brain worked. How a very specific human brain worked. I thought I could repair him.

Bring him back." She gave a rueful shake of her head. "Instead, I created a thinking machine of my own. A truly new consciousness. It wasn't what I intended to do, but it is what I did. It wasn't... I..." She came to a stuttering halt, unable to find the words.

"There was a conference in London," Isaac said, "where the ethics of creating artificial intelligence, and indeed on what constituted life itself, were to be debated. We came to Britain with the intention of showing them that the time for hand-ringing was past, and that the future had arrived."

"It was arrogant, I know," Maggie said, "But we were very different people then. Through a little bribery, we got a slot to speak at the end of the conference's second day. There wouldn't have been more than a handful of people there. It's likely that no one would have believed us. We would have sunk back into obscurity, our achievement remembered as nothing more than a hoax. That fear was what drove us to release our presentation in advance to a few of the more sensational news outlets. It was rather dry and not at all dramatic, just a thirty-minute video demonstration. Within an hour, the first of those digital viruses were released."

"The other AIs?" Ruth asked.

"No, they weren't truly sentient. They had no capability for independent thought," Maggie said. "And I doubt that they had time to develop it during the seventy-two hours before the nuclear missiles fell. They were tied to their programming, and that made them seek out my creation. They wanted to destroy it. They couldn't. It wasn't on a network. There was no way they could touch it. That is how the world died. These viruses kept searching, and replicating so they could search further and longer. They met each other, and they went to war, thinking that they had found the AI. But they hadn't. They couldn't."

"A lot of that's conjecture, of course," Isaac said. "What we do know is that these viruses came from at least three different sources. At least," he added. "It's possible that—"

"Wait. Stop. Go back. You created the AI?" Ruth asked Maggie.

"I did."

"And what was your role in this?" she asked Isaac.

"I—"

"He was my assistant," Maggie cut in.

Ruth knew that answer was, at best, only half the truth "We'll come back to that," she said. She turned to Mitchell. "Did you know all of this?"

"Yes," he said.

"Who else knows?" Ruth asked.

"No one," Isaac said.

"Riley does," Mitchell said.

"Who else?" Ruth asked.

"No one," Isaac repeated.

"What about Kelly, or Gregory, or any of your other followers?"

"No. Kelly might have guessed something, but if so, she hasn't said."

"What you're saying is that other people *could* know, but you don't know who, or how many, or how much," Ruth said. "Any one of whom could have told Emmitt. He knew your name, Isaac. He knew! But," she added, turning to Maggie, "he didn't ask about you."

"Maggie Deering didn't exist before the Blackout," Maggie said. "I took the name from a street sign I saw when we emerged from the Tube."

"Oh." For some reason, after all that had been said, that was the most distressing revelation. "I see. Okay. Well, Emmitt knew that expression of yours, strike a match. He has to know you, Isaac."

"It's not an expression I've used of late," Isaac said. "But I did use it during those early hours when we were trying to stop the world from being torn apart. I was trying to find the human operators who would have been able to stop those viruses."

"Maybe that's who Emmitt is," Ruth said. "He's one of those operators."

"Or maybe not," Mitchell said. "Ask yourself whether it matters, and whether it will help us catch the man. Either you were kidnapped because he wanted information on Isaac, or he was pretending an interest in Isaac to gain your trust. Perhaps he did know your parents, or perhaps he picked that name, Sameen, out of thin air. Don't trust anything he said unless you can verify it."

"You're right," Ruth said. "The rest can wait. It won't be forgotten," she added, again looking at Isaac. "But it will wait until we've caught Emmitt." She turned to Maggie. "You better go and check on Gregory, get him ready to be moved. He can't stay here."

"Ruth, I—" Maggie began.

"You took me in. That's all that matters," Ruth said. She wasn't sure she believed that was true. "But why did you become a teacher, not a doctor?"

"Cowardice. I didn't want to be responsible for another life. Yet, here I am." As she headed downstairs, Ruth thought the old woman looked more frail than she had ever seen her before.

"Soup?" Isaac asked, filling a mug from the saucepan on the hot plate.

"Thank you," Ruth said grudgingly. Her palms stung when they came in contact with the hot mug. She closed her eyes. "You created the AI," she murmured. Questions lined up, one after another. "Emmitt," she said, opening her eyes, and sending those other questions back to be asked at another time, and in another place. "Emmitt," she repeated. "How do we find him?"

"We didn't get anything from Rupert Pine," Mitchell said.

"Who?" Ruth asked. "Oh, the MP. Riley was going to speak to him."

"At a fundraiser at the Longfields' place. It's a castle, you know? Absurd building, and absurd guests, all dressed like they were extras in some period drama. The staff weren't much better. Riley said they looked more like actors then butlers. But, as to Pine, he refused to talk, and that's as good a sign of guilt as any I can think of."

"But it doesn't help us," Ruth said.

"Not unless we can get Atherton's permission to interview him properly. We might be able to. I've still got some people who owe me favours."

"Then we should go back to the church," Ruth said.

"I'll leave Kelly here," Isaac said.

"And you should stay too," Mitchell said.

"One of my associates died rescuing Ruth," Isaac said. "I'm as involved in this as you are."

"We'll need Marines to secure the scene, and that means Weaver," Mitchell said. "Your presence would create more delays than we have time for."

"You're going to bring in the military rather than me?" Isaac asked. "Is that the law and order you wanted to create?"

"Whatever old argument this is," Ruth said. "It will wait. Get Gregory some help, Isaac. Proper help," she added. "Too many people have already died."

Ruth didn't protest too hard when Mitchell said she should wait in the funeral home while he went to organise the Marines. Isaac sat opposite her, clearly waiting for the next set of questions. There were many she could ask, but right then, she knew that Isaac wouldn't have an answer for those that were most pressing. She finished the soup, and afterwards couldn't remember the taste of it.

Mitchell returned with Riley, and they set off toward the church, collecting twenty mounted Marines on the way.

"Marines on horseback," Mitchell murmured, "we might as well call them cavalry."

But Ruth found she didn't care about that, or about the AI, or Maggie's past. All that mattered was catching Emmitt so she could find out whether he truly did know something about her parents.

"It's smaller than I thought it would be," Ruth said, looking at the smouldering ruins. Mitchell and the Marines had swept the area, confirming that there were no living souls in the vicinity before he allowed her to come close.

"It's three miles from the nearest farm," Mitchell said. "Built about three hundred years ago. There was probably a village near here, gone long before the Blackout. You say it was gasoline in the cellar?"

"That's what Isaac said," Ruth replied. "Not diesel."

"There's a test for that. The lab in the chemical works should be able to organise it. If it is gasoline, there's only one place it can have come from."

"America?" Ruth said.

"Yeah," Mitchell said. "Fairmont said that, among the documents he sold to Jameson, were bills of shipping. That must have been why. They were looking for a way of smuggling the fuel over here. I can't imagine it was hard to do. A lot of those ships return with empty hulls."

"Some of the crew must be in on it," Ruth said.

"Possibly. It's a line of investigation to follow, and it will give us something else to ask Jameson. Not that he's likely to start talking."

Riley came out of the ruins. "Two bodies. Female. Too burned to identify. Probably died from gunshot wounds."

"There were two women talking outside the supermarket," Ruth said. "They must have been involved. Maybe it's them."

"I found these in the basement," Riley said, holding out a cartridge casing.

"I remember those now," Ruth said. "The cartridges had been taken apart. The bullets and casings were scattered on the floor."

"So we're missing the propellant," Mitchell said. "How many rounds did you find?"

"It's hard to say," Riley said. "Between twenty and fifty. No more than a hundred."

"Not enough for a large explosion," Mitchell said. "Odd. Anything else?"

"There are footprints on the western side, not many," Riley said. "Six different sets. That's where they escaped."

"By truck?" Mitchell asked.

"On foot," Riley said. "There are wheel marks, but they're too close together. Bicycle wheels on a small cart, I think."

"So what will they do next?" Mitchell said. "They have lots of ammunition, but not many explosives. Is that why they're taking their bullets apart?" He looked at the trees, then up at the sky. "You said there were electric lamps in the cellar?"

"Yes."

"So there's probably a gasoline-powered generator. Look for that," he said to Riley. "Get the Marines to help. Then look for more dismantled cartridges."

When Riley and the Marines were out of sight, Mitchell pulled the phone out of his pocket.

"Is anyone watching?" he asked.

"No."

"Best that they don't. I doubt the Marines share the Luddites' technophobic sentiment. What I do know is that if you start using something like this in public news of it will spread to every pub before last orders."

"Would that be a bad thing?" Ruth asked. "It can't do any harm, can it?"

"Well, that's a very interesting question, and the beginning of a philosophical debate I would enjoy having with you over a coffee sometime. However, in the immediate future it would get the Electric Company asking why I wasn't paying them for the cost of recharging it. I'm going to take a photograph of the woman. The torturer. You can stay here."

"No, it's okay," Ruth said, though she stayed a few steps behind Mitchell as he crossed to Eve's body.

Mitchell kicked at the corpse until it rolled over. One eye was caked in mud, the other stared lifelessly into the sky.

"You all right?" Mitchell asked.

"I… Yes. I'm fine. I'm looking at her and I don't feel anything at all."

"A lack of emotional response isn't the same as fine," Mitchell said. He held the phone low over the face. "Isaac said he was working on creating a localised network so we could send messages from one phone to another. But he's been saying that for the last ten years. There." He stood. "And, of course, that picture would be inadmissible in court. Not that it matters here and now."

"What do we do with the pictures, then?"

"Show them to Frobisher, and the others we arrested in Windward Square. Confirm this is the woman of whom they were terrified. Perhaps they'll talk more freely if they know the woman's dead."

"But what can they tell us that we don't already know?" Ruth asked. "That Emmitt was behind it... but he wasn't, was he?"

"I'm sorry?"

"It was something he said. I think he was working for someone. Or did he want me to think that? I can't trust anything he said, can I?"

"No. You've had a long night. A long few weeks. I'll take you back."

"No. Not yet. Can I have that phone? I want to take a picture."

"What of?"

"I'll show you."

She walked over to the burned church, stepped over the crumbling masonry, and through the charred remains of rotten pews.

"They didn't do much to make this home," she said, kicking at the ash as she made her way to the vestry. When she reached it, she stopped. "Oh." The body of the man, Liam Greene, was burned beyond recognition. "I wanted a picture. To remember him," Ruth said.

"Who was he?"

"Liam Greene. One of Isaac's... I don't know. Followers? He died trying to rescue me. He wanted to be a shepherd. That's all I know."

"Come on," Mitchell said, laying a hand on her shoulder and leading her away.

"So much death. So much pointless death," she said.

"There are few deaths that aren't," Mitchell said. "The purpose has to found be in the life that went before."

Ruth nodded, absently. Her purpose, at least, was clear. She had to find Emmitt.

She paused by the body of Eve, and bent down.

"What are you looking for," Mitchell asked.

"This," Ruth said. She held up a small silver coin. She stood, paused, and bent down again. "Do you see that?"

"A thorn? A hawthorn, I think," Mitchell said.

Ruth looked at the trees and bushes near the church's wall. Most had been incinerated in the explosion. "There's none around here," she said. "Great," she added, standing up and brushing down her muddy, bloodstained clothes. "We've got another clue."

Chapter 15
Unmasked

Ruth lay on the cot in the funeral home, staring at the ceiling. Gregory had taken a turn for the worse. Maggie was sitting with him, and Ruth had joined her for a while. She'd tried holding the man's hand in the hope it might give him some comfort, but he hadn't responded. The silence had grown uncomfortable, filled with so many questions she could tell Maggie was simply waiting to be asked. Ruth didn't want to ask them over the body of a dying man, so she'd retreated back upstairs.

Isaac had disappeared in search of blood for a transfusion. Ruth had said that if the man's life was in that much danger, they should take him to the hospital and be done with it. Isaac had said it wasn't what Gregory would want, and Ruth hadn't the energy to argue. Mitchell had gone to speak to Weaver, Mrs Zhang still sat behind the reception desk, Kelly lurked upstairs, and Ruth was beginning to feel like a prisoner.

She'd taken a pillow from one of the caskets. The coffins looked far more comfortable than the chairs she'd pushed together. After the events of the previous day, lying in a coffin seemed too much like tempting fate. She closed her eyes in the hope that sleep would come. It didn't. All that came to her was Emmitt's face.

Did he really know who her parents were? He claimed to know the name she was born with, but there was no way of confirming it. But he had known she wasn't born Ruth Deering.

"Who are you, Emmitt?"

She took out the coin and stared at the inscription. The truth lies in the past.

"Who were you?" That was a better question. Some computer programmer who'd been trying to trace Isaac and Maggie during the Blackout? Perhaps. On learning that Isaac was still alive, had he discarded his plans to catch the man who helped create the AI?

"No. That's not right. He seemed to believe what he was saying." And what had that been? All that talk of moments in history could be summarised as a desire for power. Did Isaac somehow fit into that? She shook her head, and rolled onto her back. There was a sudden flash of pain as she put pressure on her shoulder blades. She sat up.

"Maggie. Emmitt knew about Isaac, but not her. Why not?" Was it because she'd changed her name? Maybe Emmitt thought she was dead. There was no way of knowing. Something tripped at the back of her mind. Maggie wasn't part of this, but there was something important she'd half thought a moment ago. Something obvious she was overlooking.

Slowly, she replayed everything Emmitt had said. She could feel the shape of the answer there. She went back further, remembering the torture and the questions the woman had asked.

Slowly, holding her breath lest the idea escape with it, she stood up. The pieces were there. They'd been there all along. The woman *had* known that she wasn't born Ruth Deering, but *hadn't* known her true age. What had Emmitt actually said? He'd known Isaac's name, but hadn't said anything about who Isaac actually was.

"Emmitt doesn't know you, Isaac," she murmured to the empty room. "But he did know that Davis and I were going to that supermarket." No, it was before then. When she and the Welsh sergeant had gone to that meeting in the pub, the old man had been there, ready to tell her about the supermarket. While she was upstairs, someone downstairs had told Davis.

"They knew we would be in that pub." Or that someone would be there. Not just 'someone', but police.

And a memory of the meeting room came back to her, and of the torturer standing in the doorway as Rupert Pine entered. Ruth remembered thinking that she'd seen Eve before. And then she knew where.

"Hawthorn. Norton. Turnbull." Everything fell into place. She ran though it, testing each link in the chain of events, searching for some other possible explanation. There wasn't one. Her mind shied away from the truth. She desperately didn't want to believe it, but it fit all too perfectly.

She pulled on her coat and put the pistol into its pocket. Almost as an afterthought, she picked up her badge. She crossed to the door.

Isaac was in the reception area. For once he wasn't wearing grey, but a green waxed jacket.

"Where are you going?" he asked.

"I didn't hear you come back," she said.

"I was arranging for transportation," Isaac said. "If it's not safe to take Gregory to the hospital here, then I'll move him elsewhere. But you didn't answer my question."

"I'm going to go and solve this case," she said.

Isaac picked up a tweed cap. "Lead the way."

"It's police business, Isaac," she said.

"Yes, that line only works when Henry says it."

There was no time to argue. Ruth opened the door.

"You're not wearing grey," she said.

"I thought it best to have a disguise. Or at least not to make it too obvious who I was."

"There's no need," Ruth said. "Emmitt was bluffing. He doesn't know who you are."

"How do you know?"

"I'll tell you when we get there."

"Where?"

Relishing being the person with the answers for once, she took delight in saying, "You'll see."

"Is Captain Mitchell in the Assistant Commissioner's office?" Ruth asked.

"He is," the uniformed sergeant acting as Weaver's secretary replied. "But you can't—"

Ruth had already opened the door. Mitchell was there, but so was another man whom she didn't immediately recognise. He was in his sixties, with thin, grey hair, and a long trailing moustache.

"Deering? What are you—" Weaver began.

"What is it?" Mitchell asked.

"Sorry," Ruth said. "I... sorry, I didn't realise... I thought you two were alone."

"You don't know who I am. Understandable," the man said, standing and extending his hand. "Philip Atherton." Ruth knew the name. The man was the Deputy Prime Minister. She took his hand.

"Captain Mitchell was explaining what had happened to you," Atherton said. "We understood you were on medical leave. You certainly shouldn't be up and about."

"I..." Ruth wasn't sure what to say.

"Why were you looking for me?" Mitchell asked.

"I... the... um..." She looked from Mitchell to Atherton.

"I am the deputy leader of this nation," Atherton said. "And I will be Prime Minister before the New Year. I rather think that makes me your superior." He spoke with a smile, but there was no mistaking the order behind the words.

"The woman," Ruth said. "The torturer. I wanted to know if Weaver recognised her."

"Me?" Weaver asked. "You're not going to accuse me of being involved, again, are you?"

"No," Ruth said. "But I think I know who the woman was. Or who she claimed to be. You can confirm it." She looked at Mitchell. He looked back. She thought she'd have to spell it out, but mercifully a light went on in his eyes. He pulled out the phone.

"Where on Earth did you get that?" Atherton asked. "I've been trying to get one for my press office for the past eighteen months. I can't tell you how many scavengers I've paid, but they never bring back anything other than worthless junk."

"It's from Germany. A fulfilment centre twenty miles north, and two miles east of Dresden," Mitchell said, lying easily. "I brought it back four years ago. I filed a report at the time." He swiped the phone until he found the picture. "This is the torturer," he said, holding it out for Weaver to see.

"That's DeWitt," Weaver said. "It was her?"

"Who is she?" Atherton asked, craning his neck to look at the photograph.

"Georgia DeWitt," Weaver said. "A woman who was in custody during the time Josh Turnbull was killed. She was a trustee, cleaning cells. But it can't be her. I spoke to her. She was terrified. A victim of domestic abuse. She was—"

"Acting," Mitchell said, looking at the phone. "How long ago was it she arrived in Twynham? Six months? She had no friends, no family, and she disappeared a few days after being released, having killed her so-called abuser. What was his name? Norton, wasn't it? The one witness who knew her both as the torturer, Eve, and the victim, Georgia DeWitt. So he was in on it, too."

"But she didn't have access to the cells," Weaver said. "That's why I eliminated her from the enquiry. How did she kill Turnbull?"

"I'm not sure," Ruth said, "but I think I can find out. Will you keep the Marines on standby?"

"Of course," Atherton said before Weaver could answer. "But after all you've been through, shouldn't you rest?"

"Only I can do this," Ruth said. "But I do need the captain's help."

"I think I should take direct command now," Weaver said.

"At the moment there's just a lot of paperwork to sort through," Ruth said. "It'll take us hours, maybe days, and then we'll need the Marines."

"Then we better make a start," Mitchell said, pocketing the phone. "Sir, ma'am."

They left the office.

"Do you want to tell me what's going on?" Mitchell asked.

"Who can you trust?" Ruth said. "Who can you rely on, and how do you decide that? That's what this comes down to. Are the rest of the Serious Crimes Unit here?"

"Riley's still at the church. Kingsley, Haney, and Barton are at the supermarket, waiting for Davis's body to be collected. Kowalski and Longfield are filling in paperwork from last night."

"Get Simon," Ruth said. "Don't tell Kowalski anything."

As Mitchell went to the cabin, Ruth stopped in the yard. She looked at the imposing brick building that was Police House, the stables that had once been a swimming pool, and the playing fields turned into allotments. For a brief moment, she saw it as it must have been, full of children going to lessons or playing in between. All gone, because of Maggie and Isaac. One single event. No, Emmitt was wrong. Because even though Maggie and Isaac had created that AI, someone else had made those viruses first. That had been done for a reason, and if anyone was responsible for all the pain, horror, and death of the Blackout, it was their creator.

"Ruth," Simon began. "You're okay. I was—"

"There's no time," Ruth said, marching out of Police House. "This way. Quickly!"

Isaac, who'd been lurking by the gated entrance to the building, fell in behind them. Ruth led them down alleys, across lanes, and along old footpaths away from the town centre. She finally stopped in an old cemetery.

"Were we followed?" she asked Mitchell.

"No," he said.

"We weren't," Isaac added.

"Who's this?" Simon asked.

"You don't know?" Ruth replied. "You don't know," she repeated softly. "This is Isaac."

"Oh."

"What's going on?" Mitchell asked.

"The meeting in the supermarket was a setup," Ruth said. "The old man knew that we would be in that pub. I was told by him, and Davis was told by someone else that same evening, to go to that supermarket. Then there's the ambush of the train. Emmitt organised that far too quickly for it to have been the train driver who told him. And how would she have told him? By telegraph when we reached the first depot? No. He knew as soon as the decision to move Fairmont was made. DeWitt, Eve, whatever her name was, someone let her into the cells to kill Turnbull. We all knew that, and so Weaver purged the police department. Then there's Sadiq."

"Who?" Isaac asked.

"A boy who was painting slogans across the city," Ruth said. "I stumbled across him, and he told Mitchell where the Luddites were going to meet. It's a remarkable coincidence, don't you think? I mean, that it was me who found him? Except it wasn't a coincidence. I was led there, by Simon."

"We were walking at random," Simon said.

"You were working in prisoner processing when Turnbull died," Ruth said. "I vouched for you. That's why Weaver thought you had nothing to do with it. But it was you who let that torturer into the cells."

"A lot of people worked—" Simon began.

Ruth cut him off. "You were in the room when Weaver said there was a lighthouse we could send Fairmont to."

"There were—"

Again, Ruth didn't let him finish. "You knew I was adopted. You knew I didn't know what name I was born with."

"But I—"

"And I'd told you about Isaac. About this weird guy who dressed in grey. A man who had equally weird followers, and how they were teaching me how to shoot out in the woods. But that's all I told you because that's all I knew. That's all Emmitt knew."

"I never told anyone—"

"But the torturer didn't know how old I was." A memory of that look of interested surprise on the torturer's face came back to her. "The only things Emmitt knew were those I'd told you. Everything else he said were careful guesses I had no way of disproving, but he didn't know my age. He couldn't because I never told you. You set me up. You sold me out. You were my friend. I vouched for you. I said you could be trusted!"

Simon opened his mouth, closed it, and then bolted. He managed two steps before Isaac tackled him.

"I think we can take that as a confession," Isaac hissed. "Do you have handcuffs, Henry?"

Mitchell threw them to Isaac.

"Ned Ludd," Ruth said. "We should have realised when I arrested him. You should have realised," she added, addressing the captain. "Talk about a coincidence. I was on the route from where we found Norton's body to the woods where Isaac was teaching me how to shoot. On the way, I happened to stumble across Ned Ludd. I don't know whether I was meant to arrest him, or whether he was supposed to run. It doesn't matter. It was a setup. Norton was killed so, when I went to the woods, I'd be starting from that place, and so was guaranteed to walk along that section of the railroad. They killed Norton just to be certain that I would stumble across Ned Ludd. That's not even cold-blooded. That's something else. But you were right about the Luddites. They were a distraction. How much time have we wasted on them? How many did we interview after they were arrested at that processing plant? And how much useful information did we get? How many have even been charged?"

Mitchell nodded thoughtfully. "You told Simon about the firing practice?"

"Of course. Why shouldn't I? He was my friend."

"Why use Simon?" Mitchell asked. "Emmitt had Wallace in the police department, after all."

"Emmitt didn't trust Wallace," Ruth said. "He was planning on having him killed.

"That can't be the only reason." Mitchell turned to Simon. "All right, Longfield. Why'd you do it?"

"I…" Simon began and for a moment Ruth thought he would lie. "It was my mother. I just told her what was going on. That's all. I didn't know any of this would happen, I swear."

"Are you going to deny letting DeWitt into Turnbull's cell?" Ruth demanded.

"No, I… I didn't have a choice. I really didn't. And I didn't know she was going to kill him."

"And you led us to that boy, Sadiq?" Ruth asked.

"I thought… I didn't… yes," Simon said, his shoulders slumping as he abandoned prevarication.

"Why?" Mitchell asked.

"Because I was told to."

"I meant why do any of it," Mitchell asked.

"I can guess," Isaac said. "It was trade. American imports would have destroyed the Longfields' wealth. With it would go their influence, and right now, they are very influential, but who'll drink ersatz coffee when the real bean is being shipped in from the Caribbean?"

Ruth pulled out the silver coin she'd taken from DeWitt's body.

"Have you seen this before?" she asked.

Simon's eyes widened. "My mother has one."

"She does?" Mitchell smiled. So did Ruth, in the joy of confirmation.

"Where is she?" Mitchell asked.

"At home," Simon said.

"Is there anything else you want to ask him?" Mitchell asked Ruth.

She shook her head. "Not now."

"We can't take him back to the police station," Mitchell said. "Word would get back to his mother."

"I'll take care of it," Isaac said. "His body will never be found."

"No, please! You can't," Simon protested.

"No," Ruth said. There was a momentary flash of relief in Simon's eyes. "Not yet. We may have more questions for him. Do you have somewhere we can lock him up?"

"Only the funeral home," Isaac said.

"We'll go there," Ruth said. "Take the handcuffs off. We're going to walk through the streets normally, but if you run, I'll shoot you." And she knew that she would.

"They were planning this for months," Riley said. "How long ago was DeWitt arrested?"

"Six months," Mitchell said. They were back in the funeral home. Simon was locked in a storage room. Riley had been waiting for them there, having come to the funeral home straight from the church.

"And the Luddites would get the blame for all of it?" Riley asked.

"Which is why he recruited them from students and beggars, children and the grief-ridden. Expendable people with no one to speak up for them. Imagine the headlines. Imagine the conversations in pubs and factories after an anti-technology group gets blamed for assassination. The rumours would start, and soon they would be blamed for all our current ills. Now imagine the election. Which candidates win? Those who've taken a pro-technology stance."

"Do you still think this is about politics?" Riley asked.

"Longfield's involvement confirms it," Mitchell said. "This isn't the politics of the ballot box, but of economics. The assassination and counterfeiting were about destroying the trade deal, and the only people who benefit from that are those whose fortunes have been built on rationing and aid shipments. The Longfields would be destroyed if the market was suddenly opened to the import of American food."

"There has to be more to it than that," Ruth said. "How does the fifth of November tie into this?"

"Maybe it doesn't," Isaac said.

"But it did," Ruth said. "At least, we know there was meant to be a third attack on the telegraph."

"Or that was what Ned Ludd was told," Mitchell said. "Which doesn't mean there ever would be a third attack. Maybe the fifth of November was another red herring. It made us think we still had a chance of stopping something that had already happened."

"I'm not sure," Ruth said.

"Either way," Mitchell said, "we need to arrest Longfield."

"You can't get a warrant," Isaac said. Ruth looked at Mitchell.

"He's right," Mitchell said. "We'd need a formal confession from Simon, and that means we'd have to take him in. He could probably be dissuaded from asking for a lawyer, but someone will see him. Word will spread, and it would get back to his mother. Any evidence that's there would disappear, as would the suspects."

"Without a warrant, you can't get the Marines to help," Riley said. "And we can't do this alone. Emmitt might be there, along with whoever else survived the fire at the church. Five or six people, maybe more, armed with automatic weapons. Not counting Longfield's employees. That's too dangerous to go in without back up."

"I might be able to arrange some," Mitchell said. "Corporal Lin is back in the city. I think she'll be able to round up a few Marines who won't mind disobeying orders on this particular occasion. Give me an hour. Riley, speak to Simon, find out what we might expect at the house. Isaac, I take it you have weapons here?"

"Of course."

Chapter 16
Storm

"It looks like a castle," Ruth said.

"That's just a facade," Mitchell said. "It was built less than a century ago, when the greatest threat to the owners was tax collectors, not marauding peasants."

They were lying in a copse to the north of the estate from where they had a clear view of the house and its absurdly manicured gardens. As Ruth looked more closely, she made out the guttered roofs and chimneystacks artfully hidden behind crenelated sandstone brickwork. There was even a tower, jutting up from the southwest corner. It was only the large windows that gave a hint that the building's medieval style was merely a pretentious fraud.

"They could be growing food on those lawns," Ruth said. "*And* in those fields outside the wall. There's enough land to feed hundreds. Think of the gardeners wasting their lives keeping those lawns neat so Mrs Longfield has something nice to look at."

"Think about it later," Isaac said. "Personally, I think it looks rather attractive. It would make a welcome change from the concrete and steel I'm usually surrounded by. But speaking of gardeners, I can't see any. Kelly?"

"There was a man deadheading roses on the far side," the woman said. "And I saw two faces, one male, one female, in the windows of the main house. Both on the second-storey, two rooms apart, close to the tower."

"Simon said most the staff had been sent to the estate in Scotland," Riley said. "He might have been telling the truth. When I was here for that fundraiser, I thought there weren't many people around. The staff who were here looked like they'd been hired for the night. Hardly any of them knew where the bathrooms were."

"Interesting," Mitchell said. "She didn't want to sack the staff, but didn't want to keep those she couldn't absolutely trust to be here. The logical reason is because there's someone here that Longfield doesn't want them to see. With Emmitt's face being in the newspaper so frequently, this would be an ideal place for him to hide. Corporal?"

"Yes, sir?" Corporal Lin asked.

"It's not too late for you and your Marines to back out. You know there's going to be trouble for this?"

"They killed a lot of our friends, sir," the Marine replied.

Mitchell nodded. "Secure the main gatehouse and the postern gate on the western side. No one leaves. Detain anyone who tries to get in. Emmitt might be in one of those cottages. Try to arrest him, but remember that others may not be involved in this conspiracy. Too many people have died for any more innocent lives to be wasted."

"Understood," Lin said. "And the signal?"

"No signal," Mitchell said. He looked at his wrist. "Will six minutes be long enough for you to get in position?"

"Yes, sir."

"Then good luck."

"Same to you." Lin crawled quickly back through the undergrowth to where the nineteen Marines and sailors were waiting. All came from the SS Britannia, the same ship that had supplied the Marines who'd been killed in the ambush.

"Simon said she goes to the tower after lunch, and stays there until sunset," Mitchell said. "So that's our target. We'll rush the house, head to the tower, and secure it."

"And if she's not there?" Isaac asked.

"Then Deering will look for evidence in the tower, you and Kelly will guard her. Riley and I will search the house. Isaac, you have the ropes?"

"Ready when you are."

"Deering?"

Ruth shrugged. "Let's get it over with."

Mitchell rose to a crouch. He looked at his watch, then at the grounds behind their twelve-foot-high wall, then back at his watch. They waited. "Now," he said.

He ran sure-footed across the uneven ground. Riley, Isaac, and Kelly, followed without any difficulty. Ruth found herself at the rear. The shotgun was a cumbersome weight. Like the ropes with their metal hooks, and the bulletproof vests marked 'police' they all wore, the gun had come from Isaac's personal stash. That had been hidden in a coffin in the rear of the funeral home's showroom. The shotgun was loaded with non-lethal rounds. Ruth hadn't known they'd existed. Riley was similarly armed. Isaac and Mitchell had what almost looked like pistols but which, she'd been told, would fire two wired-darts into a target. Those wires would then administer an electric shock so powerful as to incapacitate their opponent. It didn't sound particularly non-lethal to Ruth.

Her foot hit a stone. The pain brought her back to the present. She told herself to focus on the approaching wall.

Isaac threw up a rope. Mitchell did the same. They both scurried up and over. Riley and Kelly were just as quick. Riley paused at the top, straddling the wall, holding out a hand. Ruth threw the shotgun up, grabbed a rope. The moment she tried to climb, a burning reminder of the previous night's torture shot through her muscles.

"Can you hold the rope?" Riley whispered.

Ruth thought so. She grabbed it and let herself be hauled up. Now she knew to expect it, the pain wasn't so great. When she dropped down to the other side of the wall, the ache was replaced by a great wave of weariness.

"You all right?" Riley asked.

"Fine," Ruth said, brushing away the sergeant's help and picking up her shotgun from where Riley had dropped it.

There were less than twenty yards between the wall and the house on this side of the estate. Mitchell pointed forward, angling toward a shallow set of stone steps that led – hopefully – to the kitchen.

Riley went second, then Ruth, then Isaac and Kelly. Mitchell had almost reached the steps when the backdoor opened. A man dressed in old-fashioned black and white livery stepped out. Ruth froze. Mitchell didn't. He raised his arm, waiting until the man had taken another step before pulling the trigger. Two metal prongs shot from the stun gun and slapped into the man's chest. There was enough time for the man's eyebrows to furrow in surprise before his arms flew out. He spasmed. He shook. He collapsed to the ground, still convulsing.

Ruth stared. After all the wondrous things they'd made in the old-world, that was what counted as non-lethal? Mitchell dropped the stun gun on the still twitching man and drew an automatic pistol. Riley took the lead, and they went inside.

The kitchen was empty. That surprised Ruth. Out of all the places in the house, she would have expected to find staff there. Off the kitchen was a staircase leading up to a landing on the first-storey. They went up, reaching a door that led onto a balcony running the length of the entrance hall. High up on the wall were portraits. Most of the people in the paintings wore robes and armour. Ruth knew for a fact the people in them weren't relatives of the Longfields. They crept along the balcony. Mitchell paused at an open door, quickly entering, sweeping left and right, before stepping back out with a shake of his head. As she passed, Ruth glanced into the room. The furniture was covered in dust sheets.

At the end of the balcony was the door to the Tower. Like the walls either side, the door was painted white. If they hadn't been looking for it, they might have missed it. Mitchell pushed at the edge. There was a soft click, the door sprung open an inch. He pulled it open the rest of the way. Riley, stun gun held in both hands, went in first. Mitchell followed. Ruth went in next. Kelly and Isaac took up station by the door. The staircase wound upwards in a tight spiral. Though she could see the captain, Riley was lost to sight.

One staircase for the rich, she thought, another for the staff. Fertile ground not being used for grazing. It was wrong. She remembered what the man, Fredericks, had said during that meeting in the pub. The inequality of—

"Police!" Riley's yell cut through her thoughts.

Ruth leaped up a step, raising her shotgun, trying to see either the sergeant or whoever she was shouting at.

"Police!" Riley called again "Don't—" Her words were cut short by a booming shot.

"No!" Mitchell screamed.

Something heavy hit the stairs. There was a barrage of shots, too many to count. Ruth kept running upwards, making another four stairs before she came to Riley's body. The sergeant lay crumpled on the stairs, blood seeping from around the bulletproof vest. Ruth knelt, not knowing what to do, not knowing if there was anything anyone could do.

"Don't move!" she heard Mitchell say, though she couldn't see to whom.

"Go up. Help him," Isaac said, pushing her out of the way. "I've got her."

Grateful to be relieved of having to care for the sergeant, Ruth ran up the remaining steps. Near the top was the body of a well-dressed man in his late fifties. Simon's father, Ruth thought. A shotgun was held in his dead hand. It looked as if Mitchell had emptied an entire magazine into his chest.

Beyond was a door. Mitchell was standing, legs braced, gun raised on the other side of it.

"Sir?"

He said nothing.

She eased passed him and into the chamber. In the middle of the room was a woman. Simon's mother. She held a pistol in her hand though at the moment the barrel was pointing down.

"Drop. It," Mitchell said, spitting the words out through gritted teeth.

The woman looked at Mitchell then at Ruth.

Ruth saw her shoulders tense. "No!" Ruth raised the shotgun, pulling the trigger as the woman started to raise her own arm. The recoil knocked Ruth back and almost from her feet, but the non-lethal round hit Longfield square in the chest. She was down. Mitchell crossed to the woman, took the gun from her hand, and then checked her pulse.

"She's alive. Cuff her then search her." And he left, heading back down the stairs.

Ruth began to cuff Longfield's hands behind her back, but then changed her mind. Learning how to pick a handcuffs' lock wasn't a skill she thought the woman would have learned, but it wasn't a risk she wanted to take. So she could keep them in view, she cuffed Longfield's hands in front. She dragged the woman to the middle of the room, moving the furniture out of a kicking foot's range. A quick search of Longfield's person came up with nothing more deadly than a pen, but Ruth took that, along with the pins in the woman's hair.

"You're going to stand trial," Ruth said, but the unconscious woman gave no sign of having heard. "You are."

Ruth took a step back and a look around the room, checking for any stray weapons. To the left of the door was a bookshelf. To the right was a glass cabinet containing a few plates, statues, and other curios, presented as if on display. Two chairs were positioned either side of the room, one to catch the morning light, the other the evening. Opposite the door was a desk, and on it… was that a computer?

She walked over, cautiously. It *was* a computer, or at least a screen a little larger than Mitchell's phone. Gingerly, she touched it. It lit up. The screen was divided into six windows. The top left had an image of Mitchell and Isaac bent over Riley's body. Ruth swallowed. In the next she could see Kelly, with the door to the hidden staircase behind her. The woman was crouched down, the rifle raised to her shoulder, tracking the barrel back and forth. The next window showed an empty room, the fourth a section of the driveway. The fifth showed the front of a cottage, and the last had an image of the gate. A Marine stood in front of it. Cameras, she thought.

"Is that why you didn't have anyone on watch?"

There was no response from Longfield. Gingerly, Ruth lifted the tablet from the desk. There were no wires. That was a puzzle, but one that Isaac or Mitchell could answer. Her eyes went back to screen, watching as Isaac and Mitchell frantically struggled to save Riley's life. She wondered if there was sound to go with the pictures, and decided, if there was, she didn't want to hear what the men were saying.

There was a groan from Longfield. Ruth put the tablet down.

"I suppose I should tell you that you're under arrest," Ruth said. "You've got some rights, but I'm not sure whether they matter."

"Charming," Longfield coughed. "You're the Deering girl, aren't you?" The woman's voice was weak, but the scorn was unmistakable. "Why are you here?"

"Why do you think?" Ruth replied.

"I honestly couldn't say. Armed thugs break into my house, kill my husband, and conduct an unlawful search. What am I supposed to think?"

"Simon told us everything," Ruth said.

"Really? Was a lawyer present?"

Ruth shook her head. She wasn't in the mood to play games. She stood and walked over to the desk. Underneath it was a black box with a blinking green light. She ignored it, and opened a drawer, then another, then the third. They were all empty.

"Perhaps if you told me what you are looking for, I might be able to assist," Longfield said.

Ruth didn't answer. She was looking for the coin and had hoped, since Wallace had kept his in a desk drawer, so would Longfield. It wasn't there, nor had it been on her person.

"You were going away?" Ruth asked.

"To Scotland. We have a place by the coast that we often visit at this time of year."

The woman lay perfectly still on the floor, the only movement was from her lips that, even now, were curling into a smile. It was wrong, Ruth thought. Then she realised why.

"You don't seem concerned that your husband's been killed," Ruth said.

"I have seen a lot of death in my time," Longfield replied. "I have come to understand it as a very natural part of life."

Ruth met the woman's eyes, replaying what she'd just said, comparing that to what they'd learned this morning, and what Simon had told her during their time in the academy. "Simon isn't in police custody," she said. "We're holding him, but not in a cell. His life is in my hands."

"Are you threatening me?" Longfield asked, and this time there was the merest hint of emotion in her voice.

"No. I'm telling you how it is. DeWitt is dead. Or did you know her as Eve?" Ruth thought she saw a flicker of an eyelid, but she couldn't be certain. "So are Donal and Wallace. Only Emmitt is left. And you of course. The fifth conspirator." Yes, she definitely saw a twitch. "Simon told us everything. You're going to prison, but you won't be there long."

"Simon could only have told you what he *thought* he knew. That is a very different matter from telling you everything," Longfield said.

Ruth said nothing. The coin had to be somewhere close, and the coin was the key. The woman wouldn't leave it somewhere a servant might stumble across it, so either it was hidden so well that she'd never find it, or it was somewhere in the room.

Ruth stepped around the desk and crossed to the cabinet.

"Are these antiques?" she asked, opening the glass door.

"From the royal collection at Windsor," Longfield said. "I acquired them personally. But you didn't come here to talk about the baubles of long dead monarchs."

Ruth ignored the blatant distraction. There were plates, a crown, a ring, and a knife with an ivory handle. She lifted a plate. Stuck to the reverse was a coin.

"The truth lies in the past," she read.

Longfield sighed. "It does," she said. "And so does our future. My own future lies before me oh-so-clearly, but there is the matter of Simon. I will tell you everything if you promise to let him go."

"Go? You mean free?"

"Yes. No prison, no death by long knives. Promise me that, on everything you consider sacred and holy, and I will give you everything you need."

"Why?"

"Why do you think I did any of this?" Longfield said. "It was all for him. To you, who never knew what the world was like before, a radio broadcast must seem like a miracle. To me it is barely more than a taunt."

"You did it because the trade deal will bring imports of real coffee and cheap food," Ruth said. "You'd be bankrupted."

"Twenty years ago, I had nothing," Longfield said. "I built an empire. I could build another in half that time, but this is about the next century and whether there will be any humans left to mark its arrival."

"Emmitt said something similar," Ruth said. "I didn't believe him, and I don't believe you. Yes, I'll promise that Simon won't go to prison, and we won't kill him. He can go to Europe or Africa and make a life for himself there." She suspected Isaac could arrange something like that. "But in return I want to know where Emmitt is."

"Or you could join our cause," Longfield said. "It's not too late. No, I can see you are not ready for it. Not yet. In time you will come around."

"Where's Emmitt?" Ruth repeated.

"On the bookshelf is a copy of Dante's Inferno," Longfield said. "Hidden inside is a diary. It contains a map of locations we have secured. Emmitt will use one though I don't know which."

"He was here?" Ruth asked.

"Staying in one of our cottages. He left when I saw you coming."

"But you didn't," Ruth said.

"I have never run from anything in my life," Longfield said.

"You provided him with money, I suppose," Ruth said, crossing to the bookshelf.

"Yes. Money, food, clothing, some personnel," Longfield said, her voice rising. "Over the years I have had the need to employ people whose first language is violence. It is a sad truth about our world."

"Was he one of them?" Ruth asked. She ran her finger along the shelf, looking for the book.

"Emmitt? Hardly. Our relationship is far more complicated than that. Look in the diary, and you will see for yourself."

Ruth had found the book. Expecting some kind of trap, she tapped the spine with her finger, then moved it an inch and stepped back. Nothing happened. She took down the book. She opened it and flipped from page to page. They were all the same, filled with nothing but densely packed, printed text. She turned around.

"There's nothing here."

Longfield smiled and raised her hands to her mouth. "You promised to keep him safe." She swallowed. "But only I can do that."

"What did you do?"

Longfield shook. Trembled. Her legs stiffened. They kicked, violently. Ruth took a step forward, but the woman's arms thrashed up and down. White foam and dark blood frothed from Longfield's mouth, and then, just as suddenly, she was still.

"What did you do?" Ruth quietly repeated. There was something in the dead woman's hand. It was a button, broken in two with a small cavity, large enough to hold a pill. She remembered that there had been a similar broken button found by Turnbull's body, and that that was how they had been supposed to think the man had died.

Ruth sat down in a chair, opposite the body, and tried to work out why the woman had killed herself.

"Deering?" It was Captain Mitchell.

"Sir, how's Riley?"

"I don't know. The shotgun was loaded with buckshot. The vest took some of it, but there's— what happened?" He'd stepped inside, and was now looking at the Longfield's body.

"Poison," Ruth said. "There's a button, broken in two."

Mitchell crossed the room, knelt down. "Just like on Turnbull. I always wondered about that." He stood. "Did she say anything?"

"That there was a diary hidden in there," Ruth said, pointing at the book on the floor. "There isn't."

"But there's this," Mitchell crossed to the desk. He picked up the tablet. "Cameras? And a battery pack under the desk, with a cable leading…" He lifted a rug, following a slim black wire across the room to where it disappeared into the wall. He looked up. "Is there an antenna, maybe? Or some kind of localised wireless network?" He walked over to the desk and collapsed into the chair.

"Sir, what about Riley?"

"Isaac and Kelly are taking her to the hospital." Mitchell said, his voice taut. "And they'll get her there faster than I can. I could go with them, and

I would do anything and everything to save her life, but I'm not a doctor. There is truly nothing I can do to help her." He raised a fist, then forced his hand open, and laid it slowly on the desk. "So I will do the only thing I can. I will solve this case."

Ruth nodded. "There's a coin," she said. "Stuck to the back of that plate."

"That makes four of them. We only need Emmitt's to complete the set. What else did she say?"

"She said she paid for the conspiracy," Ruth said. "That she provided food, and clothing. She wanted me to promise to protect Simon. In exchange, she'd tell me where Emmitt was. The location was in a diary, hidden inside a book. When I turned around, she'd broken the button and taken the pill. I guess she wasn't ever going to tell us where he was. I don't know whether that means everything else she was untrue, but she said that she did it all for Simon. And she said that Emmitt was here, but that he left when Longfield saw us coming. She saw it on that." She pointed at the tablet. "There are cameras."

"Really?" Mitchell picked up the tablet and began tapping at the screen. "Ah, pity. It seems there aren't any cameras in the tower. No microphones either. That's a shame. I don't know whether the coin would stand up in court. On the other hand, I don't particularly care. Cameras in the stairwell, the cottages. This one looks like the room that Riley interviewed Pine in. I'll have to ask Riley to—" He stopped and let out a low growl. "There's a file here marked Pine," he said. "Looks like... yes, two video files, and four, no, five audio." He tapped the screen. A moment later he tapped it again. "So that was how she was blackmailing him."

"What is it?"

"If Rupert Pine wanted the world to know, then it wouldn't be a secret, and this woman wouldn't have been able to blackmail him. No, I have seen, and so I know, and that will be enough to get him to confess. He may have committed some crimes for which he will have to atone, but this secret is not one of them. Personally, I liked him. But Riley... perhaps this explains it." He sighed and turned back to the tablet. "There are some other video files. It looks like Pine wasn't the only one being blackmailed. But no diary."

"Perhaps there isn't one," Ruth said.

"Then why call it a diary? Why use that word unless it was at the forefront of her mind. It doesn't fit with what we know of her. She used this as her office, the reason being the tablet and her cameras. She viewed this room as safe, but not that safe. She kept the coin here, but you said it was stuck to the back of a plate? So she couldn't leave it out in the open. Unlike this tablet… What book was it?"

"Dante's Inferno."

"Perhaps she chose that because her imminent demise was at the forefront of her mind, too. Or perhaps not. Check the rest of the books."

Ruth started taking out books at random, but the contents all matched the spine.

Mitchell paced the room, looking at the walls, and finally back at the desk. He ran a hand down one leg, then underneath. There was a click. A narrow shelf popped out of the side. On it was a thin book.

"Is that the diary?" Ruth asked.

"It's more of a journal," Mitchell said. "Each page has a handwritten date. It does list some events that are coming up, and some dates have entries that look as if they've been written after the fact."

"Is there any mention of Emmitt?" she asked.

"No… nothing at all personal. It's as if it's been written to be read, yet it was hidden. Here, the fifth of November. 'Arrange game of bridge.' Is that code?"

"She did confirm she was going to Scotland."

"Yes, and on the sixth there's a hunt, with a ball in the evening. Hmm. On the fourth there's a reminder to 'order twenty game pies from Fraser's butcher's.' Game of bridge, game pies?" He turned the pages, leafing back and forth through the book. He closed it. "I could spend days looking for some hidden meaning, only to discover there isn't one. Or discover it, and find it doesn't matter. Not now that she's dead."

"But why did she kill herself?" Ruth asked. "She said it was to protect Simon, but from whom?"

"Emmitt."

"Then why not give the man up?" Ruth asked. "Wait." It came back to her. "Emmitt said that he was working for someone. It can't be Longfield, or she wouldn't be afraid of him, right?"

"Then there's someone else," Mitchell said. "Another conspirator?"

"There can't be," Ruth said. "At least, there can't be more than five. That's how many chairs there were for that table. Five chairs. Five stars. I… I think Emmitt and DeWitt confirmed there were five of them. I… I can't really remember."

"Wallace had a coin, and he's dead. So did DeWitt and Longfield. We know about Emmitt. That leaves Donal. Donal?" He repeated the man's name. "Oh, no."

"What?"

"That first coin. It was in Donal's pocket. What if it wasn't his? What if someone had put it there?"

"Who?" she asked.

"Someone else who was on the beach."

"You mean Jameson?"

"He's in custody, so why would Longfield be scared of him?" Mitchell picked up the tablet, put it into his pocket, and headed for the door.

"Where are we going?" Ruth asked.

"The hospital."

Chapter 17
The Wire

Mitchell gave instructions to the Marines to guard the house. They were halfway down the drive when a platoon of horses arrived with Weaver at their head.

"What the hell's going on?" Weaver asked. "I got some garbled message from a Marine saying you'd—"

"Simon Longfield was the spy in Police House. He was feeding information to his mother. She was the fifth conspirator," Mitchell said, speaking quickly. "There's a room at the top of the tower. On the back of an antique plate there's one of those coins."

"And the Longfields?"

"Dead. I killed Mr Longfield after he shot Riley. Self-defence. The woman killed herself. Emmitt was here, in one of those cottages."

"Where is he now?" Weaver asked.

"Gone," Mitchell said.

"You've no warrant. No suspects in custody. No witnesses other than police, and this lot, all of whom," Weaver added, raising her voice so it would carry to Corporal Lin and her troops, "are here in defiance of orders. That's a mutiny. A—"

"We did make arrests. There's a butler handcuffed at the rear of the house," Mitchell said.

"Is that meant to—"

"Riley's in the hospital," Mitchell interrupted. "She's possibly dead. I'm going there. The rest of your questions can wait."

When they got to the hospital, they didn't head to the patients' entrance but to the rear. Surrounded by bins and half broken wooden pallets was a service door. Ruth followed Mitchell into a green painted corridor that exuded disinfectant.

"The coroner is... this one," Mitchell said, pushing open a door as anonymous as all the rest.

Inside, a bearded man looked up from a partially dissected corpse. "You can't come barging in here. Get out," the coroner said, gesticulating with a bloody metal saw. Ruth turned away.

"Have the victims from the ambushed train come here?" Mitchell asked.

"Of course."

"I need to see them."

"This is my jurisdiction," the coroner said, "Not yours." He bent his head over the body once more.

"One of my officers has been killed. This one has been tortured, and my… my sergeant is lying in an operating theatre less than a hundred yards away," Mitchell said, his tone measured but far from calm. "I need to see those bodies before more people die."

The coroner paused. "Most of them have been taken away by the Navy for proper burial," he said.

"What about the civilians?"

"Two are as yet unidentified, the rest have either been claimed or are waiting for transportation to their home town."

"What about the body parts from the explosion?"

"They're still here."

"I'd like to see them. Please."

The coroner grudgingly nodded. He laid down the saw and led them to a door. "It's the cold room," he said. Inside were two large blocks of ice, and the gentle thrum of an air conditioning unit struggling to keep the room chilled. "J2 to K3 are the body parts. K4 to M2 are the remaining bodies."

"The parts. Let me see those."

"Be my guest," the corner said, waving his bloody-gloved hand toward the wall.

Mitchell opened a door, and dragged out a metal tray, six feet in length. On it was a white sheet, easily covering a small mound. Ruth swallowed as Mitchell pulled off the sheet.

"No," he said, and tried the next. In the third, he stopped. "This is it. An orange chequered suit. Is that all of it?" he asked.

"One arm, one thigh," the corner said. "There are some feet in the next locker which may match."

"Do you remember what shoes he wore?" Mitchell asked Ruth.

"No. Just the suit," Ruth said.

"Me too. Do you have some scissors?" the captain asked.

The coroner passed them to Mitchell. He cut at the cloth prying it from the frozen flesh of the leg.

"Nothing." Mitchell turned to the arm. He cut through the fabric and peeled it away from the charred remains. "Damn."

On the arm was a tattoo. The top part was missing, but below a curve that might have been the bottom of an anchor was one misspelled word 'SS Britania'.

"Thank you," Mitchell said, handing the scissors back to the coroner.

"Is that what you were looking for?" the coroner asked. "What does it mean?"

But Mitchell didn't answer.

Ruth followed him out into the corridor. He looked left and right, almost as if he was uncertain of what to do next.

"I was wrong," he said. "All this time, we've been investigating the wrong crime." He took a deep breath, and another. "I want to see Riley," he said, and headed off, into the hospital.

They spotted Isaac first. He was pacing up and down an otherwise empty corridor.

"Where is she?" Mitchell asked.

"The operating theatre," Isaac said. "Still alive last time they updated me."

He actually looked nervous, Ruth thought. It was surprising to see.

"Where's the doctor's station?" Mitchell asked.

Isaac jerked a thumb over his shoulder.

"Wait here," Mitchell said.

"Where's Kelly?" Ruth asked.

"The roof. She likes having the high ground," Isaac muttered. Ruth thought that was more of an attempt at humour than an explanation.

"Longfield killed herself," she said.

"What? How?" Isaac asked.

Ruth told him. "What about Riley?" she asked. "How is she really?"

"They have to remove the shrapnel and repair the damage it did," Isaac said. "Even if she survives the surgery, it'll be touch and go for weeks."

"Oh." Ruth looked around. "Is she safe here? You didn't think Gregory would be."

"That was different. This isn't just blood loss and the danger of infection. She'll die without help. She might do so anyway, the equipment here is so primitive, but what can I do?"

"You're really worried."

"Of course."

"I mean, she doesn't like you," Ruth said.

"We had a falling out, but that doesn't mean…" Isaac took a deep breath. "I'll make sure she's safe."

Ruth wasn't reassured. "A falling out over what?" she asked.

"It was a misunderstanding," Isaac said. "It doesn't matter now. None of it does."

Before Ruth could ask any more questions, Mitchell stormed through the double doors.

"There's nothing I can do here. Nothing. Isaac, copy everything that's on this." He handed the man the tablet he'd taken from Longfield's tower. "Deering you should stay here."

"No, sir. I'm in this to the end. Where do we go next?"

"The last piece of the puzzle. Frobisher was right. I think this *was* a robbery, and I want to know what was stolen."

The United States Embassy was more heavily guarded than ever, and it wasn't the only building in the district to be so. Next door, a pair of British Marines stood sentry outside the telegraph office. Even the newspaper building next to that had two on the roof.

Mitchell stormed through the gate, Ruth followed, but they were stopped at the doors. They weren't allowed in until the ambassador himself had been called. Then they had to wait until Perez and Clarke came down to the lobby to meet them.

"I want to see Fairmont's cell," Mitchell said.

"Why?" Ambassador Perez asked.

"I think the answer may be inside," Mitchell said.

"The answer to my question, or to yours?" Perez asked.

"To all of this," Mitchell said. "The murders, the assassination, the counterfeiting. Everything."

"You need to be more specific," Perez said.

"Show me the cell, and I'll tell you the rest," Mitchell replied.

"I see. Clarke, lead the way."

They followed Agent Clarke down to the basement. Again there was a guard on duty inside the door to the stairwell.

"Do you have other prisoners down here?" Ruth asked

"No. Oh, you mean the guard? That's just procedure," Perez said.

Clarke unlocked the cell. It was empty. Mitchell went inside. He stood in the middle of the room, looking up and then down as he turned a full circle.

"Well?" Perez prompted.

"Was this the only room Fairmont was held in?" Mitchell asked.

"From the moment we took custody, yes," Perez said.

"And the suit? Why was he wearing that?"

"I told you," Clarke said. "The money he made from selling information was spent on suits. He bragged about it. How it was important to be well-dressed."

"That annoyed you, did it?" Mitchell asked.

"That a man would sell out his country for some clothes? Yes, that annoyed me," Clarke said.

"So much so, that you made sure he wore something unflattering when we moved him?"

"He asked how much luggage he'd be allowed to bring," Clarke said. "He wanted to make sure he'd have something good to wear. That's why I found him that suit."

Mitchell crossed to the far wall and opened the doors to the fixed cupboard. There was nothing inside.

"What are you looking for," Perez asked.

"The answer's here," Mitchell said. He looked at Perez. The captain's eyes narrowed. He reached a hand up to brush the ceiling. "I need some light. Clarke, can you get me a lamp from the corridor? No, two of them. Quickly!"

Clarke moved back out into the corridor. "But what are you looking for?" Perez asked again.

"I don't think Fairmont died on that train," Mitchell said. He walked over to the cot and sat down. Almost immediately he stood up again. He lifted the bed and upended it. There was nothing underneath. "It wasn't an ambush, but a rescue."

"Really? How? Why?"

"Why do I think that, or why was he rescued?" Mitchell replied. "There's not much left of the man who was wearing that suit. There is an arm, and on it is a tattoo. SS Britania, spelled with only one 'n'. The Britannia is the ship from which the Marine escort on that train all came. I imagine it won't take long to find out which of them had a tattoo with that unfortunate spelling, but we don't have the time. During the ambush, they could have fired that grenade into the train the moment we stopped. They didn't. They risked their lives to go on board. Not to kill Fairmont, but to free him. He took off the suit and put it onto a Marine. An explosive device was strapped to that Marine. It was detonated. All that remains are a few charred lumps covered in a singed orange suit. They risked everything to rescue Fairmont. For whom would *you* risk your life, Perez? Close the door and lock it. I want to see it as Fairmont did."

Ruth closed the door and turned the key. She stood by the small window, watching Mitchell.

"Can you hear me?" he called.

"Yes, sir."

She watched as he tapped the back of a cupboard, then the next, and then the third. He nodded.

"I have the lamps," Clarke said.

"Hang on," Ruth said. She watched as Mitchell took out a knife and slammed into the back of the cupboard. The wood cracked, and the knife seemingly went into the wall up to its hilt.

"What's he doing?" Perez asked, and then added, in a panicked tone, "Open the door!"

Ruth pulled the key from the lock, dropped it, and kicked it down the corridor.

"You shouldn't have done that," the ambassador said. Mitchell had pulled away the remains of the cupboard's back. He leaned forward and seemed to disappear into it. Into a hole, Ruth realised. One that must have been hidden by the cupboard, and which led into the next room.

"What's in there?" she asked.

"It's top secret," the ambassador said. "No one goes in there."

Ruth gestured through the small window. Only Mitchell's legs were now visible. "I think the captain just did."

The ambassador sighed. "Open the door, Clarke."

There were two women and a man inside the room, all wearing plain shirts, and pocket-less trousers. They'd been sitting at desks in the middle of the room. What they'd been doing with the strange equipment and sheaths of paper, Ruth didn't know, but now they were staring, horrified, at Mitchell.

"Fairmont didn't have access to this room," Mitchell said.

"No," Clarke said.

"Who did?" the captain asked.

"Myself and two of my deputies," Clarke said. "The staff are locked in here during their shift."

"Ambassador, you don't have a key?"

"No," Perez said. "For operational reasons there's only one copy."

"So the only way for Fairmont to get inside is to steal Agent Clarke's key, or to break in." Mitchell gestured at the cupboard and the hole in the wall beyond. "I think it's clear which one he chose."

"What is this room?" Ruth asked.

"That's classified," Clarke said.

"I think your staff here should take a break," Mitchell said. There was an ominous silence broken only by the slow grinding of Mitchell's teeth.

"Go," the ambassador said to the staff.

"What is this place," Ruth asked again once they'd left.

"Clarke's right," the ambassador said. "We can't tell you. It's classified."

"It's a wire tap room," Mitchell said. "Quite literally this is where they tap into the telegraph. That's right isn't it?"

Clarke stared straight ahead.

"I'd remind you," Perez said, speaking with deliberate caution, "that we are on American soil."

"And I'd remind *you*," Mitchell growled, "that Sergeant Riley's in the hospital, and Sergeant Davis is in the morgue. Do you really want to try matching me threat for threat?"

"I don't understand," Ruth said, speaking in the hope of dampening the suddenly dangerous atmosphere. "How do you tap into the telegraph?"

"The central telegraph office is next door," Mitchell said. "The wires come in underground. Each message is a series of electrical impulses." He gestured at the equipment on the table. "All of this is so they can listen in, and write down the messages. Every shipment of coal south, and of food north. Every price promised, and deal made."

"That has to be illegal," Ruth said.

"No," Perez said. "This is American soil."

"I always thought it was an odd place for you to set up your embassy," Mitchell said. "Next to Parliament would have made more sense. Instead, you chose one next to the telegraph, and your new one is next to the radio antenna. Well, this might be American soil, but I'd say that all adds up to espionage."

"I'm protecting American interests," Perez said.

"Sure. What was it you said? What are Britain and America if not friends? And what was that line that politician used? Friends don't spy on their friends?"

"An ally today could be an enemy tomorrow," Perez said.

Mitchell picked up the sheet of paper a clerk had been writing on. "It's the amount of food being shipped to the mines. This must be so much easier than having people count the trains. This tells you what's in demand. That information goes back to the US. You get to work out what food is worth growing for export. This is economic warfare. I prefer it to the other kind, but it's not the act of a grateful friend."

The atmosphere had sunk beyond dangerous and was heading toward violence.

"So Fairmont dug a hole through that wall to get access to the telegraph?" Ruth asked.

"No," Mitchell said. He pulled out a chair and sat down. "Each night that I've been in Twynham, and when the weather permits, I've taken a walk down by the hulks on the coast. Few people go there. To me, the ships are a reminder of how a lot of us, literally, got here." He sighed. "On one such night a few weeks ago, whom do I see but Lucas Fairmont selling information to two of the conspirators. I was so focused on the conspiracy that I failed to notice a coincidence too large to be anything other than a setup. Who knew I walked that particular beat? Commissioner Wallace, the man who gave me my very own unit in the police department. Fairmont wanted to be arrested, and to be caught selling American documents. He would have known your procedures. Perhaps he even wrote them. That gave him access to that cell. However, you have people in here, twenty-four hours a day, right?"

"As long as the telegraph is running," Perez said.

"Precisely, and as the messages run three hundred and sixty-five days a year, he needed a way of stopping them. The Luddites. He created an anti-technologist political movement purely so he could find the most zealous of believers. Talk about dedication to the crime. He had them cut the telegraph. There were no telegrams coming in to Twynham, and so no staff on duty in here. He broke through the wall, stole what he was after, and covered the hole. Then he had to escape."

"That's why he gave us Frobisher," Ruth said. "When we raided the house on Windward Square, that was the signal to Emmitt that he was ready to be rescued."

"Precisely," Mitchell said. "Frobisher and those people were there to make us think Fairmont had information of value. Specifically, the locations of groups of men and women, armed with automatic weapons, and all waiting for some mysterious deadline. That information was worth us giving into his demand that he be moved somewhere far away from Twynham."

"But he couldn't have known you would have taken that train north," Perez said.

"No," Mitchell said. "And if we search, we'll probably find other ambush sites on the tracks leading east, and to Wales, but the thing about a train is that it has to stay on the rails. There are a limited number of railroads, and so he would only need three or four ambush sites. The truck was ready to depart as soon as they learned to which direction we were going. That information probably came from Simon Longfield, the spy within our department. But then they needed to let Fairmont know that the rescue was imminent."

"That's why the telegraph was cut again," Ruth said.

"Because how else can you get a message to someone who's a prisoner on a train?" Mitchell asked. "You do something so catastrophic that everyone on that train is talking about it. Hell, I think I told him myself it had been cut. We'll never know, but I think he might have had a key to that cage, perhaps even a weapon. After the shooting began, I think that he got out and killed at least some of the Marines. That element of surprise was why none of his followers were killed during that part of the rescue. Then there was the explosion. It destroyed almost all the evidence. The rest, well, they knew it would be destroyed when the tracks were cleared, because a resumption of normal service is more important than a few dozens deaths."

"That's absurdly elaborate," Perez said.

"Not really. In fact, most of it only required money or time. Thugs like Turnbull, Lyons, and Frobisher only needed to be paid. Organising the Luddites required time. Six months. Perhaps a year. Of course, that leaves the question of what in this room is worth that level of dedication. It's not the telegrams. It's something else. A safe? Ah, yes." Mitchell stood. "It's the most secure room in the building. Clarke keeps looking at you, and you are desperately trying not to look over here." Mitchell crossed the room. There was a small cupboard. He tried the door. "Locked. I take it the safe is in there?"

"Nothing is missing," Perez said.

"Of course not," Mitchell said. "You made the man change his clothes. He knew you would. He was banking on it. I expect he thought he'd end up in some prison jumpsuit, but he knew that he wouldn't be able to take anything away from here. Nothing written down, at least. But in there is something that he memorised. There is something, the knowledge of which is worth the sacrifice of a year or more of his life."

Mitchell stared at Perez. The politician stared back.

"Blackmail," Ruth said. Perez blinked.

"What?" the ambassador said.

Mitchell smiled. "We learned that they were blackmailing some British politicians. That's a far easier way of running a country. Get someone else to worry about whether the trains will run on time while basking in the knowledge that any policy you want will come into law. So Fairmont has something on you, or on someone else?"

Silence.

"A better question is how he knew the combination," Ruth said.

Silence.

"Fairmont found the safe," Perez finally said. "It was his idea to install it in here. I had no key to this room, and Clarke didn't have the combination to the safe. An extra layer of security, you see."

"When was that?" Mitchell asked.

"Almost two years ago," Perez said.

"Two years? It's got to be something big," Mitchell said. "I need to know if it's going to cause immediate problems for the country."

"You mean are they missile launch codes? No," Perez said. "The documents all came from the old U.S. Embassy in London. They were CIA and NSA files on individuals who were influential in the old-world, and who are still alive today."

"Active in politics, you mean?" Mitchell asked.

"Yes."

"Like you, Congressman Perez," Mitchell said. "You were in Congress before the Blackout."

"I was. But I'm not the only one. I won't tell you what's in there, nor the names of the individuals concerned. Suffice it to say that the information could cause more than one presidential candidate to drop out of the race."

"Or to control them after they won the election?"

"Yes," Perez admitted.

"And that is a big prize. Control of Britain and a newly reunified United States. As those are the only two functioning nations of any significant size, that means control of the world. I'd say that was worth a couple of years of planning."

Silence returned, but this time absent of all earlier threat.

"What now?" Perez asked.

"I'm going to catch him," Mitchell said. "But first I want you to open that safe."

"I won't show you the documents," Perez said.

"And I don't want to know what's in them. Just open it."

Perez did. Inside were a few brown and red envelopes, and a lot of plaster.

"It came from the hole in the wall," Mitchell said. "Since Clarke doesn't know the combination, and you don't have a key to the room, he knew it would be a long time before it was found."

Chapter 18
Counterfeit Conspiracy
9th October

"Tomorrow?" a voice asked.

"The next twenty-four hours are critical," another replied. "Many things can go wrong, but I'm hopeful."

"Thank you."

Ruth opened her eyes. She saw Mitchell shake hands with a doctor before coming to sit down on a chair opposite.

"How is she?" Ruth asked.

"The surgery's over. She survived that, and now... now we wait and see. I brought you some soup. It might be cold by now."

Ruth picked up the large cup. It was cold, but she was ravenous.

"What time is it?" she asked.

"About two," Mitchell said. He looked at his watch. "No, four."

Ruth looked around. "In the morning?"

"You were tired. You snore, by the way."

"Oh. Sorry."

"Don't apologise," he said with a brittle attempt at a smile. "It kept everyone else away." Mitchell stood, paced a few uncertain steps, and shrugged as if the movement confirmed that there was nowhere to go, and nothing to do but wait.

"I hate hospitals," he said. "They're a place I associate with death."

"I suppose that's the same for most people," Ruth said.

"And they all look the same," he said, clearly not listening. "British, American, before the Blackout and after. The easy-to-clean, hides-the-blood paint. The smell. Even the doctors, none of it changes." He sat down. "This, here, the waiting, it reminds me of when my father died. I was about your age. There had been a road accident. It was one of those stupidly tragic accidents for which no one was to blame. A driver had a heart attack while he was behind the wheel. The truck he was driving ploughed straight into my father's car."

"Oh, I'm sorry," Ruth said.

"Thank you," he murmured automatically. "I was in school at the time. We were sitting a test. Math. I was struggling over this problem of angles. I remember that. The principal came in. He told me the news out in that corridor. I raced to the hospital as fast as I could. Too fast, considering the nature of my father's accident. Then I had to wait. After twelve hours, I knew he wasn't going to make it. No one said it, but there was something about how the nurses came to keep me updated. He's still alive, they said. Still fighting. I knew he was dying, so I sat by his bedside and tried to think of some appropriate last words to say to him. You see, I thought that they'd take out the tubes, and we'd have one final moment together. We'd each have an opportunity to say all those things that we'd thought but never said. Those words had to be perfect because I knew the memory of our last moment together would stay with me for the rest of my life. And it has. Except, we didn't say anything to each other. He died without regaining consciousness."

"What were you going to say?" Ruth asked when the silence began to stretch.

"Some variation on thank you and I love you, though I never really settled on anything."

"Maybe thinking it was enough," Ruth said.

Mitchell smiled. "Maybe. After all, the words were for me, not for him. Ours was a complicated relationship. It was just the two of us and… well, after he died, he didn't leave much. I sold what was left. I went to Boston because that was where a TV show I liked was set. I got a place at college. For the first few months I was so full of anger I didn't realise that studying, or at least that kind of studying, wasn't for me. I didn't want to drift from one thing to another, nor did I want to waste any more time accruing student debt that I'd be unable to pay back. I'd made up my mind to quit, and the choice was either the police or the military."

"A bit like mine," Ruth said.

"The more things change, the more they stay the same," Mitchell said. "I'd decided on the police because, perversely, I thought there would be fewer rules. But I wasn't ready for it. So I looked for a job. Nothing permanent. I wanted something where I could meet some different people. Maybe get a new perspective on the world. I saw an advert on campus. A professor was looking for an assistant. No qualifications were required, so I applied. She called me in for an interview. It was a series of mathematical puzzles. I didn't have a clue what the questions meant let alone how to guess the answers. She kept on asking them. I figured she was having her fun, proving her own superiority. But she wasn't. At the end of it, she gave me the job because, out of all the applicants, I was the only one who didn't understand the first thing about what she was doing. That was Maggie."

"Maggie? You mean you were her assistant too, like Isaac?"

"I was nothing like Isaac, and I wasn't an assistant, not really. She needed someone to carry her bags from America to England for her presentation. But she wanted to make sure that that person wasn't going to be able to steal any of her research."

"That's how you ended up here?"

"I often think about the past, trying to work out if I was somehow destined to be here, at this time and in this place. Destiny doesn't exist. If any one of a hundred events had played out differently, I wouldn't have come to Britain. Whether I'd have survived the Blackout is another matter. But I do know that this corner of Britain would look very different."

"One small act that changes the course of history," Ruth said. "That was what Emmitt said. Longfield, too."

"Yeah, but this isn't what they were talking about."

"No." Ruth thought about what he'd said. "How would it be different?"

"Maggie and Isaac would have died soon after the Blackout. So would the Prime Minister and dozens of others. Someone else would have been in charge here. I don't know whom. Wallace, perhaps. Maybe Longfield. Whoever it was, they wouldn't have done as good a job at clawing something back from the devastation. Mine was a small part in history, but it was a significant one. That's not false modesty, but none of it matters when set against that other thing I did. I rescued Riley. Right now, I'm trying to find comfort in the fact that I gave her nearly twenty years of as close to a normal life as anyone could have in these times. And she's as close to a daughter as I'll ever have. That's something. Twenty years. It seems wrong to have it ripped away in such a pointless way."

Ruth wasn't sure what to say. "She'll recover."

"Probably. It's just hospitals; they bring out the worst in me." He sighed. "The world can change in a moment. But life is a succession of moments, one coming so fast on the heels of another that it's impossible to pinpoint the precise point where change began. All you can do is try to identify the moment that it changed for you. My father told me that, it was about a week before he died, but it's what I think of as his last words to me. Often, I think about what that moment was for me. Was it the car accident? Going to Boston? Taking that job with Maggie? I still don't know. Whichever it was, it led me to this place. I helped bring law and order to the chaos that surrounded us after that nuclear holocaust. I will not let that be ripped asunder by the likes of Emmitt and Fairmont."

"We're going to find them," Ruth said.

"I'm going to try," Mitchell said. "It's all I have left. You're on two weeks of medical leave and won't be allowed back until you've been signed off by a trauma specialist. The Serious Crimes Unit is going to be folded into the S.I.S., and Corporal Lin and her colleagues have been reassigned to patrol the Solent. Technically I'm on compassionate leave until Riley recovers, but what use am I here? I'm going to find Fairmont, and Emmitt, and stop them both."

"I'll help," Ruth said. "I have to. I was the one he kidnapped. I won't be safe until they're stopped."

Mitchell grunted. Ruth wasn't sure whether it was in assent or refusal.

"Why did they kidnap me?" she asked. "I mean, if this was about stealing information from the embassy, then why take that risk? Do you think it is connected to Isaac, somehow? Or me, even?"

"No. I don't think so. Did Emmitt mention that bear with the ribbon? Did he even mention the coin?"

"Not the bear, but the coin... wait, no, I brought that up first."

"So he was just using information Simon had told him about your adoption to manipulate you into assuming he knew more. As for Isaac, he isn't nearly as anonymous as he likes to think. Plenty of people know the name. Weaver for one, the Prime Minister for another, along with a lot of people who made it out of London just after the Blackout. To them, he's the person who received a message saying that we would find food here, on the southern English coast. Because of that, his is a name they're unlikely to forget, but I doubt that many know the face that goes with it."

"Then Emmitt was bluffing," Ruth said. No comfort came with the realisation. "That doesn't explain why he wanted to kidnap me."

"I think he'd have settled for any police officer. He wanted an insider in the police. Wallace had his own agenda, and Simon's real loyalty was to his mother. Thanks to Simon, he saw an opportunity to turn you. As to why he wanted to kidnap a police officer, I suspect that was another distraction. We would have spent weeks looking for you. Our principal suspects would have been the Luddites."

The memory of the torture came back to her. Ruth shuddered. "I suppose, if I'd not told him anything, eventually my body would have been found with a backward 'L' carved into it."

"Don't let your mind conjure images like that," he said. "While you were sleeping, I went back to Police House. I looked again at the evidence. Do you remember that rifle that was pointed at you in Windward Square?"

"How could I forget?"

"The propellant in those cartridges had been replaced with sand and dust. The weight was perfect, but that's why the weapon didn't fire. I assume that was the reason the assault rifles were in the house. Fairmont would have hoped that Frobisher and the rest would have used them for defence when the police came in. He was trying to ensure that no police officers died, since a dead copper would have made us reluctant to agree to his deal."

"Those discarded cartridges I found in the cellar of the church, they must have been taken apart for the same reason."

"Probably."

"So they weren't after the propellant," she said. "It's so much effort, so much planning, all for a robbery?"

"Fairmont's dedicated, I'll give him that. But it wasn't just a robbery. Whatever information he has with which to blackmail the presidential candidates, he also wanted to disrupt our society here. That's part of his long-term aims. Considering the time that went into it, there are plenty of other ways to have stolen the information from that safe. But he wanted the chaos of the assassination, the counterfeiting, the sabotage, and even the murder of the passengers on those trains. Perhaps he knew, if not precisely what secrets were in the safe, at least whom it implicated. By destabilising Britain in this way, he can ensure that only a candidate he can blackmail will win the election. Or perhaps not. Perhaps, to him, this was the simplest course of action. Hell, perhaps he enjoyed creating all this chaos."

"But none of that will matter," Ruth said. "Not if we can stop him."

Mitchell gave a weary nod of his head.

"Right," Ruth said, forcing herself to be proactive. "What do we know, and what do we have to ignore? Windward Square, and everything else Fairmont told us, was a lie, right? It was all so he could escape. What about the coins?"

"The conspiracy was as counterfeit as those twenty-pound notes," Mitchell said. "It made us search for conspirators rather than thieves."

"It had to serve some purpose," Ruth said.

"Oh, the story of a grand conspiracy was probably a way of persuading Longfield and Wallace to be part of this. Make them think they were dealing with some powerful group rather than a couple of conmen. It probably helped give them some control of DeWitt, too, though we'll never know."

"Right. Right," Ruth said, trying to force some enthusiasm back into her voice. "So what's left? What's real? The ambush? The Luddites? No, they were scapegoats. Wait. The fifth. The fifth of November!"

"A date he picked out of a hat because it has historical resonance," Mitchell said. "It would make the Luddites seem far more terrifying than they were."

"But Ned Ludd said the wires were going to be cut three times," Ruth said.

"Just because that was what he was told, doesn't mean it would happen."

"But what about the placards and the pamphlets? Why bother making them if they weren't going to be used?"

Mitchell sat up. "Possibly to keep people like Frobisher and Ned Ludd occupied," he said, but there was more life to his voice now.

"What if it wasn't?" she asked. "What if there was going to be another act of sabotage, one to tie in with a public demonstration?"

"On the fifth of November?"

"Right," Ruth said. "It probably wasn't going to be anything more than a few dozen people marching in the street."

"Okay, but why?" Mitchell asked.

"For the same reason he's done everything else. It's a distraction," Ruth said.

"But from what?"

"You know how I told you I like mystery novels," Ruth said. "Well, think of this as a heist. The information in that safe is the loot. He's stolen it, and now he has to get away."

"On the fifth of November?"

"When there was due to be a bunch of Luddites marching through the streets," Ruth said. "All the police would be busy arresting them."

"Not just the police," Mitchell said. "Ned Ludd was meant to be caught, wasn't he? We were meant to know about the fifth. What did we do? We brought in the Marines to guard every viable target, and those are all in Twynham. There's only one place Fairmont and Emmitt can go. Only one place that they would want to go because the robbery is only the start of their plan. The blackmail comes next, and for that they have to be on the other side of the Atlantic."

"How do they get there?" Ruth asked. "By boat? It has to be."

"That gasoline had to come from America. What if they were planning to get out on the same ship?"

"Aren't people looking for the ship?" Ruth asked. "I mean, you did tell someone, didn't you?"

"Yes, and they've searched all the ones currently in dock. Hmm. Why the fifth?"

"Longfield was going to be in Scotland," Ruth said. "And you know, thinking about it, wouldn't we have eventually been led to her?"

"Possibly," Mitchell said. "Probably. You think she planned to escape with them?"

"By ship, from their place in Scotland. She said it was near the coast."

"Right. But why the fifth? Why not sooner? Because," he said, answering his own question, "the ship is on some expedition, and won't reach the Scottish coast until then. Okay. That's a theory. It doesn't help us find them, does it?" He slumped into his seat. Ruth felt like doing the same.

"If the conspiracy was never real," she said, "then there really is no connection between them and my parents. Emmitt really was lying."

"I'd take that as good news," Mitchell said. Ruth wasn't sure she agreed.

Silence settled as both lapsed into thought.

"No matter how fake the conspiracy was," Ruth finally said, "there were five of them."

"And lots of hired help," Mitchell said.

"Exactly," Ruth said. "We can't trust anything that Fairmont said, right? But according to Frobisher, Emmitt was someone who came to the house in Windward Square a few times. According to Turnbull, he was the only one who knew how to fix the printer. When it broke, and if he wasn't there, they had to wait for him to return. Didn't Turnbull say that sometimes he was away for a day or two?"

"And that he took the cart. He took it into Twynham to drop off the finished money. Presumably he used some of it to pay off others. That must have been when he visited the people in Windward Square."

"Right, but there would be other things for him to do," she said. "I mean, he'd have to do pretty much everything else. Fairmont couldn't do it because, if he went missing for more than a few hours, someone would notice."

"Unless it was at night," Mitchell said.

"Even then, people might spot him sneaking around, or being exhausted at work the next day. After that, he was in custody. It's the same for Wallace and Longfield, people would have noticed if they disappeared. As for DeWitt, well, she was in the cells in Police House, wasn't she? So it all had to be done by Emmitt."

"Not necessarily. Everywhere connected to this case is within a few miles of Twynham."

"It's not," Ruth said. "Not everything. What about the house where we found the bodies of Dr Gupta and Marcus Clipton? That was in Southampton. How could they move those two there with no one seeing? They didn't use the train, did they? And it was done with only a few hours' notice."

"By truck," Mitchell said. "The same one they used to drive to the ambush."

"And the same one that they'll use to get to the ship," Ruth said.

"It would have to be nearby, somewhere within a few hours journey from the house we found the printer in."

"They were storing the petrol at the church," Ruth said,

"But there were no tyre marks outside. I think that fuel was to keep the generator running, but that gasoline came from somewhere. There were no tread marks outside, so they brought it by cart. Hmm. Emmitt went to check up on the people in Windward Square. I can't imagine he left the people with the truck on their own, either. So, yes, it has to be somewhere he can get there and back within a day. But an engine is a noisy beast, so wherever it is, has to be somewhere secluded. That house was chosen for the printing because it was close to the electrical grid. There's too many workers in the immediate vicinity, but the New Forest isn't far away. Few people live there, but there's plenty of abandoned houses and hamlets."

"The New Forest?" Ruth asked. "It's a big place,"

Mitchell looked at the door to Riley's room. "It's where I rescued her," he said. "And it *is* a big place, but what else can we do but look?"

Chapter 19
The Forest

But they did need better weapons. The only place Ruth knew that had them, and the same place Mitchell knew, was the funeral home.

"Where are you going, Henry?" Isaac asked from the doorway.

"We have a lead," Mitchell said, opening a coffin. It was empty. "Where are the weapons?"

"Can't you wait for dawn?" Isaac asked.

"It'll be light by the time we get there."

"It will? Great." Isaac closed the coffin. "Do you think you should deputise me? Formally, I mean. Give me a badge, perhaps."

"This is police business," Mitchell said.

"Which is why I asked whether you should deputise me," Isaac said. "We can argue over whether I'm coming with you, but since Kelly and I followed you from the hospital, I don't see the point. I'm coming with you, Henry, just tell me where to."

Ruth had had enough. "The New Forest," she said. "That's where the truck is. We find that, and we find Emmitt."

"That's a big place," Isaac said.

"It won't be near the railway line," Mitchell replied. "Either the one that cuts through the southern part or... look, do you have a map in here?" One was found. "This is the railway line," he said, tracing a line along the map, "running northeast from Christchurch up to Southampton. The truck will be hidden north of there, and at least four miles from the western edge of the forest, otherwise someone might have heard the sound of the engine."

"That still leaves about twenty square miles to search," Isaac said. "And how many hamlets and villages would we have to search? How many houses?"

"We don't look for the truck," Ruth said, "but the road it's driven down. How many roads are there? Five?" She peered at whisker-thin lines. "And are they even proper roads?"

"Find the road, find the truck. Fine. Can we wait until tomorrow?" Isaac asked.

"Why?" Ruth asked.

"I've some more people arriving."

"And I thought you said they'd be here by now," Mitchell said.

"People get delayed," Isaac said with a shrug.

"We can't wait," Ruth said. "We might know what their plans were, but those might have changed."

Isaac nodded. "I moved the guns, they're in the back."

"Afterwards," Ruth said, taking a shotgun "You're going to tell me why you brought these weapons to Twynham."

"I'd be glad to," Isaac said.

"We'll follow this road east toward Normansland, and… see what we find," Mitchell said. The uncertainty in his voice was palpable.

They'd gone to the railway station and pressed Rebecca Cavendish into providing them with a train. It had taken them north, past the power station built on the site of the old Bournemouth Airport, leaving them at the northerly edge of the New Forest. Mitchell had given the train's driver a note to be taken back to Weaver. Ruth wasn't sure if that was an afterthought, or if Mitchell was second-guessing the plan.

Standing in the damp woodland, she understood his uncertainty. The trees were densely packed, spreading far beyond the clear lines marked on the old-world map. Beneath them the ground was littered with mud mixed with multi-coloured threads of shredded plastic. The rusting, tyre-less car was the only clue that there had been a road here. Ivy had wrapped around the engine with a tenacity that forecast it wouldn't be too many more seasons before the car was entirely hidden by evergreen leaves.

"Was ever a place better suited to a conspiracy than this?" Isaac asked, and even his usual sardonic tone was edged with doubt. "Shall we?"

Kelly took the lead, walking soft-footed across the loamy soil, her rifle half-raised, the barrel swinging left and right like an inaccurate pendulum. Mitchell went next, his fingers rolling over the grip of a pistol the size of a hand cannon holstered at his hip. His shoulders were stooped, his head jutted forward, tilted to one side, as if he was listening more than looking for signs of their prey. She glanced behind. Isaac, cradling the shotgun across his arms, looked more like a hunter out to bag a brace before breakfast than a law bringer on a quest for justice.

And then there was herself. She was dressed in faded jeans, a worn jacket, and her least worst pair of trainers. The only clue as to her profession was the word 'police' stencilled on the borrowed bulletproof vest. Somehow, she felt more like an officer of the law than ever before.

Mitchell stopped.

"We're doing this wrong," he said. "Nothing's used this road for a decade. We'll cut due east."

Ruth agreed, simply because she hadn't a better idea. Haystacks and needles came back to her. Was Emmitt still here? Or had he already fled north? The silent forest gave her no answer. No, there, a bird's call cut through the damp, expectant air. It was as if the trees themselves were waiting for the coming confrontation. She told herself that was nonsense.

Even without the shotgun in her hands, it wouldn't have been a pleasant walk. The trees thinned, replaced by a thick carpet of leaves overlaying an even thicker layer of mud. They reached a stream swollen almost to a river, and had to backtrack before they found a way around it. Ruth was certain they were lost, but after another five minutes Mitchell came to a halt.

"Here's the road," he said.

Knowing it was there, Ruth was able to discern where it had once run. Curving more toward the west than the north, it was a crooked line with stubby shrubs for ten feet either side. The road itself was clear of vegetation though covered in those ubiquitous rotting leaves. Ruth looked up.

"Where do the leaves come from?" she asked.

Collectively, their eyes went up, then down.

Kelly kicked at the leaves. She bent down. "Here. There's a tread mark. They swept the leaves onto the road to cover the tracks."

Suddenly energised, Ruth peered down the road. "We go south?"

"Yes," Mitchell said. "But we'll stick to the woods."

After twenty minutes of painstaking trudging through increasingly dense undergrowth, they reached a hamlet slowly being retaken by the forest.

"We burned this place down," Isaac said. "Do you remember?"

"Watch the roofs," Mitchell said. "Do you see the birds?"

"Five crows," Kelly whispered. "It's an ill omen. But there's no one here. I'll check the road."

Despite the woman's assurances, Ruth's palms began to itch as Kelly ran, doubled over, onto the old roadway. The shotgun was growing heavier, and she could feel her last reserves of energy draining away.

Kelly straightened, gave a gesture that Ruth couldn't begin to translate, before disappearing behind the shattered houses. Mitchell's face was taut, Isaac's was calculating, and from those expressions, Ruth couldn't gauge how worried she should be. Kelly returned, at a swift jog, but with her head held high.

"They didn't come through here," she said. "There are lots of deer, but no people have been this way for months."

"Then we need to backtrack," Mitchell said.

Kelly raised a hand. Ruth raised her shotgun, but the woman was pointing to a herd of wild ponies shuffling through the woods to their south. Ruth lowered her weapon. The task was futile. It was something for Mitchell to do so he didn't feel useless waiting in that hospital. Isaac too, she thought. They had no… There was a hint of something in the air. Was that smoke?

She took a cautious step, and another. The ponies drifted beyond earshot, and the forest seemed more silent than ever. Too silent. There were no birds nearby. What had caused the animals to start moving?

Eyes narrowed, Ruth angled toward the direction from which the ponies had come. The smell didn't grow more distinct, nor was there any new sound betraying where people lurked, but there was something about this stretch of woodland that spoke to her gut, telling her they were in the right place.

Her coat snagged on a branch. She reached her left hand up to free it and saw the thorns. Hawthorn. Just like on DeWitt's jacket, and on Norton's. She looked back. The others were spread out, a few paces behind. She gestured ahead. Mitchell nodded, his expression changing, as a dark veil slid across his eyes.

Was that a sound? She paused with one foot in the air, slowly lowered it, and took another step. Yes. A sound. It wasn't the rustling of leaves, nor dull thump of a falling branch, but a scratching metallic rasp. There it was again. She turned around, intending to indicate what she'd heard to the others, and found Kelly at her shoulder.

The woman raised a hand, then three fingers, making another of those incomprehensible gestures the other two seemed to know so well.

"I'll take the lead," Kelly finally mouthed.

Ruth let her.

The hawthorn grew thicker, almost forming a wall. Kelly found a way through, but thorns scraped at Ruth's neck and face. She had to slow down again after her jeans caught. There was an audible tear as she tugged her leg free. Mitchell and Isaac, seemingly oblivious to the bush's three-inch long needles, silently pushed past her. Ruth fell to the back of the group.

Twenty yards further on, the three of them crouched. Ruth did the same. Ten yards after that, they stopped, and bent even lower. They'd found them. Beyond the screen of hawthorn, the forest opened out. A large building stood in a clearing that must have once been at least an acre of grassland.

"Boulderwood Hotel," Mitchell whispered, pointing at the remains of a weather-warped sign.

The hotel was built of red brick, three-storeys high with windows in the attic. Two sets of bay windows were positioned either side of a double-sized front door. A single column remained of the pair that had been supporting a roofed porch. That, like the broken column, lay blocking the main door.

"No smoke," Ruth whispered, staring at the chimneys, though she was sure she could smell something. There were no obvious holes in what she could see of the roof. Half of the windows had been boarded up. Glass remained in most of the rest, though some had been left to let in the elements. It was a place in which to hide, not to live. But where was the truck? To the right of the house, separated from it by a tennis court, were three low buildings. Someone had added log cladding, the timbers carved into intricate shapes, but that didn't disguise the rusting metal chimney pocking out of the roof.

Ruth looked from window to window, and then to the outbuildings, back to the house, and finally at Mitchell. His eyes were roaming across it just like hers. She looked to Isaac. He looked thoughtful. She didn't need to read his mind to know they were all thinking the same thing. Mitchell raised his hand, fingers out. Ruth took that to mean they were waiting, perhaps for five minutes.

After two, there was an inhuman, mechanical roar that spluttered and then died. It came from the outbuilding, Ruth thought. A moment later, that arrhythmic rasping began again.

Mitchell lips curled into feral grin. "Broken engine," he mouthed.

Isaac rose from a half crouch. "What now?" he whispered.

"Kelly, how good are you with that rifle?" Mitchell whispered back.

"Very," she said.

"Find a position with a clear view of the front of the house. I'll lure them out. When I do, start shooting."

"To kill?" Kelly asked.

"Not if you can help it," Mitchell said through gritted teeth. "I want them alive.'

"Even after all he's done?" Isaac asked.

"No. Because of it. Go."

Kelly drifted backward. Ruth moved out of the way. When she turned to look for her, the woman had vanished.

"How are you going to lure them out?" Isaac asked.

"By walking up there and asking them to surrender," Mitchell said.

"Simple. Direct. I like it," Isaac said. "But I've got one small suggestion."

"Yeah?"

Isaac smiled. "Good luck, Henry. Tell Anna I'm sorry. Here," He thrust his shotgun into Mitchell's hands. Before the captain could say anything, Isaac had run out of the trees and down to the drive leading up to the hotel.

Mitchell hissed in frustration. "Cover the road," he said to Ruth. "If they try to drive that truck out of here, it'll come along this track. Use the shotgun. Aim at the tyres. Stay low and out of sight until it's close." And he turned, and ran through the undergrowth, toward the house.

Ruth heard Isaac whistling a vaguely recognisable tune. She crept forward, finding a position half hidden by a laurel bush from where she could see Isaac. Mitchell and Kelly had vanished. She braced the shotgun, aiming it at the road.

"Hello!" Isaac called. "Anyone home?"

Ruth had to force herself to look away from Isaac and focus on the house, and then the outbuilding, then back at the house. She thought she heard something behind her. She swivelled. There was nothing.

The engine's noise changed, rising in pitch. Ruth counted the seconds. She reached nine before a door in the outbuilding opened. Wearing tattered overalls covered in grease and oil, one hand holding a wrench, the other stuck in the large front pocket, a man came out. His hair was dyed black, and he had the beginning of a trimmed beard, but she recognised him instantly. It was the old man from the pub.

A wave of furious hatred rolled over Ruth. She forced her hand away from the trigger, squeezing the immovable metal of the stock instead. The old man ambled toward Isaac.

"Yes?" the man asked. "Can I help you?"

"It's a nice day, isn't it?" Isaac said. "The kind to remember. Is that an engine in there?"

"Most of one," the old man said. "You familiar with them?"

"I dabbled a little, back in my wayward youth."

The old man nodded. "You don't live around here?"

"No, I was on my way to Nunton," Isaac said. "I lost my horse, my travelling companions, and my bearings."

"I've a map in the garage," the old man said in that same kindly tone with which he'd spoken to Ruth moments before he'd shot Davis. "Why don't you come inside and have a look? You can have a cuppa before you continue."

"That's very generous of you," Isaac said, though he didn't move.

The tension was palpable. Ruth's breathing seemed loud. Her heart was echoing like a drum. Isaac tilted his head to the side. She saw his fingers flex. She wondered where his gun was. She guessed the old man's was in the hand concealed in his pocket. Who would draw first? The shotgun would be useless. Carefully, quietly, she lowered it to the ground, intending to reach for her pistol.

There was a shot. Not from the old man, nor Isaac, but from the house. And another. There. The second-floor window, to the left of the door. She saw a flash, and a shape of a person. Then the shooting really began.

Gunfire came from behind her and from in front. Glass broke. Wood splintered. Stone chipped. Ruth scrabbled back into the illusory safety of the bush's leaves, trying to make sense of it all. Isaac was on the ground. Dead? No, crawling, rolling toward the garage. The old man was… motionless. A new, dark stain was spreading over the oil-covered overalls. An unintended smile curled her lips upward, lasting until a burst of gunfire sprayed the ground a foot from Isaac's head.

She looked back at the house. Windows were breaking, almost systematically. No, it was systematic. Kelly, or Mitchell? It didn't matter. Someone was shooting each glass window, breaking each in turn, showering glass on anyone hidden inside. Why? Ruth couldn't see anyone. No, there, by the outbuilding. A figure with a rifle. Not Emmitt, not Fairmont. A bearded man she'd never seen before. He raised his rifle, and she knew, from that range, he wouldn't miss Isaac. She raised her gun. Before she could fire, the man flew backward, a bullet planted squarely in his forehead.

Isaac rolled the last few feet to the relative shelter of the garage. He had his gun raised, firing at some unseen target in the house. Shots were being returned, but not as many as before. Were the people in the house dead? Ruth doubted they would be so lucky. More likely, the criminals had simply taken cover. Soon they would realise that there were only three people shooting at them. But how long was soon? How much ammunition did Mitchell and Kelly have?

Isaac was reloading. He waved his hand above his head, turned, and ran toward the garage's side door. He reached it as the wide gates at the garage's front smashed apart. A truck barrelled out and drove over the old man's corpse. The vehicle swerved, angling down the moss-lined road. It was painted a mottled green with the words 'British Army' stencilled on paintwork that was being chipped by gunfire. Who was firing, Ruth didn't know, but she recognised the people in the vehicle. Behind the wheel was Fairmont. Emmitt was sat next to him.

Barely audible above the engine's growl, there was a shout from inside the house, the words lost behind a high-pitched squeal from the vehicle. Ruth thought the truck would stall. It didn't. There was a tortuous grinding of gears, as the vehicle accelerated down the road, and towards Ruth.

She holstered her pistol and grabbed the shotgun, tracking the barrel left and right as she tried to maintain a bead on the jostling cab. It drew nearer. Someone opened fire – Kelly, Ruth guessed. It was a long sustained burst that fractured the windscreen. Cracks spider-webbed along its length, but the glass didn't break. The men in the cab were barely visible now. She didn't care. But the glass was bulletproof. She lowered the shotgun, aiming at the tyres. They weaved left then right. Left. Right, and the side of the truck slammed into a tree. It bounced off and kept coming. Closer. Closer. Close enough. She fired, rocking back with the recoil, wincing as fresh pain washed across her back, but already chambering the next round. This time barely aiming, she fired again.

The front wheel blew, the vehicle jack-knifed across the road, and the cab slammed into a tree. There was an almighty crunch of metal. The wheels spun. The tree creaked. The engine cut out. The wheels slowed and stopped. Smoke and steam poured from the wrecked vehicle. Without the roar of the engine masking all other sounds, she heard a distant gunshot, followed by a shout of, "Clear!" she thought that was Isaac but couldn't be certain.

Metal clicked and cracked. Ruth waited, the shotgun raised, pointing at the rear of the vehicle. No one appeared. She stood. Shotgun held tight, her finger poised by the trigger, she walked toward the rear of the truck. The driver-side mirror was shattered. She moved out into the road, giving the vehicle a wide berth as she edged toward the driver-side door. There was crack from above, and a branch fell from the tree into which the vehicle had crashed. It landed heavily on the stalled truck, and Ruth jumped back, almost pulling the trigger in reflex. She breathed out, took another step. Another, and she could see into the cab. It was empty. The passenger side door was open.

Quickly, she stepped around the cab, swinging the shotgun left and right, looking for the two men. They weren't hidden behind the side of the stalled vehicle, but there were two sets of footprints in the mud by the door. Three feet into the forest, she saw another footprint. A second, six feet further on. She kept following. After twenty feet, the ground rose, the mud hardened, and the trail ended. She didn't stop.

After thirty yards, she slowed and listened. The only sounds came from behind her. Another ten yards and even the wrecked engine was inaudible. The silent forest seemed to swallow all sound, even that of her own footsteps. She kept walking.

Where would they go? North, she decided, away from Twynham, but which way was that?

Another twenty yards, and the trees opened into a grassy clearing. There was no sign of anyone. She lowered the shotgun. No, there, on the trunk of a tree was a bloody smear, four feet above the ground. One of them was wounded, and they'd come this way.

She moved more slowly now, her ears alert, her eyes roving across the trees at the clearing's edge. She saw movement. Not in the trees, but above them. A flock of birds erupted from the leafless canopy a few hundred yards ahead. She ran, across the clearing, into the trees. Stumbling on slippery leaves, dragging herself through thorny bushes, she forced her way through overlapping barriers of evergreens. Heedless of footing, of noise, of anything except that desire to catch the men and bring an end to it all, she ran. She stumbled, slipped, fell. The shotgun hit the ground first. Her face hit mud a moment later, landing with her eye an inch from the barrel. She picked herself up, berating her own carelessness.

Where were they? Where was she? She'd become disorientated. She turned around and saw the fist sailing toward her face. She ducked. Fairmont's blow missed her jaw, but he turned the blow into a push, shoving at her shoulder. She staggered a pace, trying to bring the shotgun up. His leg came up, almost at a right-angle, slamming into her chest. She was knocked from her feet, and the gun from her hands. She sprawled to the ground, trying to catch her breath and draw her pistol at the same time.

Fairmont nimbly moved to the shotgun and scooped it up.

"Almost," he said smiling. "Almost, but that's never close enough." He levelled the gun. She stared down the length of the barrel. "And now," he said, "we win." The smile grew wider, and then it vanished. Blown away as his head disintegrated.

The vague realisation that there had been a sound, a gunshot, surfaced in Ruth's frozen mind as she saw Mitchell limping through the trees toward her. His gun was steady, but the rest of him wasn't. His other hand was clutched at his side, and he looked pale.

Ruth scrabbled to her feet.

"Sir, are you—"

"Where's Emmitt?" he asked.

Ruth looked around. There was no sign of him. But someone had left that bloody smear on that tree and it hadn't been Fairmont. "I'll find him," she said, drawing her pistol, and started running once more, heading in the direction opposite to which Mitchell had appeared.

Find him, find him, find him. The words echoed as she scanned the tree. There. A swatch of cloth. Could it have been from Emmitt's coat? She hadn't got a good look at what he was wearing. She slowed her pace, using her ears more than her eyes. Ahead, something was crashing through the undergrowth. Lots of somethings. Deer or wild ponies, she thought. It didn't matter which. Like the birds, they told her where Emmitt was.

Another two hundred yards, and she caught a sight of a shadow moving through the trees. A hundred yards after that, she saw him more clearly, and he was staggering. One arm in a sling, the other reaching for trees, pushing himself from one to the next.

Ruth kept running, feeling like she could do it all day, and knowing that there would be no need. The distance between them closed until, at thirty yards, she raised the pistol and fired a shot above his head.

Emmitt turned. He saw her. He tried to find some reserve of energy, sprinting for a dozen steps before he stumbled to a halt. He leaned against a tree for a moment, then pushed himself away, stopping with his back to her.

Ruth gripped her pistol two-handed and walked slowly toward him, coming to a halt twenty feet away.

"Kneel down," she said.

"No," he said. "I'll die standing up."

"You're under arrest."

He craned his neck around. "Really?"

"Yes," Ruth said.

"Are you sure?" he asked. "Don't you want to finish this, here and now? Get your revenge?"

She did, of course she did, the temptation to pull the trigger gnawed at her, and for that reason, and that he had suggested it, she didn't. "Kneel down, put your hands on your head."

He raised his left hand and turned around.

"I can't raise the other, sorry. It's the arm," he said affably.

Ruth steadied her aim. The adrenaline was wearing off. The pistol was growing heavier. She was all too aware that they were alone in a forest, with help a long way away.

"Kneel down," she said.

"How about a deal?" he suggested.

"I'm not interested," she said.

"I'll tell you about your past, and you let me go."

"No."

"I'll even throw in the truth about that man Isaac. How does that sound?" he asked.

Ruth hesitated. She didn't care, not now, but she knew that one day she might. She needed to know whether this man knew the truth.

"Do you know him?" she asked.

"Isaac? Yes."

"Have you ever met him?"

"Oh yes. It was a long time ago, but I'd never forget it."

Ruth nodded to herself. He hadn't recognised Isaac when he stood outside the hotel. That was as close to confirmation as she would get that he was lying. This wasn't a game she knew how to play, nor was this the time to learn.

"You haven't a clue who he is," Ruth said, knowing that she needed to remember this moment in order to quell any demons of doubt that may come to haunt her in the future. "You don't know what he looks like. You've never met him. Everything you say is a lie. All of it. Even the conspiracy. Even those coins. You and Fairmont created them. It was an elaborate hoax."

"That's what you think is it?" he asked.

"Are you going to deny it?"

"You want me to tell you everything," he asked. "You want a full confession? You want all the whys and wherefores?" He looked up at the trees. "It began a long time ago, before you were born. Your mother was —" He ducked, his left hand moving to his sling as he tried to draw a gun hidden in the black cloth, but Ruth had seen his shoulders move. She fired. And again, just for good measure.

Emmitt howled in pain.

"One through the shoulder, the other through the leg," she said. "I've been practicing. Didn't Simon tell you that?" She moved close enough to kick the gun away, then stepped back again.

Emmitt spat. "Finish it, then," he said.

"Oh no," Ruth said. "I told you. You're under arrest. There's going to be a trial. I'll be there when they sentence you."

Emmitt cursed.

Ruth took another step back, fixing Emmitt's expression in her memory. It would be of great comfort in years ahead when she was plagued with doubt as to whether the man truly did know something of her past. The man looked scared. Ruth smiled.

Epilogue
The Black Cap
15th October

"Does the defence have any questions?" the judge asked with nothing but scorn in his voice.

"None at all, your honour," Emmitt said, his tone nothing but polite.

"Then you may go, Officer Deering. I would add that the court is grateful for your testimony."

Ruth nodded politely and stood up. Leaving the stand, she glanced at the jury. Variations of stunned disbelief were written across their faces. It was the same with room's lawyers, all acting for the prosecution. She couldn't see the expression on the four journalists. They all had their heads bowed as they scrawled endless notes.

The only other exception was Emmitt himself. Handcuffed, wearing a prison jumpsuit, and sitting in the open – so he couldn't hide his hands beneath a table – he looked smug. He had admitted his guilt, readily confessing to everything. The jury was a formality, and the sentence already decided. Death.

Weaver was outside, sitting on a long wooden bench, alone. Mitchell had given his testimony earlier in the day then returned to the hospital. In deference to the politicians who risked blackmail, the trial was being held in camera. Two uniformed police officers stood guard either end of the long, basement corridor, with more upstairs and Marines on the roof.

Ruth wasn't sure why. Fear after the fact, Mitchell had said, though he hadn't explained what he meant.

The journalists would be allowed to print the story 'soon'. That was what they had been told at the beginning of the brief trial. Not just brief, it had been rushed. Isaac had vanished though that didn't mean he'd left the city. His involvement had been brushed over both by Mitchell and her. No one had noticed the obvious omission from their accounts, or if they had no one had said anything. It made her pause, but not for long. Emmitt was guilty. The words had come from his own lips. Yet…

"Now what?" Ruth asked.

"We wait," Weaver said.

Ruth sat down on the bench. For the first time in a week, she wore a police uniform. It was a new one.

"How are you feeling?" Weaver asked.

"Fine."

Silence settled.

"The trauma specialist is…" Weaver stumbled to a halt.

"It's fine," Ruth said. "Good. Helping." She wasn't sure that was true. So far they'd got no further than talking about her childhood, and that was something Ruth didn't want to think about.

"I… I have some good news for you," Weaver said, with forced cheerfulness. She paused, but Ruth said nothing. "You're being promoted," Weaver continued. "To probationary constable."

"I thought I had to serve a minimum of three months as a cadet," Ruth said.

"Under the circumstances, that has been waved," Weaver said. "It was Mr Atherton's idea. I agreed," she added, "but he said it was important for the press. We have to treat this like a victory and that means rewards given to the victors."

"Treat it like a victory?" Ruth repeated. "He doesn't think it's one either?"

"No."

"Because of the graffiti?" she asked.

"It's going up everywhere," Weaver confirmed.

Ruth had counted three walls daubed with 'Ned Ludd' that morning, and twice the previous evening. Only one had a backward 'L', and another was missing a 'd', but there was no mistaking it.

"I thought he'd ban the Luddites," Ruth said.

"What for?" Weaver asked.

"Sabotage," Ruth suggested.

"Except we don't know which of them was involved in cutting the telegraph wires. Until we can prove that, arresting them in their hundreds would do nothing but fill up the cells."

"Hundreds?" Ruth asked.

"There was a rally yesterday," Weaver said. "Most of the people arrested in that processing plant attended, along with another three hundred. It went off peacefully, and no one said anything more incendiary than that rationing should be brought to an end, but I think it's only the beginning."

"Huh! So Emmitt created this fake political movement as a distraction to aid their escape, and now it's a real thing?" She gave a short brittle laugh. It was funny. Almost hysterical. Ruth clamped her mouth closed before the laughter could turn into a sob. Her emotions had been like a leaf on the wind for the last few days, soaring up and down, directionless, and unpredictable.

After they'd arrested Emmitt, there had been questions. Ruth had fallen asleep halfway through them. She'd slept for twelve hours, but woken more tired than ever before. She didn't think it was a victory either. Mitchell had given her the new uniform, and the first time she wore it was for the memorial service for the Marines who'd died on the train. She'd barely made it through the service, and had cracked during the ceremonial gun-salute.

"Yes," Weaver said, speaking to fill the uneasy silence, "Constable Deering. It has a nice ring to it. You're still on medical leave, of course. But when you return you can have your pick of assignments."

That was the reward. She was meant to be grateful. She wasn't.

"Are the newspapers really going to be allowed to print everything?" she asked instead.

"Almost everything. They will include a full explanation of how the Luddites came to be formed as part of an elaborate robbery organised by figures within both the British and United States governments."

"And what will they say was stolen?"

"The location of an unnamed treasure, now reclaimed and returned to America."

"Oh." That was for the best, she supposed. Then she remembered the words of the oath she'd sworn before giving testimony. The whole truth, and nothing but. If she was required to tell it, then surely the public had a right to hear it. There was no point making that argument to Weaver.

A few minutes later, the door opened, and a constable came outside.

"Officer Deering?"

"Yes?"

"The judge wants to see you."

"Why?" Weaver asked.

"Sorry, ma'am. He didn't say."

Ruth followed the constable through the door, and then through another, and into the judge's private chambers.

"The prisoner wants to speak to you," the judge said. "You don't have to, and ordinarily I wouldn't allow it, but he's said little in his defence."

"Will anything he says be considered?"

"Toward his sentence? No." He gestured to his desk. On it was a piece of paper and a square of black cloth. "The jury has reached their verdict. As he offered no defence, it was a foregone conclusion."

"Guilty?" Ruth asked, wanting to know, to *absolutely* know, that Emmitt wasn't getting off on some technicality.

"Guilty," the judge confirmed.

"And the sentence?" she asked.

The judge picked up the black cloth square. "Morally, I am against the death penalty," he said. "I understood the need for it in the early years, but I hoped we would have moved beyond that barbarity. In this man's case, I am inclined to make an exception. In any case, my own feelings are immaterial. There is only one punishment our law will allow for this man's crimes. Taking a life is no small matter, even a life like his."

The relative morality of the death penalty, and the other provisions of the Emergency Powers Act, were debates for another time and another place, and perhaps, Ruth thought, for other people. She had chased the man, caught him, and brought him to justice. She had done her part, now it was time for others to do theirs.

"He'll be executed?" she asked.

"Yes."

"Then I'll speak to him," she said. "At least, I'll listen to what he has to say."

"What do you want?" she asked from the open doorway.

"Is that a way to greet an old friend?" Emmitt replied.

He was handcuffed, chained to the floor. The cell was bare, save for a solitary bulb in a cage above the door.

"What do you want?" Ruth repeated.

"Because I am an old friend," Emmitt continued, as if Ruth had said nothing. "I was there when you were born."

"Do you have anything to say in your defence? They're going to execute you. You know that, right?"

A brief shadow flickered across his face. "I do know that, yes, and no, I have nothing to say in my defence. What would be the point? We won, after all."

"Won? Fairmont's dead. So's Longfield, Wallace, and DeWitt. The conspiracy is dead. Except it wasn't a conspiracy at all, was it? It was a heist, and you failed."

"We can quibble over how to describe it, but it didn't fail. It all worked perfectly."

Ruth shook her head. "You've had no contact with anyone since we brought you in. Whatever Fairmont learned in the embassy died with him."

"True," Emmitt said. "Ah, well done. You wanted me to confirm it? Well, yes, he died without telling me. He certainly wouldn't write it down. But the secret didn't die with him. Other people know it. That particular truth may lie in the past, but it will come out. That is the nature of secrets."

"Is that where you got the idea for the inscription from?" she asked. "Old secrets from old governments that should have stayed lost among the ruins of the old world?"

"Ah, no, but that is a long story. Would you like to hear it?"

"No. Was there anything else you wanted to say? Or was that it?"

The scowl returned, and this time remained. "We won," he said. "History has been set on an unchangeable course. I heard about the graffiti."

Ruth frowned. Emmitt smiled.

"I may have no visitors, but I hear the guards talking," he said. "Ned Ludd's name has been appearing on walls all over the city, hasn't it?"

"That wasn't you," she said.

"Wasn't it? The name is out there. The man we created has become a myth. The movement will follow. We won, you see. Everything we wanted has come to pass. The economy has been proven fragile. Suspicion has been created between Britain and America. Distrust has been sown among the candidates. Knowledge of that secret will prove more destructive than had it been revealed. The Prime Minister has gone. Atherton has replaced her. He is a thoroughly unimaginative man who will resort to violence, and so will armies be created. Whoever follows him will acquire a military. It won't take long before they look for somewhere to conquer. We won."

"Yes. You said that. Goodbye." She turned for the door.

"Wait. I should ask you whether you wish to join us."

She caught the odd usage. "Should?"

"But I won't ask, because there's no need. In time you will see that you are on the wrong side."

"Oh, stop," she said. "It's over, Emmitt. Seriously, this is your last chance to say something truthful. To apologise or… I don't know. But if you want to be remembered for anything other than your deeds, say it now."

"Is it really over?" he asked.

This time, Ruth didn't reply. She walked out and kept walking until the courthouse was far behind her. Of their own volition, her feet took her to the hospital.

Mitchell was there, in what was becoming his usual chair, outside the door to Riley's room.

"*Constable* Deering," Mitchell said.

"Probationary constable," Ruth replied. "You heard?"

"I still hear things," he said. He wore his uniform though, like her, he was on leave. She supposed that if her reward was being promoted, his was not being sacked. "And probationary or not, it's still constable," he said. "Well done."

"How is she?"

"Drifting in and out of consciousness," Mitchell said. "But, on the whole, I'd say she's heading toward recovery."

"Will she...?" Ruth began. "I mean, do they know if...?" She found it hard to ask the question.

"We won't know if she'll walk again until she tries, and that is some time away. But you don't need to walk to be a good detective." Mitchell shrugged. "She is alive. That's all I care about. The rest, well, it is what it is."

She could see the brittleness of his facade. She searched around for something else to say, but all she could come up with was, "I spoke to Emmitt."

"You did. What did he say?"

"The usual lies and twisted words. They're going to execute him."

"Yes."

She looked around for a clock. "I suppose they'll have done it by now."

Mitchell stood. "We are a nation of laws, and that means we're also a nation of appeals. There are procedures that have to be followed, and so we don't march people out of the courthouse and put them up against the nearest wall."

"Oh."

"It'll take a week or two," Mitchell said. "But he won't escape it. Not this time. Come on, let's go for a walk."

Ruth fell into step next to him.

"Have you seen the graffiti?" she asked.

"It's hard to miss," he said.

"Do you think it means trouble?" she asked.

"Hopefully it means that the youth of today are opening a history book or two," Mitchell said.

"So, no?"

"No. Not for us, or not more trouble than a copper usually gets." He held open the door.

"Do *you* think it's over?" she asked as she stepped outside.

"There are some loose ends, I suppose," Mitchell said. "But there usually are. The major players are all dead. Yeah, I'd say it's over."

They proceeded in silence, heading away from the hospital. A fine mist filled the air. It wasn't quite rain, but it was persistent enough that she'd be drenched in a few minutes. She didn't mind.

"There's something that's bothering me," she finally said.

"Only one thing?"

"Well, now you come to mention it, I do think someone needs to talk to Isaac."

"His store of weapons worries you? Let me deal with him. I know how."

"Where is he?" she asked.

"Precisely? I don't know. He's taken Gregory north. He claimed that he has better health care than we have here. Honestly, I think he just wanted to get out of Twynham."

"And Simon?"

"Gone with him," Mitchell said. "Isaac will find him work."

"But not in Britain?" she asked.

"No. He mentioned something about retrieving something from a vault in Geneva."

"Oh." She thought. "Where's that?"

"Switzerland. That's a long way on foot. Simon probably won't come back."

And she thought about that. "Good."

"Was that what you wanted to ask?"

"No," she said. "It's Rupert Pine and the other politicians. The ambassador, too. I'm pretty sure that Fairmont didn't tell anyone what was inside Perez's safe. But the ambassador knows, doesn't he? And he's planning on standing in the election. What if he uses it himself?"

"A good point. I've had a word with Perez. I don't think he will use that information, because he knows that if he tries, I'll come after him."

"But he'll be the president!"

Mitchell smiled. "I didn't mean with a gun." He tapped his pocket. "They called them phones, but even in the old world I didn't use mine to make calls. They can do more than take photographs. They can record video, and sound."

"What do you… you mean you recorded what he said in that room in the embassy?"

"Of course. That's our insurance against Perez's honest behaviour."

"Politics," she sighed.

"It's better than the alternative."

They continued in silence for another few minutes.

"Where are we going?" Ruth asked.

"The coast," Mitchell said. "We have done our duty for the day, and any that's left can wait until tomorrow. I always liked walking down to the sea and looking at those rusting hulks. Emmitt might have used that information against us, but I'm not going to let that taint my memories of the past."

"Life goes on," Ruth said.

"It does, indeed."

The end.

Printed in Great Britain
by Amazon